KEVLAR

SKYE MCNEIL

HOT TREE PUBLISHING

A Bad Boy Romance Trilogy

Appointed by Fate

Exonerated with Love

Credence

Atlas Series

Hearts Abroad

Oceans Away

Macha MC Series

Doc T

Kevlar

For information, contact the publisher, Hot Tree Publishing.

www.hottreepublishing.com

Editing: Hot Tree Editing

Cover Designer: BookSmith Design

E-book: 978-1-922359-48-3

Paperback: 978-1-922359-49-0

To the women who shatter glass ceilings, no matter the size.

Author Note

Thank you for purchasing Kevlar, book two in Macha MC. In order to write this story, certain liberties were made when it came to the FBI procedures and WitSec (Witness Security/Witness Protection Program). I address these now, fully aware that it is unlikely for this to happen in reality. I so badly wanted to write these characters and overlooking procedures and protocols was necessary to see how these characters intersect in a way that intensifies the twists and turns in motorcycle club and suspense romance. Enjoy the ride.

Skye McNeil

Fifteen years ago

"You can't walk away from your family. You'll come back, *mija,* and you'll stay by my side. You will always be an MC princess."

Nikita Morales stared into the hollow, black eyes of her father. They weren't filled with sorrow, despite the judge's final words of condemnation. They were dark, gleaming orbs of prophecy.

Nita stepped closer to the man adorned in an Armani suit, his equally expensive attorney by his side. Both were purchased with blood money. It made her sick to her stomach.

"No, *Papi.* The MC destroyed my life. I won't ever return to it." She straightened her shoulders. "And

I'll never see your face again." She inhaled once, the scent of his Spanish cologne one that'd never escape her memory. "But you'll see mine every day you spend rotting in that prison cell."

Nikita turned on her toes and released a shaky breath. The prison guards clicked the handcuffs in place, the jingling of the shackles resonating in her ears. He called out to her; his voice strained the further she walked. It was over. The trial of the decade was complete, and the boss of the Diablos MC wouldn't see the light of day beyond prison fences for the remainder of his life.

Shivering, she recalled the long days in court filled with gruesome photos and chilling testimonies. Estevan Morales was the monster beneath the bed, and yet, she'd never seen the truth. *Not until it was too late.*

The courthouse hallway ended and her mother, Rose, stood huddled between two US Marshals. After years of being under his thumb, Nikita expected her mother to finally step into the light. Sadly, her mom did the exact opposite. She constantly looked over her shoulder, fearful of what Diablos may do to her now that their president was an incarcerated murderer.

"*Mamá*, you don't have to be afraid. He can't get

you." She grabbed Rose's hands in hers. They were ice cold and clammy. Searching her mother's light brown eyes, Nikita sighed. It'd never be the same for them. They couldn't stay in New York any longer. They couldn't live in the mansion the family purchased with dirty business ventures.

"He'll come for us someday. We betrayed him." The arctic words trickled from Rose's lips in a whisper that sent goose bumps up Nikita's arms. Rose believed it with every fiber of her being.

"No." She shook her head and eyed the two marshals. "We change our names and start over. No more Diablos. We'll live a simple life, *Mamá*." She tried to smile, but it came out more like a grimace. Returning to finish her freshman year of college wasn't possible. New York City would be the first place her father's minions would look for them.

Her heart continued to break at the thought of never seeing her college boyfriend again. *Tucker can't know about any of this.* She'd kept him in the dark about her father but didn't regret it. She couldn't say goodbye to him. There was nothing she could say that would help him understand why she had to leave. The boy who always got into trouble would be her past. Her future couldn't involve the tattooed soldier.

The marshals escorted them from the court-house and to the waiting SUVs in front. Her mother's shaky legs tripped down the stairs, and Nikita swore silently. *I'll never let a man destroy me like my father did.* She cemented the thought in her heart, mindful of dredging up this memory whenever she second-guessed herself.

"I'll hunt down the MCs, Mamá," she promised as the vehicle lurched to life. She stared at Rose's black dress, a gift from her husband. "And I'll make them pay."

Chapter One

KEVLAR

Present

Fog surrounded him from the moment he stepped outside the Macha clubhouse. Tucker "Kevlar" Dorous grinned at the sight. Having the clouds so close he could physically touch them gave him a sense of awe. Living in Colorado had many perks, but this was one of his favorites.

After lighting a cigarette, he inhaled the smoke and let the exhaust swirl among the clouds at his feet. A hint of the sunrise beckoned over the easterly mountain range. Sweat dripped from his forehead and disappeared somewhere on the ground. Chest still heaving from his recent workout, Kevlar eyed his cigarette and chuckled. *Damn thing probably isn't the best idea after ten miles at this altitude.*

He took another puff, then dropped the remainder of the cigarette to the ground, snuffing it with his black boot. It was a habit the Army enhanced over the years. The constant battlefields and aura of danger could only be silenced one cigarette at a time. He'd quit eventually. When, he wasn't so sure.

"Damn, Kevlar, what're you doing up this early?"

Kevlar glanced over his shoulder and noticed Hawk at the clubhouse door. The man, slightly shorter than him, sported a similar shirtless attire, torso covered in ornate Macha tattoos, the symbolic goddess spreading across his wide chest. She kept Kevlar safe, just like his Kevlar vest.

"I've been up for a while. Had to get my run in before the sun." He offered the other man a cigarette.

The door slammed behind Hawk, and Kevlar couldn't help but notice the other man's unzipped jeans riding low on his hips. It wasn't abnormal for the single club man, but with the sweet scent of perfume lingering on his skin, Kevlar guessed Hawk spent the night with a club nymph.

A recently added silver and black tattoo gleamed

in the morning light as Hawk stepped away from the building. The old-style motorcycle was never one to go out of style on the tattoo artist. "Never got a chance to really catch up with you." Hawk rested the cigarette between his fingers, the act natural after years of the habit.

Kevlar swept a hand over his military cut hair. After his last assignment, he wasn't sure he wanted to rehash the details of his missions in the Arabian deserts.

"Still decompressing," he replied, hoping the other man would let the subject drop.

Hawk nodded once and lifted his hand to his mouth, the bright orange from the cigarette the only color in the white world around them. "The nymphs are useful for things like that."

That, he disagreed with. The club whores—or nymphs in Macha MC—did help. At first. After successfully defeating the Twelve Brothers a month prior, Kevlar had his fill of the assortment of nymphs. Redheads, blondes, brunettes, and every color in between. They helped satisfy his body but didn't alleviate the constant nightmares or quiet the sense of danger that followed him.

"Well, shit, I thought I was ahead of the game."

Kevlar grinned when a tall man filled the space

next to Hawk. Rubble, his old military chum, stood with a disappointed expression on his bearded face. The bright red beanie cap kept his bald head covered, but Kevlar knew the tattoos that lay on his skull.

"You're never ahead with me around." He grabbed Rubble's hand and the two chest bumped.

"Yeah, yeah, asshole."

"You should join me sometime. I only go ten miles."

Rubble rolled his eyes, one blue, one green. Years ago, it'd freaked Kevlar out. Once they'd spent hours on end in the never-ending sandbox of the Middle East though, Kevlar changed his mind about the man's anomaly.

"Fuck you and your ten miles." Rubble passed on the offer for a cigarette. "I usually hit up the shooting range in the mornings." He squinted at their surroundings. "But with this shit, I'll wait until it clears."

The sun's bright rays bit through the blanket of fog, illuminating the trio outside. The warmth spread over Kevlar's skin, a sharp contrast to the cold sweat drying on his tattooed body.

"I missed Colorado."

He didn't care if it made him sound like a pussy.

Colorado was home. The better parts of his life were spent amid the tall pines and the scent of fresh mountain springs. His teenage years may have been spent at a military school out East, but his heart remained in the densely wooded mountains of Colorado.

"We all miss home eventually," Rubble chimed in, eyes focused on the horizon.

A pang of regret hit Kevlar. He'd missed home, sure, but there was something else he missed. *Someone else.* He hadn't seen *her* since they were love-struck kids in college. Soon after spring break her freshman year, Nikita Morales disappeared, never to be heard from again. It tore him up inside every day. It was the one mystery he hadn't solved. Years overseas hadn't lessened the burden either. He needed to uncover where she went and why. Until then, he couldn't release the hold she had on his heart.

Grabbing another cigarette, he lit it just in time for three more club members to stumble outside and watch the sunrise. Watching the sunrise didn't happen often, but the sense of brotherhood was strong with Macha. It was why he'd patched in the first place. Now that he was officially retired from the Army, he could settle into a normal life. *If a motorcycle club is normal.*

It wasn't, but it was better than living out of a green duffle. Whatever the next years brought, Kevlar had to remind himself of that. He was home, and he'd defend his home with his brothers until the very end if it came to that.

Chapter Two

NIKITA

GUN POISED FOR ACTION, NIKITA STOCKDALE followed the stench of death down the hallway. She was close. She could feel it in her gut and her gut was never wrong. Over the years, she'd learned to trust it more than the myriad of fellow FBI agents she'd met along the way.

The light overhead flickered, the sound buzzing in her ears. Her blue FBI jacket rustled slightly when she came up to a door and cleared the room. The five agents behind her followed at a similar pace, though the last man lagged a bit.

The scent grew stronger the deeper they moved into the lair. Adrenaline coursed through her veins, the sensation a familiar high for her. It was one she lived for over the years. Being stuck behind a desk wasn't who she was. A field agent was the only life she envisioned from day one.

"Stockdale, don't blow this," a voice griped in the earpiece of her left ear.

Despite fifteen years, her government-assigned surname didn't feel right. It didn't sound right. She gritted her teeth—her boss was constantly on her ass about one thing or another. She was the best in her unit, but Randy Penn had it out for her ever since she rejected his not-too-subtle offer to suck his dick to get a promotion.

Obviously, she'd turned the narcissistic asshole down. Ever since, Randy tried and failed to catch her in a compromising situation so he could swoop in and save the day... with his dick. She rolled her eyes, never once allowing the attractive yet pompous man to get the upper hand. She'd learned her lesson young. *Gracias, Papi.*

A closed door beckoned to her at the end of the last hallway. *This is it.* Sweat trickled down her neck, the sweltering heat from the motorcycle club's drug grow house an oven with her current duds. A body sat crumpled on the left side of the hall, his blood pooling on the floor. She checked for a pulse just in case but found none. It was a sad occurrence and one she saw too often in the MC world.

Motioning to her crew, she nodded once and waited for breach. The door swung open, agents filing into the greenhouse. Gunshots rang out upon entry. A bullet whizzed by her face and she dropped to the floor.

Gripping her gun tighter, she glanced under the table and spotted the feet of the MC members scurrying away. Acting fast, she let off five shots, each hitting one of the bikers' legs.

"Aw, come on, Stockdale, can't you let us get one?" The whiny voice of Mandi Riggs met Nikita's ears.

Popping up from her hiding spot, she preened at her best friend of five years. "I'm not even sorry."

Mandi shook her head, walking over to one of the injured bikers and cuffing him. "I mean, you've collared the last, what, five motorcycle clubs? Can't you share the satisfaction of shooting them? You know I like to do that."

Nikita pulled the man off the ground and handed him over to one of the other agents. "Nah, there's no fun in that. Plus, I'm a better shot."

This time, Mandi flipped her off, a smile on her oval face. "You talk big."

Not bothering to watch the FBI swoop in on the rest of the Grow MC members, Nikita perused the greenhouse. Marijuana plants abounded for as far as she could see. This wasn't why she singled out this particular MC. Their side business of cocaine and heroin was the real culprit.

She walked through the tables, eyeing the varying types of marijuana. The plant didn't bother her. After all, she'd experimented in college like everyone else in her dorm. Rounding the last table, she found what she was looking for. What she'd staked her career on. A lone laptop sat just off the room, the screen filled with numbers and bank accounts.

"Yo, Wells, get over here." She motioned to the IT man in her unit. She'd dragged him—quite literally —from his cozy hovel at headquarters because of her gut.

The curly-haired man cautiously avoided the detained bikers on his way to her. "What'd you find?"

She picked up the laptop and unceremoniously handed it to him. "I believe this will substantiate my theories about this MC laundering drug money. I have a hunch you'll see Diablos in there somewhere."

Agent Wells pushed up his glasses and furiously typed. After a few seconds, his eyes widened, and he started nodding. "Whoa, they *are* here. How'd you know?"

Keeping her cool, Nikita shrugged. "It's what I do." She walked backward. "Let me know when the full specs come back. I need to hear about it ASAP."

She didn't wait for Wells to nod before turning around and all but skipping out of the room. Nothing could get her down after this.

"Agent Stockdale, please report to my office when you return."

She grimaced at the voice always in her ear. *Except that.*

"Yes, sir." She pulled out the earpiece and handed it to the tech controller on her way out the building. After her morning, she'd earned a latte and croissant.

Thirty minutes later, she waited for the elevator doors to open to the fifth floor of the FBI building in Boston. The exact location was kept under wraps, but anyone who watched the block could see agents filling in and out of the exits.

"Way to go, Nikita. I heard you reeled in a big one."

"Thanks, Kathy." She smiled at the receptionist and handed her a bag with a warm blueberry muffin inside. It was their routine. She'd bring Kathy a pastry after she took down the latest MC and the older woman helped her now and then with office work.

Her black boots clicked on the recently waxed floor. Any other female field agent wouldn't dare wear heeled boots, but she wasn't like the rest. She staked her reputation on her career and wouldn't allow her fashion to suffer because of her job title.

Moving her motorcycle helmet from under her left arm to her right, she nodded at a passing FBI agent. Riding her rebuilt Harley in the winter didn't happen much, but a slight reprieve in the weather gave her the perfect opportunity to feel the rush of adrenaline only a bike could offer.

The modern artwork on the wall led to a secured door. Using her card badge, she swiped it along the black box and waited for the green light. The door buzzed, and she pulled at the handle, mindful not to let anyone else enter with her.

A maze of cubicles greeted her, the scent of burned coffee lining the air. Most of the employees here were desk techs. The clump of cubicles near the back of the room was for field agents. She spotted Mandi's desk across the hall but steered toward the office on the other end of the large space.

Knocking lightly, she brushed back her midnight black hair. "You wanted to see me?"

Randy Penn lifted his head, green eyes astute. "Nikita, yes, please shut the door."

She did so begrudgingly and sank into the chair opposite his desk. It was uncomfortable and probably meant to be so people didn't linger. "What's up?"

Randy finished typing his email then focused on her. It'd take an imbecile not to notice the way his eyes brazenly fixed to her breasts beneath the gray shirt. She didn't shrug back or try to deviate his gaze. After working predominately with men, Nikita had grown a thick skin. Thicker still than the one her criminal of a father forced on her.

"You're aware of the recent breach to our online servers."

"I am."

His left cheek twitched. "It appears a few personnel files were taken."

"That's it?" She glanced to the clock then back.

"Yes, but very specific personnel files."

This made her perk up. She watched him closely and put the pieces together. "Mine, I take it? Why?" She knew the answer before she finished speaking.

"Your identity has been compromised, Agent—

Nikita." He straightened his tie. "It could be nothing, or it may have been an intricate rouse to get marshal files. Those were the ones taken, mind you—about twenty in total. We've already scrubbed the active files and taken care of those assets. Which means the only file open is you."

Nikita bit her thumbnail. The marshals warned her this could happen. An FBI agent under marshal identity was a target any of her enemies would want. "I see."

"You have two choices the way I see it. Either stay in your current identity or allow the marshals to create a new one for you."

"Hell no. I've worked too hard in this job. I'm not giving it up."

"I assumed as much, which brings us to our next topic. We need to discuss your upcoming assignment." He swiveled his chair to the computer and clicked the keyboard. "You've been digging into a motorcycle club in Colorado, is that right?"

Her pulse quickened. She'd been working on the case for the last six months, never able to crack into it until last month when she'd managed to secure an inside man—or more appropriately, woman.

"Yeah, the Greenback Cutthroats. I suspect they're working with Diablos MC." Her amber eyes darted from his computer to him. "Why? You're not going to bury it, are you?" When he didn't immediately answer, she stood and paced. "Because I have an inside woman there. She's in deep too. Almost didn't agree to be my CI."

"Calm down, Stockdale. I'm not burying anything." Randy grabbed a folder from his stack and handed it to her. "I received this information today. I think it could be useful."

Opening it, Nikita scanned the contents. Photos of battered women and children of all ethnicities soured her stomach. It was exactly as she thought. "So they *are* trafficking people." She cursed loudly. "And you're sure it's the Cutthroats?"

"Very." He shuffled some papers on his desk and finally read one of them. "A local from Waverley, Colorado, sent those photos and verified the motorcycle gang had the Greenback Cutthroats emblem on their jackets."

"Holy shit." She tried not to get excited. People were being mistreated and that was nothing to celebrate, but the chance to shut down another motorcycle club was always reason for her. *Especially one potentially working with Diablos.* It was another hunch... but she knew it was legitimate.

"Since this is your find, I've contacted the Denver office. They're expecting you this week."

"All right, great."

"But I should warn you—" He paused and eyed her warily. "If this is only about Diablos—"

"It's not," she quickly interrupted. It was no secret she was Diablos MC. Everyone in the department was aware of the manhunt that never panned out. Just when she thought she'd had them, they'd escaped. No one, except her bosses and the marshals knew the true reason she focused on her father's MC.

"The jet will take you there whenever you're ready." He handed her a hefty manila envelope. "You've been begging to go undercover again, so here's your shot. If you nail this, it'll get you on the map."

Nikita nodded. While she didn't want her face splashed on the national news, she did want a promotion. Being in witness protection had its perks, but the marshals warned her what a life in the FBI would do. It kept a target on her back. One that Diablos may try to hit. Thus far, none had. The recent office break-in put her on edge. Anyone could want marshal files to sell to the highest bidder.

Pushing the fear aside, she focused on her latest assignment.

"You can take an agent to be your second," Randy said, interrupting her thoughts.

"Mandi Riggs."

He smirked. "I figured as much. I'll let you tell her the good news."

"Thanks. I'll finish my report from today and we'll leave tomorrow." She hurried from his office before he could attempt more conversation.

Hurrying to her desk, she opened the top drawer and grabbed her passport. It served her no purpose at home when she often plane-jumped with her job. Stuffing it in her jacket pocket, she typed up her report from the day's bust and emailed it off to her supervisors. Mandi hadn't returned from lunch yet, but that didn't stop Nikita from texting her.

Nikita: Pack your skis. We're heading to Colorado.

She grabbed her helmet and set off toward home. Her bag was ready to go already, and she was more than eager to leave Boston for a few weeks.

***

The private FBI jet soared higher, and with it, Nikita's anxiety. As a child, she'd always flown private. She nervously cleared her throat. Mandi smiled over at her, flipping through a case file. The luxury on the FBI jet was much different than what her father insisted upon. Her mother didn't give a damn about such frippery. At least that's what Nikita always thought.

She pushed up her long sleeves, a myriad of tattoos coming into view. The small rose on her wrist made her think of her mother. Rose was somewhere safe. That's what she said the last time they spoke. That'd been nearly five weeks ago. Making a mental note to call, she slowly traced the tattoos covering both arms with her gaze. They weren't a rebellious statement or a phase. The tattoos were her past and present. Each one represented something important to her. The black and white hues reminded her that life was just the same. Black and white. No room for gray. No room for color.

The plane bumped slightly on a pocket of air, and Mandi gripped the arm of her chair. She'd never been fond of flying. She insisted on driving whenever possible. Nikita, on the other hand, would rather fly than drive anywhere. The shorter woman pulled out her earbud and listened to the hum of the airplane for a moment before returning to the reggae music. Nikita hid a smile. Her best friend didn't go anywhere without earbuds or music.

Pulling out her own case file, she scanned the photos, both black and white and color. She preferred the black and white snapshots. Just as she preferred black tattoos over colored ones. Her tattoo artist always tried to convince her to add a little blue or green, but she refused. Her life was black and white. There was right and wrong. She didn't color outside the lines. Not like her father had.

She turned to the next page of the folder. Every now and again, memories of her life before witness protection flooded her. Bright colors were her father's favorite. He used to bring home the latest fashion from Paris for her, and they always had plenty of color involved. Nikita looked down at her standard black pants and gray FBI sweatshirt. She wore colors, sure, but not ones her father approved of and preferred.

The last page of the report piqued her interest, a photo taken from a long distance of a Cutthroat and another man. She squinted, trying to read any part of the second man's jacket. It was leather like the Cutthroat's, but there was something familiar about it.

Grabbing the small magnifying glass she always carried on her keyring, she slid it over the photo. The outline of a symbol or sketch was on the back of the second man. She held it up to the light, and a devil horn came into view.

Cursing, her stomach jumped. *Diablos. I was right.* Since Estevan "*Muerte*" Morales's incarceration, her father's motorcycle club remained reclusive. Despite their low profile, everywhere she searched, the East Coast MC dominated the club market. Other MCs laundered Diablos' money and moved their drug shipments. *This time, I'll get them.*

Immediately, the past hit her hard. After finishing her FBI training, she'd been dead set on tracking down the bastards and making them pay. To her regret, they avoided her and always gave her the slip. It wasn't a coincidence. Her father knew her occupation—how? She could only guess money granted information from within prison walls, and Estevan had plenty of it—and didn't want her to catch them. She'd kept her government issued surname in hopes that no one would associate her with Estevan. No matter how much distance she tried to put between her past, it wasn't far enough. Her supervisor at the time forced her back to reality. It was then that she focused her career on organized crime, specifically motorcycle clubs. She had to take down Diablos. *One way or another, I will.*

She looked out the window. Fluffy clouds met

her gaze, along with blue sky as far as her eyes could see. Removing her father's MC meant she'd have to color outside the lines, though. Her FBI set of rules didn't apply when it came to Diablos. They were the devil that hid in the shadows, waiting for her to step out of bounds so they could capture her and take her to their leader—her father.

An entire wall of her apartment was dedicated to Diablos, with a multitude of spider webs intermingling the MCs she knew of or had taken down. After her father repeatedly tried to get in contact with her, it became clear she couldn't ignore him. Estevan Morales filed numerous appeals with the court, attempting to appear as the wronged victim and loving father. Nikita rolled her eyes. Her father was anything but innocent. He'd wanted to pull her into the MC. He'd said so before he was sent to prison. She purposefully avoided all things MC after his trial.... but the past always seemed to come back for her. She couldn't put aside her true purpose in life. *End Diablos.*

Mandi nudged her leg. "You look like you're brewing something."

She closed the file. "Maybe, I am."

Her partner sighed. "Just try and not get me

killed. My niece turns five next month. I'd like to attend her golden birthday."

"Don't worry, we'll be home before then."

She glanced to the window again, the plane entering a clump of dark clouds. The dark hue of the clouds reminded her of the pile of cuts in her storage locker. She clenched her jaw, recalling ripping the patches from the MC presidents' cuts after each takedown and pinning them up on her intricate MC board at her apartment. Trophies in a way but mostly puzzle pieces that would lead her to Diablos.

Her reputation in the bureau was solid, and she earned the respect of the men and women around her. She couldn't ask for more. Thoughts of a future and someday having a family of her own made her frown. Her workaholic reputation didn't get her any dates, but she didn't have time for that.

"You'll come back, mija, and you'll stay by my side." Nikita shook her head. She'd prove her father wrong. She wouldn't return to Diablos unless it was to take it down for good. There was a black and white tattoo with that same promise. The future could wait.

Chapter Three

KEVLAR

"Once you finish the radiator, move to the air compressor." Kevlar patted the prospect on the shoulder and walked away before the younger man could ask any more questions. He didn't feel like answering now.

Pausing at the entrance of Macha's garage, he watched vehicles zoom by one at a time. Over the last month, he'd slowly reintegrated himself with society and the club. It really didn't take much effort. The guys were the same as when he'd left. A few new faces greeted him each morning, but the tried and true kept him going.

Hawk waved at him from outside the tattoo parlor connected to the club's bar. He was out there for his usual smoke break, Legs and her man,

Snoopy, joining him this hour. Rubble cursed from within the garage, and Kevlar glanced over his shoulder and smirked toward the big man rubbing the back of his head. He was a whiz when it came to vehicles of all kinds, but clearly, his large stature wasn't made for Honda Civics.

He faced forward, a group of nymphs huddled outside the bar, their assortment of colored hair blowing in the sultry air. He recognized one of the brunettes, and the night before flashed in his mind. Scratches lined his back alongside bite marks from when the little nymph could take his thrusts no longer. He wiped a bead of sweat from his brow and turned around. The casual sex was fine. Nothing to write home about, but better than none.

"Kevlar, can you give me a hand?"

Steering toward one of the newer prospects, he helped the other man finish the tire rotation and wiped his hands with a rag.

"I'm done for the day. Let's go grab a beer," Rubble called over the hum of the impact wrench.

Tossing the rag to the prospect, he nodded. "Works for me." He gave the prospects their final jobs, then walked toward Booze and Tattoos.

Waving his big hand, Rubble said, "Nah, not ours tonight."

Kevlar lifted his brow. "Then where?"

Rubble straddled his gigantic Harley. "Greenback's."

"Wait, what?" He grabbed his helmet off the back of his bike.

"Prez wants us to do a little recon. He heard some whisperings about the Cutthroats joining up with Diablos."

The MC name sounded familiar, but he couldn't place it. "Who're they again?"

"They're an East Coast MC." Rubble pulled on his leather gloves. "Over the years, they've slowly encroached on other club territories. Some even merged with Diablos."

"Damn." He shook his head and swung his leg over his bike. "Wait, weren't they on the news? They run drugs."

"Off and on. Their president is in prison. Guess he got pinched and is serving life for multiple murders."

"Wait, he's still running it from prison?"

"As far as everyone knows. His officers run day-to-day operations."

This surprised him. Not many club presidents could maintain control over their men during incarceration. "He must be pretty badass."

A strange flicker surged in Rubble's mismatched eyes. "He's not one you want to fuck with. I heard his wife and daughter testified against him at his trial, then went into witness protection for their safety."

"He'd hurt his own family?"

"Guess so." Rubble started his bike. "Sad, isn't it?"

Kevlar followed suit. "Yeah. If the Greenback Cutthroats are in bed with Diablos, we need to know about it. Snowshoe doesn't need that kind of violence. Even if they're ten miles away."

"Hawk heard a few Cutthroat bikers talking about trafficking too."

He cringed at the thought. "Animals or people?"

"Dunno." Rubble jutted up his chin. "That's what we're gonna find out." He grinned. "Let's ride."

Easing off the ground, Kevlar followed Rubble to the MC bar in the next town over. The wind cooled him until he walked through the front doors of the Rusty Cantina. His blood surged a fire he long thought diminished. His personal heaven on earth with a dash of hell sat in front of him. *Well, fuck me sideways.*

Chapter Four

NIKITA

"That was easy." Mandi downed a shot of tequila and popped a lime in her mouth, sucking in the juice and making a face at the sourness.

"Almost too easy." Nikita glanced around the bar full of burly bikers. It was the club's main hangout and source of business in the town of Waverley, Colorado.

Mandi handed her a shot, swaying to the music. "Your contact got us in. What's too easy about that? She's one of the club's whores. I can't say I love being a fake whore, but I guess it's better than being an old lady." She eyed her friend. "I mean, honestly, who wants to be one of those?"

Swallowing her immediate reaction, Nikita opted against explaining her mother's title once upon a time. When she was a child, being an old lady seemed so exciting and glamorous. Finding out the truth about her father sent her back to square one. *Nothing is as it seems.* It was the one constant in her life. Not even Mandi knew her FBI origin story, and she'd keep it that way. The more people knew, the more they were in danger.

"How're we going to get out of, well, you know, screwing any biker who demands it?"

That was the one thing Nikita hadn't counted on. She was fully aware of the MC "doll" role in the club but didn't expect to be welcomed into the club as women used purely for self-gratification. Her gut didn't like the undercover role, but her head told her to suck it up.

"I'm sure we'll figure something out." Nikita sipped her bottle of Bud Light. Tap and canned beer weren't the same. If she had her way, they'd sip something much stronger.

"Best-case scenario, we hand them off to one of the actual club girls."

"And the worst case?" She met Mandi's gaze and shrugged. "Aw hell no, I'm not doing that."

"Oh, calm down, we won't have to act out our roles."

"Better not." Mandi swiveled around on the

barstool. "But I gotta say, there are a lot of hot guys in Colorado. Maybe I'll try out my cuffs on a few." She chewed the tiny straw in her drink. "I wouldn't mind knocking boots with a bad boy."

Following her gaze, Nikita had to admit there were a few lookers. She took a drink. But none who could tempt her for even a fast fuck behind the bar. She'd gone months without casual hook-ups and could go another few more before she got desperate.

Since arriving in Waverley, their club contact, Juliet, set them up at the Greenback Cutthroat dollhouse. It was an old hotel, complete with plenty of rooms for the girls and MC members who wanted to taste. Juliet assured them they'd be fine. New girls were a delicacy and ones the MC didn't fuck all at once. Plus, they couldn't become acting dolls until initiation. The act evidently included one full night spent with the club cabinet members. Nikita shivered at the mere mention. They'd be out of Waverley and Cutthroat control before anyone was initiated.

"Now, he is one hell of a man. Hot damn."

Swinging her gaze to where Mandi had her eyes glued, Nikita couldn't stop the sharp intake of breath. "No fucking way."

Tucker Dorous stood in the entry of the Rusty Cantina decked out in more tattoos than the last time she saw him and seemingly ten times sexier by all accounts. His chest was wider, muscles straining at each movement. The beer in her stomach gurgled almost as loudly as Mandi.

"Who is that and where can I get one?" She pinched her arm. "Um, hello, earth to Nikita. Do you know him?"

Tucker's eyes latched to her and a glimmer of disbelief scribbled over his face. The shadow on his jaw was dark and his lips held a hint of mischief. Judging from the leather cut tight across his shoulders, he was part of a motorcycle club. This was the absolute last place she expected to see him. Last she knew, Tucker was in the Armed Forces somewhere in the Middle East. The military was where he belonged not in some grungy bar in Colorado. *What the hell happened to him?*

"Yeah, I know him or knew him." Nikita reached for her bottle of beer and almost tipped it over. She managed to get a good grip on it in time for Tucker and a hulking man beside him to reach them.

"I'll be damned." He stopped shy of the barstools, his brown eyes gliding over her. "Is that really you, Kita?"

"*Kita*?" Mandi choked on her drink.

She cleared her throat, the nickname drudging

up old memories of their times together. She couldn't look away, her body heating the longer his adorable grin tempted her. "How's it going, Tucker?"

His eyes narrowed and the grin slipped from his face. "Seriously? After all this time, you're just going to act like you didn't disappear on me? Where the hell did you go? Why didn't you call me? I was worried sick about you, Kita."

Nikita took a large sip of beer, her stomach doing somersaults. "Um, I can't really talk about it."

Tucker placed a hand on the bar beside her, locking her in place. His beautiful eyes were full of pain and anger. She couldn't blame him for either one. He deserved to be pissed at her.

"You can't or you won't talk about it?" He searched her face, worry lining his brows. He looked good enough to kiss until they were both breathless.

"Both," she said softly.

He leaned in closer, brushing his cheek to hers. Nikita closed her eyes at the contact, their surroundings morphing into white noise. Nothing mattered when Tucker was around her. It'd always been that way. Somehow he made everything but them disappear.

"Well, that's a damn shame," he said, his breath cascading down her neck, tickling and turning her on at the same time. "Because I've missed the hell out of you."

He pulled away long before she was ready. The fog around them dissipated and Nikita's vision finally cleared. She was an undercover FBI agent. She couldn't let some flame from her past disrupt the mission. *No matter how hot he is.*

Crossing her arms over her chest, she looked to Mandi who looked a little too enthralled by the entire scene. Already she wasn't looking forward to the conversation they'd have later.

"Look, Tucker, I'm not interested in catching up."

"It's Kevlar these days, but that's okay. Clearly, you've forgotten how to stay in touch with people. Can't say I'm surprised since you didn't care enough to say goodbye."

Nikita's nose twitched at the obvious rebuke. She did care. She just couldn't care in that moment.

He nodded to his friend. "This is Rubble, a buddy and brother of mine."

Reviewing their cuts, she recognized the goddess when Rubble turned. He was part of Macha MC. They'd come up a time or two on her radar, but never seemed like a credible threat. It gave her a jolt of relief. Even though he was still part of a dangerous lifestyle, Macha wasn't one of the bad ones.

Three sets of Greenback Cutthroat members' eyes locked on their unexpected reunion. The men sporting ripped jeans and equally muscular arms scurried out of the booth. A glint of metal on the biggest man caught her attention. She'd recognize a gun anywhere, and hers was safely stowed under her bed at the dollhouse.

Tucker or whatever he was calling himself these days could expose her. He knew her real name. All he had to do was mutter it and the wrong person would discover why she and Mandi were slumming it as club girls. She had to get him the hell out of there before he blew her cover.

"Cool, well, unless you guys want to eat your cuts, I suggest you leave." She nodded toward the approaching men and set down her beer. She couldn't tell him what was going on, but she could protect him. It was a poor consolation, but it'd have to do. "Now, Tu—Kevlar."

Kevlar's eyes dashed to the stocky bikers and a secretive smile crossed his face. "I appreciate you looking out for me, Kita, but I can handle my own. You'd know that if you stayed in contact." Nikita opened her mouth to interrupt, but he jutted his chin to his friend and added, "And so can he."

Questions peppered Nikita's mind, but she didn't voice any of them. If he didn't leave soon, she may never know what happened to the boy who most definitely turned into a man over the last fifteen years.

"But— "

"Well, well, lookie here, boys. Two Macha bitches are ready to cause trouble," the biggest man said.

Rubble stepped forward, his stature over-whelming every man and woman in the bar. Nikita tilted her head up to see his face, something she rarely had to do with her nearly six-foot frame. His long beard looked as fierce as his unique eyes.

"Not looking for trouble," Rubble stated, looking down at the trio. "Just a beer or two."

Kevlar waved at the bartender. "Unless the Cutthroats want to turn away money."

"Have your beers but stay away from our dolls," the biker with a gray beard growled.

Rubble and Kevlar exchanged a knowing look. It was one she dreaded. *If he fucks this up for me, I'm gonna kick his ass.*

"Our nymphs are fifty times hotter than your dolls," Kevlar stated with a sneer.

The Cutthroats murmured between themselves, the statement clearly true.

"Seems you like these two," the middle man said. "Just recruited them." He slung an arm around Nikita's neck, and she held her breath at his stench of stale beer and cigarettes. "Haven't had a chance to break them in yet, though." His gaze turned to her. "How 'bout it, sweetheart? Want to prove your loyalty to the MC by sucking my dick in front of these Macha menaces? I'll bet you suck good too with those big lips." His hand slipped to her jeans. "And a very tasty ass."

Nikita's throat dried at the crass request. She'd dreaded the first lewd interaction but having her college boyfriend in the audience made it worse. Glancing at Kevlar, she recognized the possessive gleam in his brown eyes. Two sets of fists clenched, neither one trying to hide their outrage.

"Honey, you don't want her," a new voice stated with a deep rasp. They all looked over to see Juliet join the group. An inaudible sigh resonated, and Nikita felt her pulse slow.

"You know these two haven't been initiated yet. They're only for looking at until the girls and I teach them what Cutthroats want." Juliet grabbed the man's tattooed hand and led him away from the group, nodding subtly to her before they disappeared into one of the back rooms.

The rest of the Cutthroats dispersed but not before sending threatening glares and accompanying taunts toward Rubble and Kevlar.

"You should go," Nikita said, standing and pushing Kevlar toward the exit. His chest felt harder than mere flesh and muscle. Nevertheless, she couldn't trust him to not blow the operation.

"Just got here." He reached up and caught a tendril of her hair between his fingers. "And after fifteen years, I don't particularly want to leave you."

Meeting his gaze, she recognized the humor in his handsome face. "I don't think tonight is the best time to chat."

"Then tell me when and where, Kita." When he stepped forward, hints of sandalwood and automobile oil mingled in her nostrils.

"Tucker...."

"That's not my name."

Her curse caught in her throat. It'd take some time before she accepted his new role, his new life. *Then again, he knows nothing of mine.*

"Kevlar, you're in Macha MC." She shook her

head. "I'm a doll for the Greenback Cutthroats. From what I hear, we aren't supposed to be friendly, let alone friends." She took a step backward. "Leave before I make sure you aren't welcome here ever again."

Kevlar's brows rose, surprise prevalent on his chiseled features. She'd always liked the hard lines of his jaw and running her fingers along the divot of his chin.

He looked over his shoulder at the Cutthroats, then back to her. "Are you in trouble?"

"Oh my God." She rolled her eyes. "Just because I'm here doesn't mean I'm in trouble."

"I don't believe you." He lowered his voice. "My club, Macha, they wouldn't treat you like the Cutthroats. We respect women. Idolize them even."

His apprehensive tone pissed her the hell off. "You think you can come in here and save the day?" She poked his chest. If she wasn't mistaken, he was wearing a bulletproof vest. Immediately, her mind spun to the reason why. "I don't need to be saved, *Kevlar*. I can save myself."

Holding up his hands, he backed away. "All right, Kita, whatever you say. If you need anything, say the word and I'll be here for you."

She didn't release her balled hands until both he

and Rubble left the bar. The hard rock music drowned out her own thoughts, but not Mandi's.

"Girl, I know you're against getting involved with somebody in a MC, but that man would convince me otherwise."

Nikita downed the rest of her beer, her friend chattering in the background. She wasn't wrong. If he truly wanted, Tucker Dorous could shimmy her out of any pair of panties. Today, she was damned sure it would've happened again had her job not gotten in the way.

"He better stick to Macha. I can't afford any distractions."

Chapter Five

KEVLAR

"Do you wanna talk about it?"

Rubble's voice bounced between the Macha club buildings, but Kevlar didn't stop walking. His past was suddenly chasing him, and every emotion swiftly bubbled in his heart. Attaining the clubhouse door, he swung it open and whizzed past the three nymphs in the hallway, ignoring their calls to him. Sex wasn't on his mind at the moment. Only Kita was.

Finding the refrigerator, he pulled out three beers and headed toward the den. It was the one place he could count on no one being there. *I hope.* He cracked the top of the first beer and guzzled half of it by the time he reached the cool, dark den.

Letting out a sigh of relief at the emptiness, he sunk into the leather recliner and closed his eyes.

Memory after memory of his senior year at the academy invaded him. He'd met Nikita at a kegger off campus of Columbia University where she attended.

"Jesus Christ, Kevlar, since when do you stalk off like a little bitch?"

Popping open his eyes, he swallowed a mouthful of beer. Rubble plopped into the couch, a curious expression on his bearded face. It was a wonder he could see the man at all, but his shiny, bald head served as a beacon in the darkness.

"I don't."

Rubble harrumphed. "Not what just happened." He snatched one of the beers from him. "Spill."

"You don't want to hear this shit."

"Seeing how we served together, and you never mentioned that woman with a very gorgeous ass, yeah I do." He tipped back the bottle of beer.

"Nikita and I met in college. I was at the academy and she was a freshman at Columbia." He paused to see if that would appease the big man. The blank stare persuaded him otherwise.

"It was one of those whirlwind relationships you

hear about. Fell in love fast, but by the time spring break came around, she disappeared."

Rubble sat up slightly. "Disappeared?"

He sipped the beer. "Yeah. She went home to help with family drama. She didn't say what it was. After that, I never heard from her again. I went to the address she gave me, but it was a vacant trailer." He ran his fingers through his short hair, a habit he couldn't cease despite barely having any there. "Her cell phone was disconnected. The cops didn't seem to care at all about her whereabouts. Neither did the FBI." He stared off into the darkness, reliving the heartache. "It was as if she went *poof*."

"You never heard from her again?"

"Nope. I finished my year, then was sent over-seas." He finished off his bottle and grabbed another. The moment he spotted her; his gut dropped to new depths. He couldn't keep his distance either. He had to be closer to her, smell that intoxicating jasmine scent she wore. It wrecked him tonight just like it did when they first met.

Kevlar shook his head. For years, he couldn't accept that she'd simply leave him without so much as a word goodbye. But she did and he spent years pining after a ghost. He rubbed a fist over his heart, the throb there pulsing through his ribcage. Seeing her dredged up all the emotions he locked away. Letting them loose was dangerous, but he couldn't help it. "Sometimes, I think I hallucinated her."

"I saw the way you reacted tonight." Rubble lightly nudged Kevlar's boot. "You didn't make her up. You loved her."

"Once upon a time, sure, but now? I don't even know who that person was at the bar." He stood and started pacing. The mere notion of Nikita—his Kita—being with a Greenback Cutthroat tore up his gut. "She acted so cold, so rough. That's not Kita."

"It's been years, brother. We all grow up."

He took a long draught of beer. "No, she couldn't change that much."

For a moment, neither spoke. Kevlar's mind hummed at the different scenarios that could've led to Kita being a club girl. None of them made sense. She was too smart to fall prey to the vileness of the Cutthroats. Something had set her down this path and it killed him that she wouldn't talk to him. He swallowed hard, worry filling his gut more than the Irish beer.

Finally, Rubble asked the question Kevlar couldn't get out of his head. "You think she's in trouble?"

"I don't know. It's possible, but she did say she didn't need rescuing."

Rubble rolled his eyes, bottle pressed to his lips. "Women always say that bullshit."

He nodded. "From Kita, I almost believe her. She was a badass fifteen years ago. I know she can handle her own." He sat back down on the edge of the seat. "But something never felt right."

Rubble cocked his left brow. "What was her last name back then?"

"Morales."

Rubble choked on his beer. "Wait, Morales? That's the same last name as Diablos's president. "

Kevlar's mouth went dry as he quickly connected the dots. "No, that's not possible."

"Brother, Estevan Morales was incarcerated about fifteen years ago. That's right around the time Nikita went dark, right?"

"Uh, yeah, I guess so." His pulse skyrocketed. "You don't think she's related to him, do you?"

"It's a common surname, but the way she just disappeared makes me wonder." Rubble chewed on his thumbnail, brows furrowed. "Did she ever mention her parents' names when you were together?"

"No, and I never asked. I was a dumb kid. Her parents were the last thing on my mind."

Rubble rolled his eyes and smirked. "Clearly."

Kevlar glanced to his oldest living friend. The war had taken the rest. He'd made it out alive and in one piece. He couldn't say the same for the other men in his company. Rubble was the reason he joined Macha. The club members were the brothers he always wanted. But Rubble was more than that to Kevlar. He was the brother he'd never had.

Standing, Rubble left the room and returned with a six-pack of ice-cold beer. He thudded it down on the table between them. "If you think there's even an inkling that Nikita is related to Estevan Morales, we need to find out. The man controls Diablos from prison. And as you know, the rumor is that the Cutthroats are in bed with Diablos." He pointed his beer. "The same rumor we went to Waverley to investigate and couldn't get information on thanks to your little reunion."

Kevlar opened his mouth but was too slow.

"We'll circle back to Waverley later." Rubble cracked his knuckles. "Even if Nikita isn't related, she's in danger the longer she stays there."

Kevlar rolled his neck from side to side. "Yeah, I know. She's too stubborn to see it."

"Maybe you should try talking to her. A blast from the past at a loud bar probably isn't the best place for a reunion."

Thinking it over, he nodded. "True. Maybe I'll cruise the streets and see if I can run into her again."

The clubhouse sounds overwhelmed any chance of silence. In a way, Kevlar was grateful for the distraction. Kita had never left his mind or his heart. He carried her there since that rainy, spring day she never showed up at the coffee shop. She was in his skin like the tattoos covering his flesh. He couldn't get rid of her and didn't want to. No matter how many women he fucked, Kita always came to mind.

"You really loved her."

He met Rubble's gaze. "I don't think I ever stopped."

Chapter Six

NIKITA

"Okay, my curiosity is killing me. Who the hell was he?"

Nikita downed her shot of tequila, then Mandi's. "No one."

"Yeah, okay, right." The short brunette grabbed her face. "Who on God's green earth was that sexy biker who clearly has a thing for you? Judging from his tight jeans, a very big thing."

Flicking her gaze from her friend to the door Kevlar recently left, she sighed. "An old flame, all right? One I haven't seen in fifteen years."

"And you get him all riled up after all this time?" Mandi dropped her hold and whistled. "Damn, girl."

Nikita turned toward the bar and leaned her elbows on it, her pulse thumping her chest harder than the rock music over the speakers. "It doesn't matter. We're here to do a job," she whispered harshly. "No distractions."

Mandi hopped on the barstool next to her and rubbed her hand down Nikita's back. "But, he's a super-hot distraction."

Nikita glared at her. "No."

"What? Just for a night?" She reached down and adjusted her breasts, so more cleavage stood out beneath the blue V-cut. "Hell, if you don't want him, I'll ride his— "

"Stop," she growled.

Giggling, Mandi shimmied her shoulders toward an incoming bar patron. "Fine, he'll do then."

She grabbed Mandi's wrist. "What're you doing?"

"If we don't act the part, they'll kick us out." Mandi's blue eyes went toward the group of Cutthroats Kevlar and Rubble recently sparred with. Each one diligently watched their movements, almost as if they were waiting for a fuck up.

Not wanting to put the operation in jeopardy, she released Mandi's wrist and forced a smile on her face. "Fine, just don't do anything with him."

"Please, I have a stash of nighty-night drugs in my back pocket. All I gotta do is slip one in his drink, and he'll have such sensual dreams, he won't remember what happened." Mandi flashed her a bright smile—the fake one she'd practiced on their way to Colorado—and led the Cutthroat member toward the back of the bar. It was the one place Nikita never wanted to visit if she could help it.

Like that'll happen. She swallowed another shot of tequila and stood. The room wobbled slightly, and she cursed herself for drinking. Escaping the bar before a biker grabbed her, Nikita hurried to the dollhouse and locked the door to her tiny room.

Falling face-first into the bedding that reeked of cigarette smoke, she sighed. Never in her wildest dreams had she guessed she would see Tucker Dorous. *No, he's Kevlar.* She rolled over and stared at the yellow-stained ceiling. He'd always been trouble, that much her parents said when she'd mentioned him in college. They'd refused to meet him, each stating it'd never work. Back then he was just in the military.

A repetitive thumping of the headboard in the room next door didn't bug her, but the faux moans made her frown. It was clear what they were getting into when they agreed to go undercover as Cutthroat dolls. The reality was much worse than she imagined.

Reaching under the mattress, she found her FBI

burner phone. It couldn't be traced even if a Cutthroat caught her with it. Sending a quick coded message to the Denver office, she shut it down after receiving the scheduled response.

A whiff of fresh cigarette smoke made it to her, how she wasn't sure, but she guessed the crack beneath the door let in the odor. For a brief moment, it reminded her of Kevlar. Not Tucker. He hadn't smoked when they were together. But tonight, the odor was evident on his leather cut.

Rubbing her lips together, she wondered what else he did differently. *Definitely not sex.* She blushed despite herself. *He can't get any better.* Back then, she'd only had two other men to compare him to. Still, she doubted the bad boy had honed his sexual prowess any more.

Seeing him excavated memories she'd buried deep. They all included her father. As badly as she wanted to tell Kevlar why she never showed up, the marshals hadn't let her. Once she and her mother were settled three months after they'd left, she'd dialed him but hung up before she could speak.

The wound from leaving New York had scabbed but never fully healed. Not even their closest relatives knew what happened to them after her father was convicted and tossed in prison. To her gratitude, she'd never buckled to visit him. She'd been tempted several times. Mostly when a case kept her up at night because of the connection to Diablos MC. She never gave in. It was her one consolation.

Kevlar's light-brown sugar-colored eyes swam in her mind. They were the same yet so different than the last time she saw them. They were hardened by the world but also held a hint of devilry. His body had changed, hardened over the years. Even without seeing what lay beneath his jeans and MC cut, she could tell his muscles were sculpted and ready for action. His hair was the same military cut. The shadow of scruff on his jaw and around his lips was new and extremely tempting.

Blowing a raspberry, Nikita shook her head. She couldn't succumb to Kevlar, no matter how much her hormones demanded it. *He's trouble with a capital T... or is it K now?*

The sounds from next door intensified, then dropped into silence. She had to give the man props for lasting as long as he did. She'd seen the girl in the room beside hers. She'd never crossed the sexuality line before, but the blonde with perfectly sized natural breasts and China blue eyes interested even her.

Damn, I need to get laid. She scurried beneath the

covers and made a mental note to buy a pair of noise-canceling headphones. If she were going to stay here for a while, she'd need them. Hearing sex sounds day after day would grind down her desire to ever have it again. *And that would be a tragedy.* Especially with the way Kevlar looked at her.

***

The common eating room for the Greenback Cutthroats dolls left much to be desired. The long picnic-style tables were plastic and almost as cheaply made as the plates and silverware. Taking care of their club whores wasn't high on the MC's list of things to do it seemed.

"So, how long you girls been here?"

Nikita glanced up from her plate of runny eggs and well-done sausage. "Just arrived last week." She nodded to Mandi. "We wanted to try something new."

"Ha! Don't try Scuttlebutt. He'll give you the rash something fierce," a lanky blonde said across the table.

Nikita did her damnedest to not laugh at the expression on Mandi's face. "Yeah, don't worry, we'll steer clear of that one." She took a bite of hash browns. "Any new faces around the club lately?"

"Other than you?" A busty redhead walked into

the room wearing only a bra and lacy thong. The indecency didn't faze her, but the toddler following the woman did. Nikita exchanged a glance with Mandi. They'd seen their fair share of MC children, but most were kept out of the club's main houses. Then again, they were at the dollhouse, not the clubhouse.

She offered a small smile. "Yeah, other than us."

The redhead plopped onto the bench and the table wobbled. "A few new MC men showed up a few months back. They've been back a few times. Stay in the clubhouse basement and speak some fancy language I ain't ever gonna learn."

"It's Spanish, Estelle," the woman next to Mandi said, sarcasm evident in her words. "And it's not fancy. It's common. Just like how you suck dick."

Estelle narrowed her green eyes. "At least I didn't get pregnant from banging all the Cutthroats in one night and not knowing who my baby daddy is."

The room erupted into a bout of name-calling and food splattering on the walls. Nikita choked on her orange juice and ducked before a pancake hit her in the forehead.

"Maybe, you should try to talk to the bikers," Juliet said under the hum of the room.

The two undercover agents glanced over to

where Juliet had suddenly appeared. She was looking worse for the wear but such could be said about most the dolls.

"That won't get us very far," Nikita said. "We need to find evidence."

Juliet's gaze flicked to the door then back to them. "They have a room in the basement that's usually got a guard by it. I can take you there and distract them long enough for you to look around."

Mandi exchanged a glance with Nikita then nodded. They couldn't stay undercover forever. The sooner they got intel the sooner they could take down the MC.

"Lead the way."

They followed Juliet closely, dodging the dolls in the room. They reached the hallway, and Nikita ran her fingers through her hair. Wherever they looked, bikers were found.

They made the short walk over to the Cutthroats clubhouse. Voices carried from the parking lot, smoke curling alongside the curses and innuendos when the men spotted them. A few whistled and catcalled. Mandi graced them with flirtatious winks, but Nikita stayed focused. If they needed to run, she'd be damned sure both of them made it out alive. Working undercover was her favorite thing to do, and she'd never lost a partner. She was not starting now.

Opening the side door, Juliet waved them in. The stench of stale cigarettes and spilled beer met them. Nikita scrunched her nose and was grateful when Juliet steered clear of the oncoming Cutthroats. They didn't seem to notice them anyhow, too involved in their conversation about an upcoming shipment. If they had better cover, Nikita would insist on listening.

Mandi tugged on her wrist, and she turned to see Juliet pointing to a door at the end of the hallway.

"I'll stay here in case someone comes by," Juliet said, practically shoving them toward the basement.

Nikita met Juliet's eyes and offered her silent thanks. Without this woman, they'd be no closer to finding out what the Greenback Cutthroats were really into.

Following her down the steep stairwell, Nikita slowly adjusted to the darkness. "Where the hell is the light?" she muttered, feeling the wall as they moved further into the pitch black.

"Ow! Son of a bitch!" Mandi stopped and Nikita ran into the back of her. "We're at the bottom."

Running her hand along the wall, she finally

found a switch. When she flipped it up, both women gasped at the basement's treasure.

"Drugs, how original." Mandi walked over and perused the tables full of narcotics. "Not too stingy either." She lifted a small, plastic bag. "This one is meth, but I see some cocaine over there too."

Nikita walked through the maze of drug tables, the door at the back of the basement her goal. "C'mon, we don't have much time."

Mandi nodded and set down the scale with a green leafy substance.

Nikita jutted her chin to the door. "If we get caught...."

"Play the whore, yeah, I know." Mandi teased

Nikita slowly cracked open the door and Mandi peeked in. "All clear," Mandi said, walking inside the room.

Glancing at the small space, Nikita spotted a wall safe tucked behind the big office desk. "Let's see what else they're hiding." She sat in the chair and started pulling open drawers. Typical office supplies met her gaze until she reached the lowest drawer on the right side. "Got your lock pick set?"

"As if I'd leave home without it." Mandi fished out her small kit and immediately started at the lock. Within seconds, it popped open. "Tada!"

Nikita slid the drawer open all the way and grinned. A large envelope sat alone. Snatching it, she poured out the contents on the table. Ledgers and appointment dates were scribbled across some pages, while detailed routes were noted on others. She didn't have the appropriate time to review it right then. They'd send it to the Denver office for analysis and keep a copy for themselves just in case.

"Get your phone ready. The Cutthroats will be back any time."

Mandi quickly took photos of the documents. Once done, Nikita carefully put the files back in place and locked the drawer behind them. "All right, let's get out of here."

Just as they made it out of the office, footsteps sounded on the staircase. "Who the fuck left the light on? You know I hate wasting electricity."

"Shit, that's Pillar." Nikita pushed Mandi to the left side of the room. They tucked into the underside of the staircase as the club president reached the bottom.

"Let's get this done. Our friends in the dollhouse sanctum want to see the goods and I'd rather not keep them waiting."

"What the hell happened to Juliet?"

Nikita shook her head, hoping their contact

wasn't lying on the floor above them with a broken neck.

"What was that?" a new voice asked.

Nikita gritted her teeth and Mandi grimaced. She mouthed, "Shit," but the damage was already done. Within seconds, the sheet they were hiding behind pulled back and they were face-to-face with three Cutthroats.

"Look what we have here." Pillar grabbed Nikita's wrist and pulled her out of the hiding spot. "You lost, sweetheart?"

"Nah, just looking for a score," Mandi improvised.

Pillar's dark eyes searched Nikita. "That right?"

She nodded. "Yeah, we're new, and one of the dolls said we could get something to take the edge off."

The three men chuckled. Pillar brushed back Nikita's hair. "Sounds like they're hazing our new girls." His gaze dipped to her chest, then returned to her face. "But believe me, sweet cheeks, none of this is for the taking. You gotta earn it." He licked his lips. "Want me to show you how?"

"I think we can figure that out." She forced a giggle and looked to Mandi, who was sweetly smiling at the man holding her tightly. "But we're late. They said we have orientation or some shit."

Pillar gradually loosened his grip. "Ah, yes. Juliet said she brought on two new dolls." He lightly kissed her mouth. "I look forward to tasting all that you and your friend have to offer."

Too stunned to move, Nikita stared at the MC president. "Maybe next time."

He chuckled darkly and grabbed her ass. "Don't let me catch you down here again. You won't like what'll happen."

Mandi hurried up the stairs first. Nikita followed at a slower rate, unable to take her eyes off the man who she was determined to put behind bars.

Chapter Seven

KEVLAR

HE WOKE IN A COLD SWEAT. SITTING UP, HE ADJUSTED his eyes to his surroundings. He was safe. *In the States.* Wiping off his brow, Kevlar swung his legs over the bed. The time he spent overseas continued to fuck with him. He could doze off or fall into a deep sleep and the horrors from the sandbox found him, nonetheless.

The phone on the bedside table lit up with an email, and he glanced at the time. Daybreak would be soon. *Might as well get up.* He slid on a pair of sweatpants and a sweatshirt. When he couldn't sleep, he hit the streets. Hell, when anything bothered him, he hit the streets. Whether on his feet or his bike, it was a tossup dependent on the weather.

As he laced up his shoes, he opted for the route

that would help the sweat already sliding down his abs make sense. He ran every morning since he joined the Army. His officer status hadn't stopped him from being one of the fittest men.

He made it outside as a hint of sunlight glowed behind the mountains. Setting a hasty pace, he tried not to think about the military. It would've been easier if his sweatshirt didn't have *Army* scrawled on it.

After getting into trouble as a teen, his parents decided he was better suited for military life. He couldn't disagree. Well, he tried, but a thirteen-year-old didn't have much say in the matter. They shipped him off to military school after military school. Some worked, others he got himself kicked out of.

Kevlar turned onto the main drag in Snowshoe, the streetlights blinking through their color patterns. He'd hated his parents for subjecting him to the military. Until he realized how much he loved the structure, dedication, and purpose. After that, he threw himself into the Army programs. If it were his lot in life to be an officer, he'd be the best damned one out there.

The coffee shop on the corner flipped on its lights, the owner yawning from inside. The sudden urge for caffeine sent his legs faster. A good cup of coffee would wake him up but he didn't have time. *Have to get all the sweat out of me before I get clean.*

Crossing the street, he pulled his cap lower on his head. He couldn't give in to stopping yet. He had another five miles to go. The light scent of jasmine drifted from nowhere. He glanced around, expecting to see Kita somewhere. Not one soul met his frantic gaze. She wore that same scent, and it still devastated him in the best ways.

His gut dropped. Seeing her the night before made him wonder what the hell happened. She looked hella fine fifteen years older. His dick jumped at the thought of the skimpy outfit she wore and the tattoos displayed so proudly. Those were new additions. They fit her perfectly too. She was a tomboy in college, but it appeared she somehow changed that tune. *And became a Cutthroat doll.*

Kevlar shook his head. His Kita would never lower herself to drop to such standards. The Cutthroats were dickheads and treated their dolls like shit. *Surely, she knew that before she walked through their doors.*

His legs started to ache, the fitness tracker on his wrist telling him he would be over his miles by the time he turned around. Finishing the sidewalk, he took the next left and started back towards the clubhouse. Seeing Kita brought up the past and his first deployment alongside it.

He bit the inside of his cheek, trying not to remember the horrid events that made him one of the best Army officer snipers. Usually, the officers weren't at the top of the combat groups, but he wasn't like the rest. The first tour in Iraq gave him his nickname. From that day forward, wearing his Kevlar vest was a necessity. It saved his life, and in return, he had the opportunity to save his entire squad, Rubble included.

His Macha brothers initially gave him shit, but when they faced off against the Greenback Cutthroats during one of his furloughs, even Reaper insisted he carried his military nickname into the club. He rubbed a hand against his chest, the battering of bullets ghosting him once more. His ten-mile run was the only time he didn't wear the vest out and about.

Kevlar picked up his pace, sweat dripping off his nose. Kita and the Army went hand in hand. He couldn't think of one and not the other. Her memory got him through each one of his deployments. Even though he'd never known what happened to her, he'd assumed she came to her senses and opted to pursue someone more worthy of her status. She was rich. *At least she used to be.* Her role in the dollhouse didn't make sense.

The clubhouse loomed in the distance, the sun finally shedding warmth on the valley between the mountains. He squinted, seeing Rubble and Hawk outside smoking already. While he craved a hit of nicotine, a hot shower and not thinking of Kita was in his near future. But not thinking of her was harder than he thought. Especially when every-where he looked, the memory of her gorgeous amber eyes stared back at him.

***

Seven days passed since he saw Kita at the Rusty Cantina. He'd scoured the streets for her and came up short each time. *Stop being stupid.* He couldn't help it. Rubble gave him hell, and more than once, a nymph tempted him to forget her. *She's someone from the past, not someone for your future.*

Kicking down the kickstand, he yanked off his helmet and plowed past the group of prospects waiting outside the clubhouse. The time illuminated on his screen, and he shoved his phone back in his pocket before walking to the room already full of

Macha members. Taking a seat, he nodded to Doc, then Hawk. He'd barely spoken to either of them the last week, too preoccupied with Kita.

"All right, let's get down to business." Their president, Reaper, pounded a small gavel and sat. "The Greenback Cutthroats are indeed working with the Diablos MC." A murmur of grunts echoed among the members. "That being said, Rubble and Kevlar are working an angle to get some info on their operations here in Colorado."

This was news to him. He glanced to the sergeant at arms, but the big man didn't look his way. *Coward.* Being tossed into an assignment didn't bother him. The part where he'd have to hunt down Kita—who clearly didn't want his help—did.

He barely paid attention to the remainder of church. Doc said a few words, but Kevlar didn't listen. The upcoming election of the new VP came up and interested him momentarily. They all knew who'd get it. Boulder, the secretary, and treasurer was a shoo-in for the position. *Then again, so is Rubble.* The role wouldn't be voted on until spring. Plenty of time for each man to gain votes.

The meeting ended like every one before it. "May the goddess ride with you," Prez said before hammering the solid gavel on the Macha emblem carved in the wood table.

Macha's men slowly filed out of the room, chatting as they left. He hung back, waiting for Rubble. When it was just the duo and Reaper, he spoke. "Why me?"

Reaper nodded to Hawk, who shut the door behind him. "I hear you have history with one of Cutthroat's dolls."

"Ancient history."

"History is history, boy-o." Reaper's wrinkled face drew back in a grin. "When women are involved, it's better to stick with someone they know instead of a new man."

He shook his head. "You don't know Kita. She looked ready to stab me herself last week."

Walking over to him, Reaper rested a hand on Kevlar's shoulder. His light shade of blue eyes bore into him. "You've made contact with her. We're going this route."

He looked to Rubble, who merely nodded once. The decision was already made. It'd do none of them any good to argue. Just like in the military, Macha ran on following orders 90 percent of the time. It used to reassure him. Now, it pissed him off.

"Rubble's put out some feelers about this Nikita

Morales of yours." Reaper stepped back and rubbed his arthritic left hand. It was only a matter of time before he stepped down too. "If she is related to Estevan Morales, this could be huge, Kevlar."

"I don't want her to be put in crosshairs. We don't know the full story here. The Nikita I knew wouldn't be caught dead in a brothel, let alone be one of the dolls for a MC." He rested a fist to the table. "Someone's using her."

Rubble and Reaper exchanged a glance. "It's very possible, but we can't act on it." He held up his hand when Kevlar opened his mouth. "Not until we know all the facts. Macha doesn't rush in. We gather information, make a plan, and execute said plan. You know from your time with Rubble he wouldn't put your girl in danger."

He didn't bother correcting Reaper. Nikita wasn't his girl, but in that moment, it was better than the alternative. She was his years ago, and he'd sure as fuck make her his again if only to keep her safe. Under Macha protection, she was safe. Under Cutthroats' control, she was a piece of ass.

"Fine, but only I make contact with her." He met Rubble's eyes. "Got it?"

"Yes, sir." Rubble smirked. "So bossy since your

return. If you didn't have a year left on your contract when I left, I would've dragged you back myself. Let's go before you pop your top." He wrapped an arm around Kevlar's neck and gave him a half-assed noogie.

Kevlar shot a glance over his shoulder at Reaper. The older man's soft smile and nod encouraged him slightly. He didn't trust anyone outside this MC. They were his family since he'd never been very close with his own blood.

"I got the perfect way for you to get close to Nikita without the Cutthroats giving you shit."

He eyed Rubble, already knowing what the man had brewing in his big head. "She'll kick my ass before she lets me anywhere near her."

Rubble chuckled. "I'm counting on it."

***

"You know what would be super-hot?" The group of bikers looked to Hawk. "Strippers that are twins."

Isa rolled her eyes and shot back her whiskey. "You're an eejit."

Hawk laughed. "What?" He nudged Cueball's side. "Think about it. Two identical gorgeous women with big knockers all over you." He sighed. "That's the dream, boys."

Klink snorted. "Last week, your dream was Italian chicks."

He shrugged. "What? I can't have more than one fantasy?"

Isa stood, taking Doc T with her. "Maybe try a fantasy that's actually attainable for you."

The table erupted in laughter, the sassy Irishwoman sashaying away with her man in tow.

Kevlar grabbed the next round of beers and passed them out at the table. "Seriously, though, Hawk. Maybe you should try hitting up one of the girls in town." He jutted his head toward a group of Snowshoe women dressed in short skirts despite the chilly weather.

"Yeah," Rubble joined in. "I'll bet one of them will ride your dick... after ten beers."

Laughter at Hawk's expense took over until the man finally stood. "Fuck you all. I'm getting some pussy tonight." He sauntered toward the group of women, and every head at the Macha table turned to watch. Sure enough, his easy smile and charming demeanor snared him not one but two of the blondes.

"Another two bite the dust," Boulder teased, waving at one of the nymphs. "I don't know about you, but I'm just drunk enough to want a lap dance."

He waved a twenty-dollar bill at the brunette, and she wasted no time earning it.

"You think Nikita's giving lap dances over at the Rusty Cantina?"

The gulp of beer somehow lodged in Kevlar's throat. He coughed and pounded on his chest, glaring at Rubble across the table. "Fuck off."

Rubble smirked. "What? Just wondering how that ass would look shaking in my face."

Kevlar licked his bottom lip and shook his head. "Keep going, tough guy, see where that gets you."

"Oh, please. We scuffled enough times overseas. You know I'll kick your ass."

Brewer chose that moment to arrive with shots of whiskey. "Now a good time?"

"Not really, but we'll take them," Boulder said, edging closer to the dancing nymph. He playfully swatted her ass.

Three more nymphs headed toward the back of the bar, Macha's domain. The residents of Snowshoe knew better than to cross into that territory. While the club didn't condone ill-treatment of anyone, things happened after a few rounds of Guinness.

Snoopy arrived with his old lady, Legs, clinging to his left arm. "Klink, somebody's at the tattoo shop asking for you."

The other man grunted and made his way through the dimly lit bar to the attached tattoo parlor.

"Who was it?" Boulder asked.

Sitting, Snoopy pulled Legs onto his lap. "Some chick from town." He shrugged. "Had a fine pair of tits, but that was about it."

Legs downed two shots of whiskey and rolled her eyes.

Kevlar barely knew the woman, but the one thing he knew, she rarely let Snoopy out of sight for long. The duo was practically glued to each other unless they were fighting, which was a daily occurrence too.

"So, you gonna get a lap dance from your girl, Kev?"

Narrowing his eyes, Kevlar sent a silent warning to his friend. The fucker just wouldn't let the subject die. The idea that Kita probably was shaking her ass for Cutthroat scum messed with his mind, but he wasn't about to let his brothers see how it affected him.

"Nah, got plenty of girls here." He waved at a redheaded nymph, and she started swaying to the beat of the country song, her teeny waist in his face. "See? Don't need to go anywhere else."

Rubble downed another shot and stood. His hulking stature drew more than one eye toward their group of bikers. It wasn't difficult to do. With tattoos covering his bald head and standing at six feet, six inches, body stacked in muscles, and a long beard, no one would think twice about fucking with him.

"Maybe you don't, but I think I'll head over to the Rusty Cantina and see what the Cutthroats have to offer." He winked at a nymph. "Obviously not as good as our girls, but I like to see all my options."

Boulder and Snoopy nodded in agreement, but Kevlar couldn't. *Not a chance in hell.* He finished his drink and caught up to Rubble. "I'll make sure you get there okay," he said.

"Sure, you will." Rubble slung an arm around his shoulder. By the time they drove to Waverley, the place was packed. With cheap drinks and even cheaper women, the bar brought in the worst clientele of the city.

Kevlar found a booth near the side door, an urge to smoke hitting him the instant they set foot inside. Rubble chatted up the bartender, buying drinks and flirting with any woman willing to listen.

Switching his focus, Kevlar watched the Cutthroat dolls mill about the busy bar. He'd seen a few around town and even in Snowshoe, but there were more new ones. A leggy woman stepped out from behind the curtained off area, and a lump rose in his throat. *Kita.*

She was sex on heels with her fishnet stockings, low cut green tank, and black mini skirt. His pulse quickened the longer he watched her flirt with the patrons. None of them deserved even a millisecond of her time, but she handed it out anyway.

The shorter woman with her the other night wasn't far behind Kita. She was a knockout too, but he only had eyes for Kita. The dolls dispersed into the throng, laughter prominent alongside squeals from the women.

His gut pitched at the thought of Kita being touched by another man. Shaking his head, he cursed himself. She wasn't his. She'd barely been his in the first place. He took the drink Rubble offered and turned away from the crowd. Skulking in his rum and Coke would have to do for the night. He'd sure as hell be going back to Booze and Tattoos for a nymph, though. If he couldn't have who he wanted, he'd numb his mind and body with someone else.

"How long you gonna wait to get that dance?" Rubble asked, humor lining his deep voice.

"Fuck off. I'm here to make sure you don't get in

too deep." He met his friend's gaze. "Macha doesn't need to stir the pot with the Cutthroats right now."

Rubble smoothed a hand over his beard. "That much I know." He chuckled. "I'm the goddamn sergeant, boyo," he said with a fake Irish lilt.

"Get your rocks off, then let's go." He sipped the drink and winced at the strength. Never again would he bash Brewer's cocktails.

"We're not here for me." Rubble lifted his arm and snapped his fingers. Moments later, two dolls rushed over, eager to please the big man. "Nah, girls, not you. I need the really tall one."

The dolls exchanged a look, then shrugged. Kevlar held his breath when they left, and Kita returned in their place.

"Somebody call for a lap dance?" she asked cheerily, face covered in makeup. It hid her natural beauty more than accentuated it, and Kevlar clamped his lips shut to keep silent.

"Yeah, my buddy here needs one bad."

Kita's neck turned and her amber eyes met his face. Panic initially lined her features, but she quickly hid it under a smile. "No problem."

The country music in the background hushed any response Kevlar could conjure. He shot a warning glare to Rubble, but the other man didn't stop ogling Kita. He didn't blame him. The way Kita's shirt clung to her chest, revealing perfect swells of her breasts, was hypnotic. As much as he wanted to enjoy the sway of her hips, his body refused.

"Look, you don't have to."

She whipped her hair from side to side seductively, leaning close to his face. "And you don't have to be here. I like what I do, Tucker."

"It's Kevlar." He ground his teeth together at the roll of her beautiful eyes. She was messing with him on purpose, and he fell for the trap.

"Me too, darlin'," Rubble said, tugging on her wrist.

Before Kevlar could react, Kita moved to the man next to him and started her routine all over. A group of Cutthroats caught his attention behind her. Each one eagerly watching Kita's dance, their eyes alight with lust. He swallowed hard, doing his damnedest not to let it bother him. But it did. He didn't like the idea of Kita lowering herself to the likes of the Cutthroats MC. *She's so much better than this.*

"Brother, you're supposed to be enjoying yourself," Rubble said, his voice rumbling with humor.

Looking over, he noticed Rubble's big hands on Kita's hips, and his stomach lurched. "Get your fucking hands off her."

Rubble lifted his brows but did as Kevlar said. Chuckling, he tucked a fifty-dollar bill in Kita's skirt and swatted her ass.

"You need to stop," Kita said under her voice, face strained. "I can handle this."

He gave Rubble a perplexed glance. "Handle what? You're a club whore, Kita." She narrowed her gaze, and he immediately saw his mistake. No way in hell was she a doll.

"Fuck you, Tucker," she all but growled before spinning on her heels and walking away.

He should've hated to watch her leave, but he didn't. Her plump ass sashaying in the other direction and fiery response only cemented his longing for her.

"Be careful, Kevlar. She's a loaded one." Rubble finished off his drink and stood. "Let's go. I have a craving for a redheaded nymph tonight."

Following him, Kevlar searched the bar for Kita but came up empty. She purposefully kept her distance. It didn't sit right with him. Then again, not being able to touch her didn't either.

Chapter Eight

"All you gotta do is bring them back and let 'em touch you a little."

Nikita's eyes remained fixed on Juliet. The woman looked ragged after a busy night. The bags under her eyes and caked-on makeup concealed the truth behind how the Cutthroats treated their dolls. It made her gut ache at the mere thought.

"If they get handsy, slip 'em a pill." Juliet nodded toward the ones the FBI supplied both their undercover agents. "Those things will fuck with their brains but not so much they suspect you did anything other than give them a good time."

She looked to Mandi, who seemed enraptured by the entire conversation. Nikita couldn't join in. There were too many risks, and the chance that one of the bikers got forceful kept humming in the back of her mind. She and Mandi were well-versed in self-defense, but even professionals made mistakes that were life-altering.

"We're hosting a masked event in honor of our guests," Juliet continued, handing them both masks.

"What guests?" Mandi asked.

Juliet ignored her. "These should keep your identities safe in case something goes wrong." She chuckled. "Hell, you could probably wear them every night to keep the men interested."

Mandi grabbed hers and tried it on. She looked incredible. Wearing a tight black dress that hit midthigh, she'd attract plenty of attention. Their goal was simple. Extract information from the MC members who visited them during dollhouse hours. Afterward, they'd supply their intel to headquarters and hopefully make a solid connection between the Greenback Cutthroats and Diablos MC. A grainy picture wasn't enough for her. It wasn't enough for the FBI either, which was why they were undercover instead of in a surveillance van. *The mystery guests must be Diablos.*

Nikita tried to pay attention as Juliet explained more club rules, but her mind was elsewhere. It was on their mission. After sending photos of the documents they found in the basement, neither she nor Mandi had heard back from the FBI analysts. She and Mandi poured over the photos for hours, but neither could decipher them. Puzzles were usually Mandi's forte, but these figures didn't add up.

Tugging on Nikita's hand, Juliet brought her back to the present. "Sweetie, you gotta change. Nobody wants a girl in sweats."

Lowering her eyes to the gray pants, she let out a nervous chuckle. "Sorry, yeah, I'll put on something sexier."

The masked party hadn't been on their radar. Normally, the MC only hosted club-associated events. Since Halloween wasn't far off, the party made sense, but Nikita guessed something more sinister was at work. Now that they knew guests were in attendance, it became clear.

Once Juliet left, Nikita rifled through the closet, looking for a skimpy outfit. *This'll fit, I bet.*

Nikita brought it closer and hoped to God it'd been recently cleaned. The scent of starch met her, and she nodded appreciatively. "They're either bringing in new players or meeting with a partner."

"That was my thought too." Mandi stopped applying eyeliner. "Think it's Diablos?"

She took the ruby red dress off the hanger. "I hope so. Then we'll get definitive proof for Boston."

Undressing fast, she barely got the dress over her wide hips. Food was just as important as exercise, and she had her mother to thank for her hips. "We need to figure out where they're holding the women so we can intercept. I don't like the idea of people being held like animals somewhere."

Looking into the mirror, she tried not to groan. The dress barely covered her nipples, let alone her voluptuous breasts. Another trait her mother passed down to her only child.

"My, oh, my. Don't you look the part?"

Fluffing her curled black hair, Nikita had to admit she looked damned good. "Gotta love under-cover work." She applied red lipstick to match the dress and finished the rest of the makeup before the party music echoed at the Cutthroat's cantina next to the dollhouse. The Hispanic motif didn't fit the town or the club, furthering her suspicions.

"You ready for this?" her partner asked, decked in black from head to toe.

Glancing in the mirror, Nikita looked at the two of them. They more than looked the part of MC dolls. "Not really, no."

"Neither am I, but that's the job." Mandi turned

on her stilettos. "Let's get this over with so we can go home."

Nikita nodded and pulled her mask in place. Nothing sounded better.

***

Their first night was a bust. Nikita fell into the stinking bed face-first, as had become routine. She'd flirted her ass off all night. Thankfully, Juliet kept many of the men happy with her own girls. It gave Mandi and her plenty of chances to glean small amounts of information from the big-mouthed bikers.

She checked her phone to see if the FBI had cracked the documents they'd sent. *Nothing. Great.* She heard the squeaking of bedsprings all around her. Thankfully, she and Mandi weren't on the menu.

Her eyes snapped to her door and sighed in relief when she saw it was locked. Her gun was hidden beneath the mattress and could be easily retrieved, but she didn't want to screw her cover before she got anything good out of the club.

The night's events drifted through her mind. They'd both thrown themselves into the façade of slutty dolls, but something felt off about the whole night. She wanted to blame Kevlar. He kept showing up, rattling her bottom line. Nikita shook her head. Something was wrong. She just couldn't put her finger on it. Thankfully, the night wasn't a total loss. One of the drunk bikers let information slip about a drug run the following week. She sent that information on to her boss, but he merely replied they needed the trafficking details to complete the bust.

She changed into something less sexy. Easy to do with sweatpants and a tank top. Crawling under the sheets, she prayed to whatever god or goddess that her bed was bug-free. Creepy crawlers weren't her friends. In fact, they were worse than rats to her.

Once settled on the bed, Kevlar's handsome face drifted to her mind. He'd looked damned good—tall, brooding, and with enough tattoos to make even her swoon. She rolled to her stomach, the thought of Kevlar warming her to her toes. Since seeing him again, a day didn't pass without wondering where he was or how he was doing.

She rolled to her stomach and recalled the one time she'd checked on him. He'd been deployed to an undisclosed location in the Middle East. Even her FBI clearance wouldn't let her see his exact whereabouts. His future had always made sense. He was built for the military. With smarts, sex appeal, and the ability to shoot a gun better than any other man, he was the Army's best asset. *But I am a little biased.*

A manly moan pierced the night air. She grimaced. Dating wasn't a necessity in her line of work, but sex was necessary if only to relieve stress and help her focus. She could make do without a man to help her along, but it was more fun to roll around the sheets with someone who could make it worth the effort of swiping right.

Heat flooded her body, her thoughts returning to Kevlar. They'd been incredible together. But that was so long ago. She bit her bottom lip. She didn't give a shit if it was fifty years. Kevlar could still fuck her until she trembled. No doubt about it.

She swallowed the truth. Even if the opportunity presented itself, it'd put her undercover role in danger. *And I can't do that.* She huffed out a frustrated breath. *Even if it'd be so nice.*

Groaning her displeasure with her hormones, she turned over and closed her eyes. The next night, the Cutthroats were hosting more visitors. She needed to be on her A-game. Tomorrow night could bring great things for their investigation, and if that were the case, she had to be prepared.

***

Slipping out of the dollhouse, Nikita zipped her

leather jacket then pulled back her hair into a pony-tail. The keys in her pocket jingled as she walked toward the motorcycles lining the parking lot. Swiping the keyring hadn't been too difficult but finding the matching bike proved to be a bit of a challenge. Nevertheless, ten minutes later, she strad-dled the lime green Kawasaki and eased out into the dark night. She'd be back before anyone noticed their bike was missing.

Opening the engine, she grinned at the screaming sound it released into the silence. She didn't bother to stop for the blinking yellow light at the intersection. Instead, she cranked the throttle, her body vibrating as the speed increased. This was what she'd been needing. *Screw sex. I'll take the motorcycle ride any day.*

The road curved to the left and she expertly leaned into the turn. A car passed in the opposite direction, the lights mere dots at her speed. Glancing at the speedometer, she smirked and waited until she hit one hundred miles per hour before she let up on the gas. One thing her childhood taught her was to respect motorcycles but also have fun with them, and with her FBI job focused on MCs, she had the opportunity to do exactly that whenever the chance presented.

The cool air crept to her fingers, and she swore silently. She didn't have her usual gear, and if she stayed out much longer, her fingers would be useless soon. Slowing at the top of a bluff, she stopped and noticed the twinkling lights of Snowshoe. The sleepy city lay perfectly safe between the Rocky Mountains.

Kevlar is down there somewhere.

She swallowed her first urge to drive down and find him at the Macha clubhouse. The research she'd done on Macha told her they were a unique kind of club. They weren't on the news much for any reason and they stayed off the FBI's radar. That alone told her they were different. Macha had beef with the Greenback Cutthroats. When the bikers came head-to-head at the bar, no one batted an eye. The reason behind their hatred wasn't as clear. That was more common with clubs. MCs kept secrets. Sometimes they were small ones, but in her experience, they were horrific and likely to get someone killed.

Nikita shifted on the bike. Not thinking about Kevlar was harder when she looked down at his hometown. But she couldn't get involved. She knew what happened in clubs. Men rarely stayed faithful to their old lady. She'd seen that plenty in Diablos and every MC she investigated as an adult.

Rubbing her hands together, she shook her head and turned the bike. By the time she arrived back at the dollhouse, her nerves would be back to normal. She could do this OP even with Kevlar in the next town over tempting her.

Chapter Nine

KEVLAR

THRUSTING ONE LAST TIME, KEVLAR EMPTIED HIS LOAD into the nymph and let out a low growl. Fucking without feelings got redundant, but it was necessary to keep his mind clear. Clear of Kita.

He pulled up his pants, shirt still in place. He didn't fully undress with the club nymphs. It was a rare occasion when he had sex with them more than once. His eyes caught sight of the woman with jet-black hair and golden eyes. But this one reminded him of Kita. If he couldn't have Kita to himself, he'd get her out of his system another way.

"You wanna do this again?" the nymph asked, body splayed out on her bed. There was no way he'd let her into his room. That was his place to escape.

"Yeah, maybe." He offered her a small smile. She

truly was gorgeous in her own special way. *But she's not Kita.*

Stepping out of the room, he nodded at Dolly, the nymph wrangler, as the men liked to tease her. She was tattooed similarly to Kita and had the same kickass attitude that turned him on. But Dolly wasn't a nymph. Sure, she fucked the club members here and there but only at her bidding.

"Always a pleasure to see you, Kevlar," Dolly said, sipping her cup of what smelled like Earl Grey tea. "Your pleasure."

He didn't reply. Instead, he took the stairs two at a time, trying to get the recent fuck off his mind. The nymph was good. Did what she was paid to do. Nothing more, nothing less. It'd helped minimally clear his thoughts. In less than an hour, he and Rubble would visit the Rusty Cantina, and he needed to be sharp. *Seeing Kita won't be a problem.* He swore it to his president and brothers. He'd successfully lived through a war, so seeing his ex was nothing. He had to keep telling himself this, so it'd be true. The problem was, he didn't believe one word.

"Have a fun day?" Brewer teased when he walked into the kitchen.

"Just as fun as yours." Kevlar grabbed a coffee mug and filled it, grateful the dark brew was always fresh no matter what the time. "My nymph happened to mention you were having yourself a nice ménage two doors down." Kevlar smirked at the gloating in the other man's face.

"What can I say? I can please two women at once. It's a gift." Brewer lifted his cup in salute. "Dolly says you been downstairs a lot. You're not taking over Doc's role as fuckboy, are you?"

Kevlar recalled the recently patched Doc who, up until he fell for a Macha princess, had a reputation of fucking numerous nymphs in hearty succession.

"Not that it's any of your business, but no." He shook his head. "Just trying to get somebody out of my head."

Brewer snorted. "Good luck with that."

Kevlar offered him a cocked brow.

"Once a woman embeds in your brain, it's nearly impossible to get her out," the other man explained.

"Speaking from personal experience?"

"Who me?" He chuckled. "Uh, no. I don't get attached."

"That's a pity."

"It is what it is." Brewer grabbed an apple from the basket on the counter. "Try not to do anything I wouldn't tonight."

Kevlar watched the other man walk through the kitchen and start chatting with Cueball. Before long, the two were playing pool, two nymphs hanging off their poles—cue for the time being.

"You ready for this?" Rubble asked, the sun long set on the horizon.

Glancing at the other man dressed down, no Macha cut in sight, Kevlar nodded. They'd go incognito at the bar. The goal was twofold for him. Of course, there was his club role, but he also needed to pull Kita aside and talk to her. Once he figured out what the hell was going on, he could accept it. He frowned. *Probably. Maybe.* He shook his head. *Not a fucking chance.*

Chapter Ten

AN HOUR PASSED INTO THREE. NIKITA RECEIVED tidbits of gossip from the bikers and bar locals, the old ladies, and fellow dolls, but none solid enough to act upon.

The twenties-style party was complete with jazz music and plates of finger food served by club girls. None of the visitors looked familiar to her. Judging from the way Mandi shook her head, the same was said for her. They were at a loss, and the longer the MC members drank, the more dangerous the night became for them. More than one doll was ushered into one of the back rooms. The screams one of the girls made after a visitor had his fill put them both on edge.

These bikers wouldn't respect their wishes or

stop until they were sated. It was why she hated motorcycle clubs so much. The men were assholes and treated women as possessions. She'd endured enough of that under her father's hand and wouldn't allow it for others if given the opportunity.

Swallowing hard, she sipped her martini and watched the players around the room. The Cutthroats' president, Pillar, hadn't moved from his booth all night. He spoke to a man who she guessed to be a high-ranking member of Diablos. She couldn't bet on it since he wore a suit and not a cut, so she slowly made her way around the room.

Feigning flirtations with a drunk Cutthroat in the booth next to Pillar's, she picked up on some of their conversation.

"I was assured there wouldn't be any problems," the man with a thick Spanish accent said.

"And there aren't," Pillar replied. "Macha is oblivious to our plans. We'll get your shipment moved within the month, then you can see we're the right club to continue with."

Nikita's heart jumped at the words. She waved at the biker's offer for another drink. The man left and returned minutes later, sliding around the crescent-moon booth until he was directly next to her. The pressure on her upper thigh didn't bother her. The annoying jabber did. She could ignore both for the time being.

"Muerte expects no less."

"Look, man, why don't you enjoy yourself? We got plenty of hot dolls who'll love to give you some attention."

"I'm not here to ride whores, Pillar. I'm here to make sure you don't fuck up."

The handsy Cutthroat next to her slid his fingers up her dress, creeping closer to the blue thong she'd donned hours earlier. Carefully, pushing him away, Nikita offered the drunk a sweet smile. If he didn't stop pestering, she'd need to take him to the back room to avoid a scene. Bringing attention to herself wasn't a good idea. With her caramel-colored skin and midnight black hair, Pillar's visitor may want to investigate.

"Where are you keeping the shipment?"

She heard the telltale sound of a lighter and the scent of smoke wafted to her.

"Outside Snowshoe. Right under Macha's nose."

Her eyes bugged. *So that's how they're keeping it so secretive.*

"Good. If this backfires, at least we'll get rid of a rival MC."

A foreign sensation trailed her neck, slimy, and

demanding. She hadn't even felt the biker's lips until then, her mind too occupied with the conversation. Turning back to the man, she held back her disgust at the slobbering lush.

He handed her a shot of vodka and she absently took it to appease him. Cocking her head, she listened for more, but Pillar and his guest were speaking in hushed tones. The biker pulled her to him, the scent of tobacco strong on his breath. Her stomach swirled, and when her vision started to blur, she frowned. She'd drank two beers and could hold her own, but at the moment, her eyelids felt heavy. Blinking furiously, she calmed when her eyes cleared.

"Want to take this to the back?" he slurred. She absently nodded, needing to get out of there fast before she drew attention. The sooner she snuck away from him, the sooner she could hurry back to the party to hear the rest of Pillar's plan. Her pulse quickened and her tongue swelled. Something didn't feel right.

Sliding from the booth, she was disappointed but unsurprised when the man followed. Her hope of him passing out on his own didn't appear to be on the horizon. The allure of pussy did that to a man. She rolled her eyes and fought the urge to knee him in the balls when his hand drifted over her ass.

The room seemed darker, the hum from the speakers louder. The Cutthroat slung his arm around her shoulders, steering her in a different direction. The drugs in her back pocket wouldn't work without liquid. Taking a step, she faltered and held out her hands to steady herself. The one shot and beer wouldn't affect her this much. Holding her liquor was a personal feat.

Fuck, he must've drugged me. She glanced around the area but didn't see Mandi. *Shit, where is she?*

"Let's go, doll," the Cutthroat garbled, tugging her behind a curtained-off area. She didn't have a chance to convince him otherwise before his lips crashed on hers. Every muscle in her body urged her to smash his face in. He pressed her against him, his grip tighter than she anticipated for a man well into his cups. The telling sign of his arousal poked her leg, the shorter man determined to get what the MC dolls promised.

Nikita managed to pull away from his mouth. The biker responded by smacking her face hard with the back of his hand. Reeling backward, she gasped at the sudden show of violence.

"Spread your legs, doll. Your pretty pussy is in for

a treat." He pointed to the small couch and unzipped his jeans.

"Why don't we have another drink?" she offered, seeing glasses and bottled water nearby.

The Cutthroat grabbed her by the throat, and she fought for breath. His hold was much stronger than she expected. "A feisty one. Just my type."

She opened her mouth to scream, but no sound escaped. Nervous sweat beaded on her brow. All her training flashed through her mind, but the more he maintained pressure on her throat, the less it made sense. Black crowded her vision, closing in quickly. She clawed at his flesh, her attempts futile the longer he choked her.

Her body suddenly collided with the couch and cool air trailed her thighs. Whatever he put in her drink was suddenly hitting her like a diesel semi. She blinked, but he was fuzzier by the moment. Battling him, she winced when he slapped her hands away and pressed them into the couch cushion. Hands pinned, she tried to kick him, but her legs refused to obey.

"I don't mind if you scream," he whispered, running his hands over her breasts. "In fact, if you struggle a bit, that actually helps."

Nikita didn't know how to react. Her mind yelled

at her to do something, but her body had gone dormant. The familiar crinkling of a condom wrapper made the rosary whir in her mind. She hadn't said a prayer in years, but suddenly it was all she could recite.

"Get the fuck away from her unless you want your dick shot off," a deep male voice growled above her drug-induced haze.

She squinted and made out a second man in the room, pulling the Cutthroat away from her. The two scuffled, punches being thrown between them. She couldn't make out the parties, head wobbling and body heavy.

Finally, what sounded like a giant toppling to the floor met her, and she sat up. One body was motionless in the corner, the other hovering over to make sure he was down. The victor swiveled toward her and ran a hand over his head. She inhaled sharply, that act alone difficult.

"Goddammit, Kita."

Her vision began to clear, the drug's haze slowly wearing off thanks to the adrenaline coursing through her system. Now, she recognized him. "Tucker?" She coughed and cringed at the pain that caused. Her throat throbbed from where the biker had gripped her. She lifted a hand to it and winced at the bruising already forming.

A guttural sound resonated from his lips, and he easily pulled her off the couch and into his arms.

"What the hell were you...." He shook his head, his face masked in frustration. "Never mind. Let's get you out of here before another dumbass tries to rape you."

"I had it under control," she argued, the words hoarse.

Kevlar looked down at her. "Mmhmm. I see that."

She cuddled against his chest, the cigarette smoke on his shirt suddenly overpowered by a more familiar one. It was one she'd never smelled after her freshman year of college but desperately craved for years.

"What the hell happened? I turned around and you were gone," a new voice joined. "Jesus Christ, Kev, this wasn't the plan, brother."

Opening her eyes, she was surprised to see them outside. *How'd we get here?* She slowly felt the world returning to normal.

"I couldn't just let her get...." Kevlar's voice dropped off. "We'll try again."

The other man grunted. "I'm staying. You get her to the clubhouse and, for the love of the goddess, figure out what the fuck is going on with her. Macha can't have you losing your head every time this girl is around."

A door slammed—the bar door. She recognized the squeak and jazz music inside.

"Can you hold on to me?" Kevlar set her down on the back of a Harley.

"I don't know, maybe." She ran her fingers along the leather, the sensation bringing her back to reality. Her entire body ached, but she didn't feel so helpless now. Her arms locked around his waist, her head clearing the longer she was in the fresh air. Whatever the Cutthroat had slipped in her drink wasn't lasting long in her system. She couldn't send enough prayers of gratitude heavenward.

He mumbled under his breath, and before she could ask him anything else, the bike rumbled beneath her, night air tickling her face. Nuzzling her nose against his back, she let the cold air on her face wake her from the drug's stupor.

Chapter Eleven

KEVLAR

It was a dumbass move. He knew the moment he stepped into the Rusty Cantina it'd be trouble. Nevertheless, he'd gone. His club needed him to investigate. He hadn't expected to see Kita there dressed to kill. He couldn't think about what would've happened if he didn't show up.

Hours later, he watched her chest rise then fall, her pitch-black hair a stark contrast to his white pillowcase. He and Rubble arrived shortly before Nikita and her friend made an appearance. Both were knockouts, but Kita above all else in the room. She wore a mask, but he'd recognize her body anywhere. Shapely and too much shown for the sleazy Cutthroats to drool over.

He'd kept his distance, there for recon and not to

engage. One beer in him, he saw Kita sneak away to the back of the room. He followed, mindful to keep a low profile. Both he and Rubble weren't wearing Macha cuts, the goal to remain invisible. She set up camp next to Pillar's booth. An odd choice, he'd initially thought. It became blatantly clear she was listening to the conversation the MC president was having with an unfamiliar man.

Hope had filled his body. She wasn't a doll like she pretended. There was a purpose behind her madness. He just needed to figure out what it was.

Kevlar pulled apart his handgun and mindlessly cleaned it. The act soothed his nerves and tampered the urge to shake Kita's shoulders until she woke and spilled the truth. He could wait. He *would* wait.

After spending years in deserts doing exactly that, he'd built up a reserve of patience. But when he saw Kita being dragged to a back room with an extremely handsy Cutthroat, he couldn't stay idle. *Damn glad I didn't either.*

Kita stirred in the bed and his eyes darted up. She didn't wake. He was fine with that. He wasn't sure what to say when she did. The blue excuse for a dress caught the corner of his eye. The Cutthroat ripped it the night before. Thankfully, Macha's madame, Dolly, helped him with Kita when he burst through the clubhouse door with her in his arms. Dolly took over, giving him a chance to down two shots of whiskey to settle his shaking hands.

Dolly eased Kita's drug-idled body out of the dress and into his bed. He hadn't left her side since. Not even when Doc, the club's resident doctor, checked her over. The man swore she hadn't been injured, but Kevlar wasn't so sure. The purple bruising on her face and red marks around her neck made him sick. Any man who could do that to a woman didn't deserve to live.

He finished cleaning the gun and reassembled it. The time on the wall mirrored what his stomach told him. *Missed breakfast and lunch.* He'd do it every day if it meant he kept Kita safe. He counted the bullets in his gun. One of them would've ended up in the Cutthroat's head if the other man hadn't fallen the fuck down after their scuffle. He shivered at the alternative possibilities the night could've brought.

Her loopy words the night before flooded his mind. *She has a motorcycle.* That didn't shock him in the least. In college, she used to drive an old Harley. He used to think it was so badass for a girl to ride one. *I wonder if it's the same one.*

He made a mental note to ask her later. A low groan came from the woman wrapped in nothing but a sheet. Whipping his eyes to Kita, he sighed, and his anxiety lessened. She slowly cracked open her eyelids and scanned the room. When she landed on him, a little *yip* slipped from her mouth. He tried not to chuckle, but it was too damned cute.

"Welcome back to earth." He rested his handgun on the bedside table, tilting his head.

"The fucker drugged me."

"Yeah, you saw lots of pretty unicorns on the way back to the clubhouse. It was quite the trip. Literally." His smile faded. "Doc guessed it was a roofie laced with something else."

She sat up. "Who?"

"Our club doctor." He handed her a bottle of water. It was lukewarm, but she took it, nevertheless.

"Oh." She greedily drank the water, droplets trickling down her chest. He didn't bother to look away. He'd seen it all before anyhow.

Her eyes dipped to her state of undress. "Did you...?"

"No. Dolly did."

"Dolly?"

"Our club madame." He nodded to the dress. "I didn't think that thing would be comfortable while you slept."

"Thanks." She didn't scurry under the covers like

most girls. She'd never been ashamed of her body. It was one of his favorite things about her.

She used to dance around naked. The memory flashed to him and he tried to put it aside. *That was then. This is now.*

"How're you feeling?"

Kita pulled her knees up and hugged them. "Horrible headache, but overall okay." Her gaze fell to him, the amber depths another favorite thing about her. "How'd you know I needed help?"

He wiped his hands on his jeans. "Rubble and I were there for recon. We think the Greenback Cutthroats joined up with Diablos MC." Her slight frown made him study her face. The way she wouldn't hold his gaze ripped him apart. "You knew this."

She slowly nodded. "It's the reason I'm here. Why Mandi and I are here."

He frowned. "What do you mean?"

Moving to the end of the bed, she stood up with no regard for her nakedness, save a blue lacy thong. For the first time, he let his eyes graze her body. Her slender shoulders tempted him to reach out and touch, but the ornate shapes were what truly drew him in. Tattoos covered almost every inch of her skin. He frowned at the lack of color. They were all black and white. Not one colored tat. If he didn't already have feelings for her, seeing her artwork would get him there. But it wasn't merely the tattoos. Plenty of girls around MCs had them. It was one in particular he couldn't look away from.

"Kita."

She glanced over her shoulder, dark hair framing her cheek.

Getting to his feet, he crossed the small room. Slowly, he lifted his hand and traced the military dog tags complete with his service number engraved on her right shoulder blade. "You didn't forget me."

"Forget you?" Incredulous, she shook her head. "How could I forget you?" She let out a shaky breath. "You were everything to me."

Replacing his fingertips with his lips, Kevlar didn't stop after kissing the tattoo meant to remind her of him. The feelings he stored away in the vault of his heart broke free. Grabbing her hips, he continued to kiss across her back, the tattoos' stories he desperately wanted to hear.

Kita turned around abruptly and grabbed his face, pressing her lips to his. Wrapping his arms around her shoulders, he hugged her closer, his lips overwhelming her kisses with his own. It felt right. It felt like they'd never lost any time.

Sitting on the bed, he pulled her onto his lap, encouraged when she didn't break away. With her body flush to his, her breasts tempted him to break the connection. But he couldn't. He had fifteen years of pent-up desire for this woman. He couldn't unlock their lips until he was certain she wouldn't disappear into thin air once more.

Kita's fingers scraped his head, the slight pain from her nails turning him on more. She moaned into his mouth, her tongue matching the way her hips ground into him. Already, he could smell her arousal, sweet and musky.

"All righty, I'm here to check on our visitor."

When Kita broke free, Kevlar cursed Doc's timing. She fumbled off his lap to stand.

"I can come back later if you want." Doc looked at Kita, then him, curiosity in his blue gaze. There was also a hint of humor that made Kevlar frown.

"No, it's fine," she rushed to say. "Old friends catching up."

Doc snorted. "That's not how I catch up with friends." He smirked. "But then again, I don't have many old friends I'd kiss."

Clearing his throat, Kevlar looked to Kita but was disappointed when she didn't meet his gaze. Her hands went to her breasts and he was grateful Doc looked away. "I'll grab some food."

He escaped the room and awkward silence, cursing at himself all the way to the kitchen. His plan was to question her about the night before, not kiss her. When it came to Nikita, he was lost.

***

"So, you gonna tell us the story?"

Kevlar looked up from his cup of coffee and met Brewer's blue eyes. Two sandwiches sat on the coffee table, neither looking appetizing in the moment.

"About what?" He noticed Dolly step into the den, her usual high ponytail swishing back and forth in tempo with her eyes.

"About the girl you clearly have a thing for." Dolly walked over to the couch and unceremoniously sat next to him. "She's a pretty one too. I hear Rubble mention she's a Cutthroat doll."

Brewer's brows lifted. "Oh, really?" He took the recliner opposite the couch. "Tell all, brother."

Contemplating simply standing and flipping them the bird, the idea left Kevlar the moment he realized how much Kita meant to him.

He placed the empty cup on the coffee table and folded his arms over his chest. If he was going to talk about Kita, he could trust these two to keep their mouths shut.

"I knew her back in the day. Rubble and I came across her at the cantina. I noticed a Cutthroat getting aggressive so I—"

"Saved the day like a hero," Dolly finished, a secretive smile on her ruby red lips. She could pull off any shade of lipstick with her dark hair and bold blue eyes.

He smirked. "Something like that, yeah."

Brewer shook his head. "Macha would be proud." He glanced around the room. "But between the three of us, were you just scoping out the nymph competition?"

"Please, those girls have nothing on my nymphs." Dolly laughed, rolling her eyes.

"Dolly's right, of course." Kevlar nodded at the club madame. "But there's something special about Kita. She's the real thing."

He noticed Brewer exchange a glance with his sister. "Uh-oh. Somebody's thinking with his little head."

"Who said it was little?" Rubble said, entering the room, a tumbler of whiskey in hand. "Hell, I've seen it a time or two. It's not so little."

"Are you seriously complimenting my dick right now?" Kevlar shook his head, laughing.

"Fuck you. I was making conversation." Rubble finished his whiskey in one swallow, prompting Brewer to grab a bottle from the bar and return moments later to refill it.

"You like this girl then?" Dolly asked after they all had a glass of whiskey in hand.

Kevlar considered the question. He'd always liked Kita. She was feisty and one of a kind. "I'm worried about her. Anyone under a Cutthroat roof isn't good, and I know Kita's a smart girl."

"You think she's playing an angle?" Brewer asked, slowly sipping his drink.

"It's possible, but which one?" He let out a frustrated breath. "I'd feel better if she told me what's going on."

Dolly stood and moved to the door. "You don't think she's actually a doll?"

"No, definitely not."

"What happens if she really is?"

Kevlar met Dolly's gaze. "I'll deal with it. As long as she's safe and happy, that's all I care about."

"Spoken like a true Macha man," Rubble said, raising his glass in salute.

Finishing off his whiskey, Kevlar couldn't help

but wonder if Rubble was right. Their patron goddess was strict on treating women properly. With Kita, he wasn't sure how to treat her. On the one hand, he wanted to shake her shoulders until she spilled the truth. On the other, he wanted to trust that she knew what the hell she was doing. He reached for the whiskey bottle. Neither option sounded good now, but whiskey... whiskey always sounded good.

Chapter Twelve

NIKITA

"Thought you could use a fresh set of clothes."

Nikita eyed the tall man with shaggy blond hair. "Thanks."

Doc shrugged, his cut hugging his shoulders at the act. "No problem. My girl had a few that should work. You're about the same size."

She pulled out a sweatshirt and pair of jeans. They looked dead-on. "Very nice of her."

"Nah, that's just Isa. She likes to help whenever she can." His smile emitted a combination of pride and adoration. "Plus, she'd absolutely love to dress you."

"Huh?"

He chuckled, his face tinting pink. "Sorry, probably sounded creepy. She's a clothing designer."

"Oh." She offered him a smile. "I'm sure we'd get along."

Doc grinned. "I'm very certain you would. She's around the clubhouse somewhere. I'm sure she'll pop in on ya sooner or later." His expression shifted to that of a medical professional so fast she almost laughed. "Now, how're you feeling? Any soreness or pain? Kevlar was pretty animated last night when he arrived."

Heat crawled up her body. "No, I'm good. The guy got a little rough." She hadn't dared look in a mirror yet. The left side of her face seemed to have a pulse from the Cutthroat's backhand. Her throat was raw, but she couldn't decide if it was from choking or drugs.

Tenderly, Doc examined her neck and face. "You'll heal, but not as quickly as you'd like." He handed her a small pill. "This is in case the guy— "

"He didn't get that far."

"Oh, okay." He nodded and stood. "Keep it nonetheless."

"I'm not a club whore."

Doc offered her a shrewd smile. "It's none of my business, but Kevlar is. He helped save my girl, and I owe him. Just want to look out for my brother."

Nikita silently swore. No matter what she said,

he wouldn't believe her. It didn't matter. She told Kevlar she wasn't a club girl, and his opinion was all she cared about.

"Sure. Thanks for your help."

Once he left, she searched the rest of the bag. Underwear with tags was the last item. *Shower, I need a shower.* She couldn't even think about what the scumbag almost did to her the night before or how she'd been too drugged to stop it.

Opening the door, she poked her head out and looked up and down the hallway.

"Searching for somebody?" a voice asked, coming around the corner. His shock of red hair and easy smile put her at ease. Which one toppled over into comfort, she wasn't sure.

"More like a place to shower."

"Down the hall to the left. They're communal, so you've been warned." He jerked a thumb over his shoulder. "The nymphs have private showers if that's more your style." He held out his hand. "I'm Brewer by the way."

"A shower is a shower, don't care where." She shook his hand. "Nikita."

The name seemed to ring a bell. "Kevlar's Nikita?"

"Not sure I'd say that, but...." She shrugged. Once upon a time, she was Kevlar's. "Towels?"

"Closet by the showers." Brewer leaned against the wall and crossed his arms over his chest. "Does he know you're sneaking out?"

She gave him an annoyed glance. "I'm not sneaking anywhere."

"Sure."

Stomping down the hall, she smirked at Brewer's sharp inhale at seeing her state of undress. She had nothing but a thong on and sure as hell wasn't going to put on the blue dress to walk to the showers.

Thirty minutes later, she didn't want to step away from the scalding water. It did nothing to remove the memories of the Cutthroat's lips and hands on her flesh. Tears mingled with water, scrubbing harder with the bar soap she'd found in the closet. Tidbits of the night before crashed her mind, overwhelming her with regret, frustration, and anger. She could've done something different. Could've worn a less slutty dress. Could've kicked the bastard in the balls. It all hit her at once. A variable ending to a reckless operation. She was too consumed with revenge to keep up her guard.

"Kita, oh, baby."

She lifted her eyes, and fresh tears gushed at the sight of Kevlar's concerned face. He stood outside the stall, too damned perfect with his kind, brown eyes. The memories from the night before washed over her. Suddenly, she wasn't the badass FBI agent who didn't give a shit if someone saw her naked. She was merely a woman who'd been battered and almost raped. She was always strong, but the Cutthroat stole that from her. He took her confidence and choked her with it. Hot tears dripped down her chin. She'd been stripped of her control and couldn't protect herself.

"Don't look at me." She tried to cover herself, the ugly bruises from the handsy biker taking their toll in her mind.

Turning off the water, Kevlar crouched beside her. He pushed the hair plastered to her face behind her shoulders. It was then she realized exactly how she looked. She sat on the floor, hugging her knees, not giving a damn about the water burning her skin.

"Don't let that bastard win. You didn't do anything wrong, Kita," he said as if jumping into her thoughts. Pulling her up, he wrapped a towel around her shoulders. "You're safe."

Keeping her eyes fixed on her toes, she shook her head. She wasn't safe. Her role wasn't over. She had to return to the dollhouse and to the inevitable backlash from the night's events.

She didn't remember walking back to his room. Didn't remember falling into his bed or drifting off to sleep in his arms. All she could remember was what her father once said. *"If you leave Diablos, they'll come for you, mija."* She didn't want to believe it, but suddenly she did.

***

"Oh my God, Nikita, you're back!" Mandi pulled her in for a bear hug, a catchy Rihanna song blaring in the earbud hanging around her neck.

Nikita winced at the gruff embrace but patted her friend's back, nonetheless. "Of course. Where else would I go?"

Mandi held her at arm's length. "What happened? One minute you were here and the next, I couldn't find you." Mandi pointed to her face. "What happened there?"

She gently grazed the bruise she'd attempted to hide with makeup. "One of the guys got a little too friendly."

"But you're okay? Otherwise, I will open a can of whoop-ass—"

"I'm fine, Chuck Norris, jeez." She smirked. "Just need to put extra makeup on it."

She sat cross-legged on the bed. "What happened with you? Get anything good?"

The other woman started in on her escapades and what information she'd found out from the bikers. Nikita shivered, burrowing deeper in the sweatshirt. It smelled like Kevlar. The man invaded her mind at every inhale. No doubt, he'd be pissed when he discovered she snuck out of Macha's clubhouse, but she had to leave before she let herself get tangled in him once more.

Kevlar had quietly left while she napped. When she'd woken, his voice had drawn her into a large room where he and three other men played pool. For one hot second, she almost stayed. Then reality had crept back in, and she'd tiptoed out and into the darkness. She'd caught a ride from a Cutthroat returning after a night with his girl in Snowshoe.

"So, then I told the fucker to get the hell out. You should've seen his face. Priceless."

Nikita switched gears. "Then did you get any details about the trafficking?"

Mandi scrunched her brows together. "Weren't you listening?"

"Not exactly."

She barked out a laugh. "It's cool. I'm a little murky too." Mandi glanced around the room and lowered her voice. "The MC has three men rotating watch over where they're keeping a 'special package' according to one of the members from last night. What about you? Find out anything juicy?"

"Um, yeah." She cleared her mind of the assault. "Pillar said they're keeping it in Snowshoe, so if the police or Feds find it, they'll suspect Macha."

"Good, I'll call in tomorrow and let boss man know what we heard. Oh, Juliet said they're having another party tonight."

"Another one?" Her heart sank at the prompt nod in response. "Don't they ever stop partying?" She wasn't sure she could handle a repeat. Not this soon. She needed time to recover. *I should've stayed with Kevlar.*

Standing up, she found her burner cell phone and sent a message to her boss. If Kevlar kept showing up, eventually someone would get hurt. She'd never forgive herself if he was caught in the crosshairs of her war. Opening a new message, she sent a text to one of her friends at the main office. She needed to read her notes about Macha MC. If they were trustworthy, it wouldn't be a stretch to include them on the OP. Her mind spun back to Kevlar. He'd promised he could be trusted, but she wasn't sure what to believe. Neither of them was the same person as fifteen years ago. It wasn't just her life on the line anymore. She had to think about Mandi.

Seeing the encrypted reply from the tech on the other end of the text message, Nikita powered down the device. She'd have her notes by morning. Then and only then would she think about bringing Macha in on the FBI's sting. No matter what happened, she'd keep the people she loved safe.

***

"Your code has been verified. Please wait while I connect you."

Nikita stomped her boots on the pile of leaves near the convenience store. A gush of cold air hit her, and she grimaced. Cold weather she could handle. Not being properly prepared for it, she couldn't.

"Agent Stockdale, glad to hear from you." The deep voice of Zane Gibson met her ears just as a semi whizzed by the store. "What news do you have?"

"I believe Agent Riggs updated you a few days ago."

"Yes, she did. Our techs are still combing through the photos you sent. So far, they found a few similarities between the Greenback Cutthroat ledgers and an East Coast MC you took down last year. The intel about a package is circulating, but we're trying to pinpoint it exactly. Too many MCs use the same lingo unfortunately." Gibson cleared his throat. "Other than that, minimal chatter from our wiretaps."

That was what she was afraid of. Nikita rubbed her lips together. Diablos was notorious for skimming law enforcement. They'd give the FBI just enough to tap them but then avoid using those lines until they wanted to. It was a technique specific to Diablos and, more specifically, her father. She'd read plenty of audio and court transcripts over the years, and they all pointed back to her father being the genius behind Diablos' lack of member incarceration.

"All right. We'll keep digging up what we can. The club dolls aren't exactly forthcoming." She nodded at a biker passing on the street. "Or their members."

"All part of the MC life, Stockdale." He chuckled. "Hell, I had a guy undercover for two years before he got anything we could move on. Buckle up. You're in for a ride. If there's nothing else...."

"Actually, sir, there's something else I'd like to discuss."

"What's that?"

"Macha MC." She shifted on her feet when he didn't respond.

"What about them?"

Nikita watched two motorcycles pause at the stop light. Neither man looked her way, but she didn't take her eyes off them or the shimmer of metal at their hips. "I recently reviewed the file I compiled and they've stayed off the FBI's radar. Any ideas why?

Gibson cleared his throat. "They're small fish compared to Diablos."

"But can they be trusted?"

"Why do you ask?"

The light changed and Nikita watched the motorcycles glide out of sight. "Because I know someone in the club. He keeps showing up unexpected."

"And you're concerned for his safety?"

"Yes...no...in a way." She cursed under her breath. "I think Macha could be an asset to our operation here."

Nikita worried her lips together at the silence on the other end. Bringing in anyone from the outside, let alone a club, held risks.

"I'll run it up the chain and let you know."

She disconnected, the conversation clearly over. Her file wasn't full of prison records, the usual for MCs. Macha seemed to be different and they just might be the key to cracking this case. Whether or not headquarters agreed was another story.

Pulling her coat closer across her chest, she started the trek back to the dollhouse. She wasn't about ready to give up. The Greenback Cutthroats MC would give her Diablos one way or another.

Chapter Thirteen

KEVLAR

He blamed himself for Kita spiriting away like she did. It didn't lessen the pain, but he'd at least seen her since she left Macha's clubhouse. She'd been walking from the Rusty Cantina to a convenience store down the road, her friend in tow. He gave her plenty of space. Clearly, there was something bigger going on, and she didn't trust him enough to confide in him.

"You think she's undercover?" Rubble asked, killing the engine to his bike. They'd just arrived at the mountain lodge from patrolling Snowshoe. Not one lick of misbehavior which made their day much easier.

"It's possible I guess." He nodded to Brewer as they passed. "I never thought of Kita as being a cop.

She's tough as nails, but law enforcement was the last thing she wanted to do when I knew her." They reached the front door. "She was a business major back then."

Rubble entered the lodge first, the scent of pumpkin and caramel instantly invading them. The entire place was decked out in Halloween-themed wedding decorations. Kevlar had been wary at first, but Isa, the old ladies, and nymphs made the lodge their own little Halloweentown. It was the ideal amount of spooky, chic, and festive.

"I did a little digging," Rubble started, then paused when Isa—Doc's old lady to be—smiled at them in passing.

"About what?"

He chewed his bottom lip, eyes darting around the room. "Nikita's dad."

Sweat beaded on Kevlar's brow. "Tell me."

"Not here." Rubble waved him toward the den at the back of the large house.

Once they were safely stowed in the room with one wall dedicated exclusively to antlers, the big man let out a breath. "Nikita's father is Estevan Morales, the president of Diablos MC."

"You're sure?" He asked even though the look on Rubble's face said it all. He sank into one of the leather chairs and the pieces fell into place. Why he never met Nikita's parents. Why she disappeared. Why he never heard from her again. She was in hiding. Her father was the reason she disappeared.

Kevlar rubbed the back of his neck, the tension there suddenly from a new source. He ground his teeth together, filtering through every emotion he'd felt over the last fifteen years. They wreaked havoc on his better judgment and suddenly talking to Kita was the only thing he wanted to do. He needed to hear it from her sweet lips. Needed to see the truth in her eyes.

"Very." Rubble handed him a thick envelope. He hadn't even noticed it before. "It's all here. Doc's contact in Iowa has connections with an Italian mob who worked closely with Diablos a few years back."

Kevlar emptied the contents into his lap. Photos among newspaper articles stared back at him. He picked up a candid photo, and Nikita's college-aged face shone back. "Shit."

Rubble stayed silent while he went through the rest. Articles of the trial and Estevan's family weren't the worst of it. There were also trial transcripts and photos that looked to have been taken by a private investigator. They all pointed to Diablos MC. There was even a photo of Nikita wearing a leather jacket with the Diablos emblem—her young face shining pride, Estevan driving the motorcycle.

By the end, his stomach threatened to leave him permanently. Bowing his head, he let it all sink in. His Nikita wasn't so innocent after all.

"I'm surprised you never saw any of this after she disappeared."

Kevlar clenched his hands. "I was deployed not long after and the news was the last thing on my mind. Shit like this wouldn't have even interested me." He jabbed a finger at the stack of papers. "Now, a kidnapping, that would've drawn me in, but this… nah, brother."

"She's either working for Diablos or the government," Rubble finally said, placing a full tumbler of whiskey on the side table. "I hope the latter."

"But she was called as a witness." Kevlar rifled through the papers. "And so was her mom. She couldn't be working for Diablos after all this."

Rubble shrugged. "Stranger things have happened. Family is family at the end of the day."

He shook his head, not believing that for a moment. "What about her disappearance?" He grabbed the whiskey and drank half. "Where'd she go?"

"That I don't know. Couldn't find out any information about where she and her mother went after the trial." Rubble smoothed his beard. "I suggest you speak with her. It'll fill in the blanks. If she's indeed in Diablos, we'll deal with it. If not, we'll find a way to help her out."

"Not sure she wants my help."

"After the other night, I think she'll accept it." He sipped the whiskey. "If you hadn't been there... I don't even want to think about what could've happened to her."

"Neither do I, but it's all that runs through my mind." Kevlar stood and walked to the window. Prospects were outside hanging white twinkle lights for the wedding ceremony. "She went back to the Cutthroats for a reason. I don't think sheer loyalty is Nikita." He shook his head. "No, she does what's right. If not for her, then for what she believes in. Always been like that."

"Reaper needs to know."

Kevlar bit the inside of his cheek. "Yeah, he does. Can't keep something like this from him or the club."

Rubble clapped him on the shoulder. "Don't worry, I'll do the heavy lifting. You just convince her to let us help."

He smiled. "I'll talk to her after the wedding."

"Fuck that, bring her to the wedding, then you won't be daydreaming about her every second," Rubble said, chuckling.

He smirked. Rubble wasn't wrong, though he'd hoped to be a little inconspicuous. He couldn't get Kita out of his thoughts since seeing her amber eyes.

After stuffing the envelope with the contents from his lap, Kevlar followed the other man into the lodge. They had an entire day's worth of work to do before the wedding the following night. He'd go into town later and see if he was wasting his time or if there was a chance Kita was the same woman he fell in love with fifteen years ago.

***

"Kevlar, can you help with this one?" Dolly asked, handing him a string of lights.

Climbing the ladder, he hoisted the orange lights over his head. "Remind me again why we're decorating the trees outside."

"Because Doc's princess insisted." Dolly held the ladder steady, eyes sparkling mischief. "This is a very nice view by the way."

Kevlar glanced over his shoulder and noticed Dolly staring at his jeaned ass. "If I didn't know better, I'd think you were checking me out."

She snorted and smacked his left butt cheek. "Keep dreaming, Macha man."

He carefully wound the lights around the top of the tall evergreen bush. "What? I'm not your type?"

Dolly cracked her neck, her black ponytail swaying at the act. "I'm fairly certain your heart's on hold for someone else."

"Why do you say that?" He climbed down, bringing the leftover string of lights with him. Kevlar held his breath. Hardly anyone had seen him with Kita and the few that did wouldn't snitch about his former feelings about the gorgeous woman. He let out a breath. *Not all in the past.*

"Did anyone ever tell you how I became the nymph madame?"

Kevlar cocked his brow at the not-so-subtle subject change. Nevertheless, he answered. "No, I think I'd remember such a tale."

Standing on the other side of the bush, Dolly stuck the lights on the branches near her, then handed them to Kevlar to do the same on his side. "I grew up in Macha. I've seen my fair share of relationships. Somewhere along the way, I started playing matchmaker."

He chuckled. "Okay, I can't even imagine that."

She reached over and playfully punched his arm.

"Try, asshat." She smirked when he feigned pain. "I was only sixteen when I started with the nymphs."

"You set the nymphs up with people?"

"Yeah." She untangled the lights. "I didn't think it was fair that a nymph and Macha member couldn't be together."

Stooping, he finished hanging the lower lights. "I always wondered about that rule myself."

"You can argue it with Reaper. I never got anywhere with the old man." She rolled her blue eyes. "Anyway, I was tired of seeing nymphs unhappy, so I started setting them up with non-MC members. The ones who wanted it of course. Some were fine with the way things were."

"And Reaper was okay with this?"

Dolly chuckled. "Not at first." She plugged in the lights and an orange glow lit up the tree. "But eventually, he got used to it. The nymphs were happier, and we didn't have any issues with one trying to snare a Macha man."

Thinking it over, Kevlar realized he'd never seen a miserable nymph. The women were always treated well, and none even attempted to lure a Macha biker to the marriage altar. He hadn't even noticed it.

"Plus, I got to be a bigger part of the MC." She smoothed back her hair. "If my match was successful, the nymph left, new hubby in tow, and Macha brought in a new girl to take the open position.

Kevlar hid the extension cord behind the shrubbery. "So really, you're a matchmaker posing as a madame."

"In a way."

"How many Macha members know this about you?" He adjusted a patch of lights hidden too deep in the tree.

"Including you?" Dolly tightened her ponytail. "Four. Reaper, Queenie, my brother, Brewer, and you. The nymphs know of course. It's one of my biggest recruiting advantages."

When she handed him another box of lights, he held in a groan. "Then why tell me?"

Dolly pulled her phone out of her hoodie pocket, a picture of him and Kita from the other day on the screen. "Because chemistry like this is unique, Kevlar. Only an idiot would ignore such a force."

"Doll—"

"Nope. Macha's madame has spoken." She handed him the phone, and he stared at the snapshot she must've taken when he wasn't watching. They were walking out of his room. Kita looking up at him, a sweet smirk on her face. His arm protectively around Kita's hips, a similar smile on his lips.

"Thanks for trusting me with your secret." He returned the phone and climbed the ladder. "But I don't see how Kita and I work out in the end."

Lighting a cigarette, Dolly shrugged. "May the goddess have mercy on you then." She laughed heartily, her words seemingly a prophecy despite him knowing better. Kita wouldn't be his again, but he could dream.

***

Ice lined the roads in Snowshoe, flurries in the forecast, but nothing could keep Macha's bikers away from Doc T's bachelor party at Booze and Tattoos.

The rhythmic pulse of heavy rock music echoed in Kevlar's ears, eyes skimming the bar's occupants. Nymphs danced on top of the tables, each one dressed up as slutty nurses and doctors in celebration of the guest of honor.

"Can you believe this shit?" Rubble sat on the barstool next to him, whiskey glass in hand.

Kevlar took a sip of Guinness. "Kinda hard not to."

"Never thought Doc would be the next to go." Rubble downed the whiskey. "Don't get me wrong, Isa is one fine piece of ass, but settling down isn't my style."

"Oh, whatever." He nudged his oldest buddy. "You just have commitment issues."

Rubble's mismatched eyes swung to him. "And you don't?"

"Not when it's the right woman."

"Keep talking like that and I'll call you pussy-whipped again."

Kevlar finished his drink and nodded at Brewer behind the bar. The redheaded bar guru rarely drank but knew every alcohol concoction. He didn't know the man well enough to ask the personal question that hounded his mind. A bartender who rarely drank must have some harrowing history. He smirked. *Don't we all?*

They watched Doc awkwardly make his way through the horde of strippers to the bar. "Somebody needs to remind the nymphs that I'm a married man."

Dolly poured a tall glass of beer and handed it to him. "Psh, not until tomorrow, you're not." She hopped up on the bar and slid across it, bringing a nymph with her. "Now let Tisha give you a lap dance." She playfully swatted the woman's ass sporting booty shorts that barely covered anything at all.

Doc glanced at them for help, but Rubble shook

his head. "Don't look at me. I'll take that lap dance if you don't."

"Go for it."

The nymph walked over and started gyrating against Rubble. The big man shook his head approvingly, tattooed hands guiding the woman's hips.

Moving out of the way, Doc took the open barstool. He downed half his beer, eyes bright. "This all feels surreal. If you told me a year ago I'd be getting married, I would've laughed in your face."

"I think we all would." He jerked his head to the swinging doors where two nymphs were canoodling between the bar and tattoo shop. "Does your girl know what you're up to tonight?"

"Oh yeah." He twirled on the stool. "Isa's waiting for me at the clubhouse for the grand finale." A lovestruck smile covered Doc's face and Kevlar was instantly envious.

"You think you can do it?" Doc lifted his brows, so he continued. "Be with one woman the rest of your life."

"Ah, that." He threw back a shot of tequila and let out a whoop. "Yes, I do." His eyes strayed to the nymphs dancing naked now for the bar occupants to see. "I've had all that many times over." Doc met his gaze. "It felt great, don't get me wrong, but what I have with Isa... it's 150 percent better than the best fuck I ever had."

Leaning against the bar, Kevlar watched the other man's face light up when he spoke of his old lady. It was endearing, especially in club life. Every couple in the club was different. He caught sight of Snoopy and Legs making out in the corner. If he knew them—and he did—they'd be fighting in the next twenty minutes only to make up hours later. Macha wasn't perfect by any means, but the combination of varying personalities made the club work. He wouldn't trade it for any life.

"Hey, get off your arses," Reaper called, cheeks a cherry red color. "I didn't throw this party for you to sit idly by."

Doc took another shot and nodded. "All right, better go make Prez happy." He chuckled. "I don't know how the old man keeps up with us some days."

Kevlar watched Reaper's exchange with the nymphs. It wasn't one of lust but of fun instead. "He probably says the same about us." Clapping Doc on the back, he led the bachelor into the throng of dancing women. If the man was about to relinquish his unmarried status, Macha was sure to give him a night he wouldn't forget.

Chapter Fourteen

NIKITA

"Stockdale, I don't care who you have to fuck, I want this trafficking ring."

Nikita held back her initial response. Moments ago, her boss gave her the go-ahead to involve Macha MC. She and Mandi couldn't do this on their own, and it was too late to add more agents undercover. A local alliance was what they needed.

"If Macha gives us the Cutthroats and Diablos, I don't give a shit. Use them and offer immunity if you have to." Randy shuffled papers on the other side of the call. "Macha's never even been on our radar. No use in creating more paperwork."

Ten minutes later, he encouraged them to stay undercover if possible and utilize any source necessary. Having a MC behind them would help with the takedown.

"Okay, on that note, I'll check in later." She hung up before her boss could add any jokes about their undercover roles as club whores. Neither she nor Mandi liked playing dolls, but it was their only in after stonewalled attempts.

She walked the short distance to the road, Mandi by her side. "You really think bringing Macha into this is a good idea?"

Opening the car door, Nikita shrugged. "All I know is Kevlar isn't one to let something drop."

"What do you mean?"

Climbing in, Nikita turned down the radio. Mandi last drove the car, and her music choice and volume were too wild for that moment. "After my mom and I left, he looked for me."

"How long?"

"The Marshals stopped telling me after a few months. He was deployed not long after the trial." She buckled and steered the car toward Snowshoe. "Could've been longer."

"Damn, girl." Mandi popped in a piece of gum and offered her one. "Why didn't you tell him?"

She gripped the steering wheel tighter, ignoring the offer. "It would've made it worse."

Mandi let the conversation drop, and so did Nikita. She'd have plenty of time to rehash the past with Kevlar once she found him. That was the easy part. Even if she'd never visited the clubhouse, anyone in Snowshoe would help. Not only because they were friendly but also because the town appreciated the MC. It was a new sensation in her job. Most towns hated the motorcycle clubs and ratted them out the first chance they got.

Pulling into Macha's clubhouse parking lot twenty minutes later, she didn't have to wait long to see his solid form. He stood outside under the awning, smoke curling from the cigarette in his right hand. Two more Macha bikers stepped outside, and her stomach clenched.

"You sure you want to ignore that hunky guy?" Mandi asked, jutting a thumb toward Kevlar. His military haircut had faded slightly, and dark fuzz covered his head. He narrowed his eyes, and she took off her sunglasses. Recognizing her, Kevlar flicked away the cigarette and started walking in her direction.

"I'm not sure of anything anymore."

***

"Nikita, pleased to officially meet you."

She shook the older man's hand, eyes drifting to

his cut. The black leather vest said Reaper on one side and Prez on the other. His long, white beard was neatly trimmed, and his blue eyes friendly. Immediately she wondered why such a harrowing name was given to a jolly man with an Irish accent. "You too."

"While we always welcome visitors as pretty as you two, I suspect you've come for a specific reason."

Moving to a seat, she glanced over the wide wooden table. They were in Macha's inner room that much she could tell from the long table complete with the Celtic goddess engraved in the grains of the wood.

"Mandi Riggs and I work for the FBI." The collective inhale didn't faze her. "My partner and I are currently undercover in the Greenback Cutthroats, tracking a shipment of trafficked women." She slid her gaze from Reaper to Kevlar. He simply crossed his arms over his chest, face unmoving. "As it's become evident, we can't do this alone. We'd appreciate any assistance you can afford."

Rubble was the first to speak, but not to her. "Told you."

She glanced to the man he nudged but found Kevlar's face unreadable.

"I believe I speak for every member of my club when I say we'll help in any way we can." Reaper reached over and patted her hand. "Any mistreatment of women is against our laws. It doesn't surprise me that the Cutthroats have joined Diablos." He stroked his beard. "The two always seemed destined to find each other."

"How did you connect the motorcycle clubs?" Rubble asked. Her eyes slid to his cut. The sergeant at arms patch made sense. Given his build and countenance, the man could easily live up to his name and role.

"Chatter and photos got us to Colorado. The Cutthroat bikers weren't as gabby as we hoped, but I overheard Pillar and a Diablos member discuss it the other night." She searched for Kevlar's gaze, but he resisted, focusing on his president's face instead. It unnerved her the longer he remained stoic. In her mind, she imagined he'd be pissed when he found out the truth. Instead, he looked as if he expected this. Her gut rolled. *Did he react the same way when I left?* She still felt guilty about leaving him the way she did. It wasn't her idea, but she also didn't do everything within her power back then.

"The night you were attacked," Rubble filled in.

Mandi gasped and turned toward her. "What?"

"You didn't tell her?" This from Kevlar, who finally spoke up, anger lining his question.

"No."

"What's he talking about?" Mandi asked, pinching her arm.

Ignoring her, Nikita pushed on. "Pillar also mentioned they were holding a package in Snowshoe and if it was found, Macha would take the fall."

This got every man's attention. "What?" Rubble asked, his mismatched eyes taking on a harrowing gleam. "Where?"

She shrugged. "I don't know. They didn't say."

"It's all connected," Reaper said. "You got too close and they made you."

"We were there a whole two weeks." Mandi snorted. "No way our covers were blown so easily."

"Who's your contact?" Reaper asked, bushing gray brows furrowed.

"Juliet. She's one of the dolls." Mandi looked between the three Macha members. "You don't think she sold us out, do you?"

Rubble stood, phone to his ear. "Yes, I do."

He walked out before Nikita could refute his words. She couldn't be wrong. She'd vetted the woman herself.

"I don't understand." She looked to Reaper and the older man sighed.

"The dollhouse is filled with drug addicts, Nikita.

We've helped a few over the years." He paused and meshed his fingers together. "Juliet is one we couldn't. She consistently went back to the Cutthroats despite our efforts."

"So?"

"So, while she was under our care, she collected information about our club and passed it on to Pillar." He paused and sighed. "The Cutthroats ended up severely maiming one of my best men five years ago." A haunted look filled his eyes. "She isn't to be trusted."

"Dammit," both she and Mandi said at the same time.

"Don't blame yourselves." Reaper stood. "You couldn't have known. We kept it quiet."

"But if you'd been upfront with us, we could've avoided this," Kevlar said, voice strained. He also stood, his chair scraping on the floor. "And maybe we could've protected you." He pointed to Mandi, but they all knew who he meant.

"Kevlar, these things happen. She's here now and that's all that matters." Reaper patted his shoulder. "Mandi, come. I'll introduce you to my old lady. Queenie will force-feed you something delicious. We're preparing for a wedding, so there's plenty of goodies." Reaper walked to the door.

"I'll catch up later," Nikita said, eyes fixed on Kevlar's. Once the door shut, she sat back and crossed her arms over her chest. "Could you be any more of an asshole?"

"Yeah, actually, Kita, I could." He shook his head. "Why didn't you tell me?"

"Why would I? We don't know each other."

"Ouch, but valid." He wrapped his fingers around the back of the chair. "What happened?"

She rolled her eyes. "I just told you."

"No, not that. What happened fifteen years ago?"

She bit her bottom lip and stared at the tabletop, knowing the subject eventually would come up. The hope that he'd forget was overshadowed by reality. It was time to face the ugly truth. "How much do you know?"

"I know who your father is."

Her pulse jumped. "How long have you known?"

"Since yesterday."

"All right, then you can guess why my mother and I had to leave. It was for our protection." She finally met his eyes full of righteous anger. "My father will take revenge on both of us given the chance."

"How do you know he didn't just try to?"

"Not possible." She shook her head. "What

happened with the Cutthroat was a coincidence. Like Rubble said, Juliet must've tipped the scurveball off, and he targeted me."

Kevlar slowly walked around the table, his tattooed hand grazing every chair. Nikita watched him prowl closer. It shouldn't have excited her, but she couldn't help how her body reacted to him. How it always reacted to this man.

"You sure? Because now that I have all the information, I think your father sanctioned all this."

"You're crazy," she scoffed. "He doesn't even know where I am."

He paused at the chair next to hers. "Does he know who you are? Your new last name?"

"Well, y-yes." She faltered on the last word, the piecing creating an ominous picture. "Diablos has many connections. I'd be a fool to think he didn't know."

"And he's aware of your occupation, right? How you track down the worst MCs and put them out of business."

"Yes, but—"

He took another step closer. "And I'll bet he's proud of his little girl. Follows MC club busts in the local and national newspapers. I'll bet he has an inside man too telling him you're the one taking them down."

"He wouldn't...." Her refute trailed off, stomach churning at how much his insight made sense. "Actually, it sounds like him."

"He's using you to take out the competition, Kita." Kevlar's fingers brushed her arm, eyes no longer full of malice but concern instead. "He's trying to take over the weak or nonexistent clubs."

The weight of her father's connections hit her hard. She stumbled backward, shaking her head. "It can't be. Surely, he wouldn't do that."

"From what I've heard about Muerte, he would."

"Shit, yeah, he would." She blew a raspberry. "And he'd enjoy every second of it." She shook her head and closed her eyes tight. Her fingers curled automatically. The sudden urge to pommel a punching bag overwhelmed her.

Kevlar leaned against the table, giving her time to filter through everything. She appreciated his lack of smugness. She didn't deserve it after what she'd done fifteen years ago. She deserved the opposite in fact. Wracking her mind, she went over every detail from the time the Greenback Cutthroats popped up on her radar to the recent events. It all fell in place.

Sinking into a nearby chair, she laid her forehead on the table and groaned. "I played right into his game."

A gentle hand up and down her back gave her momentarily relief. "Is he that good, Kita?"

She moved her head up and down against the wood, making a screeching sound from her forehead. "He's a fucking evil mastermind, even from prison."

"Where's your mom by the way?"

She offered him a weak smile. "Europe last I heard. She moves around a lot and doesn't always tell me. It's probably better that way. She's still paranoid he'll find her."

"Ah, it's good she's safe."

She propped up her head on her fist. "Yeah, unlike her dumbass daughter who practically taunted daddy dearest to come after her."

Kevlar smirked. "Hey, he doesn't have you yet."

"Gracias a Dios."

"Damn, I missed you talking all sexy." He reached over and brushed back her hair. Nikita shivered at their connection. It'd been much too long, but it felt comfortable, safe even. "Scratch that. I just missed you."

She smirked and rolled her eyes. "You do know

Spanish is an extremely common language in the States, right?"

"Yeah, but..." His brown gaze dipped to her lips, then back to her eyes. "Nothing's common about you, Kita."

Palpable sexual tension mounted the longer she looked into his eyes. She'd left him high and dry years ago and somewhere along the way realized she'd also left her heart. Swallowing at the way his eyes darkened, her pulse quickened. She hadn't stopped thinking about him and the way he kissed her the other day. It was all she could do to stay clear of the temptation for more.

"Do you still moan in Spanish when you come?" he whispered, lightly kissing the side of her neck.

Her heart thudded loudly in her ears, his lips causing sweet havoc. "Maybe."

He pulled back. "I know I'd like to find out."

"Kevlar...."

His finger over her lips silenced the rest. "That's the best my name's sounded on someone's lips."

"This might be a mistake," she stated, mind already made.

Kevlar read between the lines and tugged her out of the chair in the next second. His lips crushed hers, the sensation painfully erotic.

Settling her on top of the sturdy table, he wasted no time ripping off her shirt and tossing it to the floor. Wrapping her legs around his waist, she only broke free from his kiss to rid him of his bullet-proof vest and shirt. *I have to ask him about that.* He bit her neck, and she arched into him. *But not right now.*

"Oh, damn," she hissed, seeing his torso. His muscles, while fabulously tattooed, were covered in scars. They were beautiful in a horrific way, windows into the past. She cupped his face. "What the hell happened?"

"War, baby." He forced a smile and unhooked her bra. "War happened."

"When?" She ran her fingers over the divots bullets and knives made. Tears formed at the ones close to his heart. Any could've killed him. Suddenly, the vest made perfect sense. Without it, he'd be dead multiple times over.

"Over the last fifteen years." He tilted up her chin, searching her face with his stunning brown-sugar eyes. "But none of that matters. It would've happened no matter what went down between us."

"I wish I could've— "

His lips cut off the rest of her blissful wish. He kissed with such resolve stars blinded her behind closed eyelids. "Don't you dare," he said, breathless from their connection.

She nodded, promising herself to kiss every scar on his body in reverence. For the time being, she unbuckled his belt and shivered at the satisfying thud of his belt and jeans.

"You sure you're ready for this after the other night?" he asked, tugging on her pants.

She nodded and stepped out of the last article of clothing separating them, then wrapped her arms around his neck, kissing him resolutely. "You won't hurt me. You never could." She paused and traced his mouth. "But I hurt you. I should've said goodbye, but I didn't. I don't know why either. I thought about it, but it was too late. Too many years went by. I'm sorry, *mi amor*."

He cupped the left side of her face, resting his thumb on her bottom lip. "Baby, I didn't want an apology. I wanted you."

He chose that moment to enter her, and Nikita's mouth dropped open involuntarily. She hadn't even heard the condom wrapper, but he'd never do anything to compromise her. Grabbing her hips, Kevlar set her on the edge of the table and thrust harder. Nikita matched his pace, the immediate friction sending sparks of pleasure through her body.

It'd been months since she'd had sex, and there was no better man to break the dry spell.

Kevlar kissed down her neck, nibbling on her collarbone and stopping at her nipples. He brought one into his mouth, sucking hard enough to make a moan escape. Moving to the second, he repeated the act, biting her gently before returning to her mouth.

"You feel just like I remember."

She kissed down his neck. "You feel better if that's even possible."

He smirked and captured her lips under him once more. "Enough talk. Show me."

Acting on his request, she slid free from him. Pulling out a chair, she motioned to it. He sat, and she wasted no time climbing on top and sliding his cock back into her warmth. Sighing at the familiar sense of fullness, she rocked her hips. Kevlar's hands drifted over her breasts, kneading and pulling them while his eyes never left her face.

Throwing back her head, Nikita ground harder, the friction hitting her G-spot again and again. She gripped his shoulders and kept his gaze. A warm tingling crept up her spine, ecstasy encasing her. "¡Dios mío!"

She shuddered, her body overwhelmed with more sensations than she'd experienced in years.

Kevlar kissed her neck, then lips, wanting a taste of her pleasure.

"Damn, Kita, you're gorgeous." His words forced her eyelids open. She stared into his lustful eyes, mischief lying underneath. Gripping her ass, he lifted her up and down on his cock, his gaze never leaving her face.

"Fuck me, Kevlar," she moaned.

"With pleasure." He stood and took her back to the table. The same table she was at not thirty minutes earlier with club members.

Spinning her, he kissed down her spine and entered her roughly. She moaned at the unexpected thrust, but it morphed into a scream when he fucked her harder, his balls slapping her ass.

She grasped for something to steady herself but came up empty. The table creaked, the legs slowly moving across the floor. Looking over her shoulder, Nikita smiled at his determined face. He'd fuck her until the table broke. That much his eyes promised.

Before she could face forward, he gripped her hair and twirled it around his fist. Bringing her upright, he lightly bit the top of her ear. "You're mine, Kita. Don't you dare go anywhere ever again."

She couldn't speak, his thrusts too brutally beautiful for any sound other than moans to make sense.

His words and actions spurred a second orgasm to take over her body. She violently thrashed at the satisfaction, screaming his name through the wave.

Kevlar dropped her hair but kept her body upright, cupping her breasts. He pumped into her twice more before he released his load into her pussy. Kita tried to catch her breath but found the air around her belonged to Kevlar. He didn't let go, merely held her flush to him, lips gently caressing her skin. His heartbeat pulsed against her back, cock fully embedded in her.

"Was it always this mind-blowing?" she finally asked.

He turned her chin and kissed her passionately. "Oh, yes, baby. Every fuck with you makes me lose my mind."

Chapter Fifteen

KEVLAR

His feet barely touched the ground. That's what it felt like after leaving the room with Kita's panties in his pocket. She almost didn't give them to him, but after eating her pussy until she came again, his Latino goddess changed her mind.

His brothers gave him odd glances when he walked by, but he barely saw them. All he saw was Kita. Kita's glowing eyes and glistening skin. All he heard was Kita. Kita's bilingual breathless cries filled his mind. He'd waited nearly two decades to hear and see those things again. And they'd happened in the most sacred of places for Macha's members. He licked his bottom lip, the taste of Kita on his tongue.

"Want us to leave you alone with your thoughts?"

Looking up from the beer in his hand, he met Hawk's knowing glance. "What?"

"Brother, the wedding starts in five minutes. Can you focus that long or do I need to hunt down Nikita for you?"

He flipped off Hawk and finished his drink. "I'm ready."

Kevlar grinned at the groom. Doc was a combination of wrecked and excited. It was funny in a way. He hadn't known the man very long, but the little he knew, Doc and Isa were perfect for each other. Doc a reformed playboy and Isa the antidote he obviously needed.

"We better get this guy down the aisle before he changes his mind."

The gathered groomsmen chuckled. He nodded to Rubble, Hawk, and Brewer. They weren't wearing monkey suits, thank God, but each had trimmed their beards, smoothed their hair, and looked overall acceptable for the night's event.

When they walked outside, the orange and white glow from the twinkle lights led them to the side of the lodge where a portion of the lawn had been set up with chairs. Halloween vibes screamed at every glance. He couldn't fault the duo for not wanting to wait until warmer weather to get married. Once upon a time, he'd felt the same about Kita.

He shook aside the slippery slope. It was much too early to think about shit like that. They'd fucked hours earlier. *That's it.* His heart told him otherwise. It was more than a chemical reaction for him.

Kita sat behind the Macha old ladies, Mandi by her side. His breath caught at her green halter dress. It was twenty times better than the blue one. This one was meant for beauty, not attention. Hell, she turned more than one male head, but it was a different kind of attention. She was oblivious to the other men, her eyes latched to him alone. A small smile played her kissable lips, making it difficult to stay at the front of the aisle with the other groomsmen.

The wedding started and ended. He barely knew what occurred in between. He'd been too distracted with Kita. She watched the wedding intently. Tears even formed in her eyes during the vows. She looked the same—acted mostly the same—as the girl he once loved. He accepted she was different. After all she'd been through, he couldn't blame her for changing slightly. The FBI role still surprised him. She'd done it to protect herself and her mother. No one could fault her for it.

Hawk jabbed him in the side, and he glared.

"Hey, don't shoot the messenger." He held up his hands. "You're literally the only one up here."

Looking left, then right, he coughed out a laugh. Sure enough, the bride and groom were down the aisle and out of sight. "My bad."

Hawk rolled his eyes. "Pussy. It gets even the baddest men."

Ignoring the man, Kevlar hurried from the lawn to the festivities inside. Stepping foot over the threshold, he smiled at the party already underway inside. Doc and Isa didn't do anything traditional, a fact he admired. There was no cake, opting instead for homemade cinnamon twists, a specialty of Doc's. Trays of mini cheeseburgers and Jell-O shots made their rounds courtesy of the Macha nymphs. Cigarette smoke curled up the vaulted ceiling, casting the dimly lit area in ghoulishness.

Each guest wore a different style of Halloween attire, him included. The pin-on skeleton holding the black rose wasn't his style, but when Isa wanted something, Doc made it happen. He sighed, leaning against the door by the kitchen. Kita wasn't like that. If she wanted something, she'd do it herself.

"You did a decent job up there."

He glanced to his right and met Kita's amber

eyes. "Thanks. It's difficult to stay focused. I get so bored."

She laughed. "Not replaying our tryst, were you?"

"Wouldn't you like to know?" A flush of red crept over her cheeks, casting her in ideal color. "But no, I wasn't. Not the whole time."

"Just partly?"

"Hey, I'm a guy. I have needs."

Kita gave him a disbelieving glance. "We had sex a few hours ago."

He cocked his head. "You say that like I don't want it every two minutes."

"Do you?"

"What?"

"Want sex every two minutes?"

Kevlar lightly kissed her, not giving a damn that her red lipstick smeared on him. "Only with you."

Another blush, this one deeper and rivaling her lipstick. "You're cheesy as hell."

"Your point?"

Kita looped her arm through his and rested her head on his shoulder. "I like it, is all. It's nice to simply be myself with somebody. I haven't done that in quite a few years."

"Working undercover can take it out of you." He kissed the top of her head, the scent of jasmine filling his nose. The same flowers as fifteen years ago sent his mind to the times they'd made love.

"So can special ops."

She gazed up at him, understanding in her eyes. She knew the struggles of keeping everything under control. Knew how difficult it was to hold everything in and never let the enemy see weakness.

"You wanna dance?" He held out his hand, and she placed hers inside it. The fit was perfect.

"I suppose, but I should warn you, I'm fabulous."

He twirled her. "I remember."

They joined the rest of the guests, swaying to the Halloween-themed dance party. He'd never liked the spooky holiday. *Until tonight.*

***

Flashes of time in the Middle East deserts agitated Kevlar out of deep sleep. He sat up and adjusted to the darkness. Heart throbbing at the memories the dreams brought, he tried to steady his breathing. The breathing techniques from the Army doctor helped bring him back to the present.

The mountain lodge. The wedding. He inhaled again and exhaled slowly. *Kita.* His eyes dipped to the woman on the other side of the bed. She faced him; her lips parted slightly. He was safe. Well, as safe as he could be without losing his heart to this woman once more.

Kevlar got out of bed, careful not to jostle Kita. Moving to the window, he looked out into the night. No hint of sunshine met his perusal. Security lights glowed, but otherwise it appeared black on the horizon.

He opened the window and leaned his torso out, inhaling the sweet scent of pine trees and the icy chill. Cradling his head, he despised how his time overseas still wreaked havoc in his mind. He'd never truly leave the Middle East. Not with the memories surfacing nearly every time he closed his eyes.

"Hey, you okay?"

Kita's arm around his waist startled him, and he hit his head on the window frame. Rubbing the back of his head, he eased away from the window and looked over at her. Not a scrap of clothing to be seen, hair covering her breasts and curling slightly on the ends. Her amber-colored eyes almost glowed in the room, searching his face anxiously.

"I'm all right." He kissed her forehead and inhaled. The scent of her instantly scared away the mortars and gunfire otherwise riddling his mind.

"How often do you have them?" she asked

quietly. "The nightmares," she added when he didn't reply.

Sighing, he pulled her into his arms, settling his hands on her perfectly full ass. He wouldn't have Kita any other way. "A few times a week at minimum."

"Oh, okay." Her lips gently caressed his chest, attempting to heal, not arouse. He closed his eyes and let her try. Every moment he spent with Kita was better than the last. She made his blood boil then simmer in the same day. It was why he loved her. Why his heart always belonged to his Spanish beauty.

"Do you want to talk about them?"

He shook his head. "No, but thank you." He tilted up her chin until her gaze met his. "You help scare the nightmares away."

She rolled her eyes, and he kissed the tip of her nose. "I'm pretty kickass, but I don't have power over your subconscious."

"Seriously, Kita. I wake up and see you beside me and my fear vanishes." He brushed her hair back, her nipples peaking in the cold room. "And it's not only your body." His hands enclosed her breasts, her pleasurable sigh encouraging him. "It's you, Kita.

You're my tether to the real world. I know I'm safe when I see you."

"Kevlar...." She laced her fingers around the base of his neck, lips cutting off her own reply.

He walked backward toward the bed, pulling Kita along with him. She settled on his lap, their connection immediate and satisfactory. He deepened her embrace, extracting a lusty moan from her ever so kissable lips. They may not be the perfect couple, but they were perfect for each other.

Chapter Sixteen

NIKITA

THE MACHA WEDDING COMPLETE, NIKITA WAS FORCED to return to reality once more. The three days she shared with the MC were pure bliss. She chewed her bottom lip. *As were the multiple rounds tangling in and out of the sheets with Kevlar.* Not thinking about him was impossible. His scent clung to her skin, a never-ending reminder.

She stirred cream into her coffee, staring off toward the back patio of the lodge. Up here, time stopped. It was the most vacation she'd had in the better half of ten years. After college, she'd been hired at the FBI, and it'd been nonstop from that day forward. She couldn't complain. She loved her job more each day. *Until recently.*

Sipping the medium blend, she walked through

the open living area and looked out the sliding doors. Kevlar was near the pool, Hawk and Rubble by his side. The trio spoke in low tones, each with a cigarette in hand. Every now and again, a deep rumble of laughter would erupt from one or all three. Kevlar's easy smile made her mirror the act behind her cup of coffee. Her stomach fluttered, flashes from their morning tryst coming to her in waves of passion.

The burner phone buzzed from the back pocket of her jeans. She didn't want to answer it, but it was the FBI. She couldn't hide from them.

"Hello?"

"Where the hell have you and Mandi been?"

Turning away from the door, she walked toward the den. "In the mountains. Cell coverage has been dicey."

Seemingly appeased by her answer, her boss cleared his throat. "You need to get back to town. We recently received chatter about the Cutthroats and Diablos moving a shipment."

This made her pick up her pace. "When?"

"No definite date. We need you and Mandi to get back in the dollhouse and figure it out."

Her pulse quickened at the idea of stepping foot back in the shack of horrors. *But this is the job.*

"All right, we'll get the information."

"Oh, and Nikita, just because Macha is on our side doesn't mean they're not in on it too."

Frowning, she paused at the bottom of the stairs. "What do you mean?"

"One of my analysts uncovered a recent betrayal by one of their own. The VP, as it turns out. He was working with the Twelve Brothers from Ireland."

That name she knew well. Her father had dealt with the Twelve Brothers on more than one occasion. She'd even visited Ireland with him as a teen, unbeknownst to her at the time the true reason for the transatlantic flight.

"All right, thanks. We won't divulge any additional details to Macha than what's necessary."

She disconnected before her boss could interject another factoid. Traitors were everywhere, no MC safe from the lure of money and power. Bounding up the stairs, she made it to Kevlar's room in time to see Mandi walking out of the room three doors down.

"Wait, isn't that Hawk's room?"

Mandi shrieked and spun around. "Jesus, Nikita, I didn't see you there."

Pursing her lips, she took in the apparel her friend wore the night before. "Yes, I can tell." She grinned. "Have a little fun with a MC man, did you?"

Running a hand through her hair, Mandi shrugged. "So, what if I did? I have needs." She rubbed her eyes. "Plus, I'm not the only one screaming through walls."

Nikita blushed. No matter how hard she tried to mute her moans, Kevlar didn't. In fact, he made it his personal goal to extract every lustful sound she could emit.

"What can I say? Kevlar likes it." She crossed her arms across her chest. "And I won't even apologize because it's so damned good."

"I'm glad." Mandi grinned. "You needed a nice release." She pulled out her phone and checked the messages. "But it looks like our sex-cation is over." She waved the android. "Work calls."

"Yeah, I spoke to Randy a few minutes ago. He wants us back at the dollhouse."

Mandi's eyes widened. "Even after—"

"He doesn't know what happened." She lowered her eyes to her feet. "I never told him."

"Nikita…."

"I know. I should've, but I don't want to be the victim." She met her friend's gaze. "I'm not a victim. I've worked my entire adult life to prove it."

Mandi reached over and laid a hand on her arm. "No, you're not, but you are human. It's okay to feel scared sometimes. If you don't want to tell boss man, fine, but you don't have to be all big and tough with me."

She nodded and pulled her in for a hug. "Thanks. I needed that."

"Anytime." Mandi stepped back. "But what about the mole in the Cutthroats? And not the one we thought was on our side. We can't go back there undercover. Surely, they've spread the word that we're feds."

Nikita chewed on her bottom lip. "Then we'll have to sneak it. This is a huge case, Mandi." She laid a hand on her stomach. "I just feel it here."

"You and your damn gut. Fine, but let's make sure Macha's with us, okay?"

"Deal."

Mandi stepped back and looked toward the staircase. "Now, I need to shower, then let's head to town. I'll bet we can get whatever intel we need without returning to the dollhouse."

Agreeing, Nikita left her to seek out the bathrooms while she stepped into Kevlar's room. Since she'd showered earlier, she gathered her hair in a ponytail and applied makeup. It was time to get back to bringing down merciless MCs.

***

"You sure this is a good idea?" Mandi asked, opening the door to the convenience store up the road from the dollhouse. They frequented it whenever they needed to check-in with the FBI or simply get away from the club. Mandi almost always bought junk food when they stopped in the store.

Nikita walked back to the wall of refrigerated beverages and scanned the bottles. "Yes. We keep striking out with the dolls outside the house, so we need to find Juliet."

"But what about—" She paused when a man walked by them. Her blue eyes followed him to the front. Then she glanced to Nikita. "Reaper said she betrayed them, and obviously, Juliet betrayed us too. We can't trust anything she says."

Opening a door, Nikita grabbed a bottle of water. "What other choice do we have?"

Organizing the assortment of potato chips, Mandi shrugged. "None, I guess." She grabbed a can of chips and read the back label. "You don't think it's weird to go back after we've been gone three days?"

Nikita had considered this, but over the weeks, they'd seen girls leave then return to the dollhouse with no excuse. Based on the track marks on the girls' arms, it wasn't difficult to guess the reason behind their disappearance. "If anyone asks, we were on a bender."

"That'll probably work." She tidied the rows and chuckled when she noticed Nikita staring at her. "What? I like things tidy. So, sue me."

Nikita laughed and swung her arm around Mandi's shoulders. "How did I ever survive without you as my partner and friend?"

"You didn't." Mandi snatched a bag of cheddar chips. "Don't worry, I won't leave you high and dry with no one to teach you good cleaning and music sense." She pointed to her paisley shirt. "Or fashion expertise."

"You and your bright colors," Nikita mumbled. Her best friend only wore mundane colors when they were undercover. Otherwise, Mandi sported the prettiest colors money could buy.

Scanning the aisles, she thought back to parting ways with Kevlar before walking to the store. He wasn't far away, he and Hawk stashed near the doll-house. She hadn't wanted to leave him. The mere notion scared the hell out of her. Getting attached to him would only spell disaster.

A pop tune came over the speakers, and Mandi swayed her hips and sang along to the words. She stopped singing long enough to say, "You know, when I die, I think I'd like a radio buried with me. It'd be too quiet without some music in the afterlife."

Nikita eyed her partner. "Jesus, Mandi, could you be any more randomly morbid?"

"Probably, yes." She stuck out her tongue and returned to her pop song.

"You two are Cutthroat dolls, right?" the cashier asked as they reached the checkout counter, eagerness scrawled on his face.

"Still in training, sorry," Mandi said, adding her chips and beef sticks to the growing pile on the counter.

"Oh, sure." The cashier grinned. "I overheard a couple dolls talking about some new MC guys in town."

This piqued their interest. "Really? I hadn't heard that." Nikita smiled sweetly. "What else did they say?"

The man started bagging their purchases, which somehow totaled thirty dollars. Nikita rolled her eyes at the stash of junk food Mandi slipped into the pile. *Never fails.*

"Something about how they'll need to learn Spanish because the guys will be in town indefinitely."

Nikita handed him the cash and Mandi grabbed

the bag. That sealed it for them. The dolls were purposefully keeping information from them. *Most likely at Juliet or Pillar's direction.* For the time being, keeping the truth quiet was the way to go.

"Anything else?" Mandi asked, opening her bottle of flavored water.

The cashier lowered his voice. "They mentioned a big job the MC is doing that'll make the Cutthroats dominate Colorado." He offered a wry grin. "But I'm sure you're already aware."

"Oh, yeah, we are." Mandi winked at him. "Just like seeing how much the town residents know."

Nikita ushered them out of the store before the cashier could suggest something indiscreet to Mandi. A forceful wind blew her hair back and chilled her bones. *I should've taken up Kevlar's offer and worn his sweatshirt.* Instead, she wore her usual black jeans and black leather jacket. Fitting in around the dollhouse wasn't difficult. Both she and Mandi wore leather jackets, but unlike the other dolls, theirs didn't have the Cutthroat emblem stitched on yet.

"You think he's telling the truth?" Mandi asked as they walked toward the dollhouse.

Nikita glanced to her left before they crossed the street. Shine from Kevlar's motorcycle met her gaze, and she relaxed slightly. Knowing he was close by somehow made the next step easier.

"I do. No way any doll would spout anything club related in public unless it's true. Juliet doesn't have that much control over her girls."

Mandi nodded. They both knew the oldest doll wasn't anything close to a madame, but the girls looked up to her, nonetheless. Juliet was the reason they were in Waverley in the first place. The sooner they could grill her about her betrayal, the better.

Chapter Seventeen

KEVLAR

FLICKING HIS CIGARETTE TO THE GROUND, KEVLAR exhaled the last bit of smoke from his nostrils. He didn't like this one bit. He and Hawk sat on their bikes, safely hidden in an alley behind the Cutthroats' dollhouse. They'd sat idle for the last hour, waiting for any sort of action from inside. Thus far, all they'd done was chain smoke.

"Why's it taking so long?" He glanced to Hawk. The other man didn't even look up from his phone. Simply sent a text message, then peered at the back door.

"Dunno. Maybe they got caught up somewhere, or maybe they're fine and taking their time." He finally shifted his gaze to him. "Stop worrying about her. She's a big girl. From what I've seen, she can more than take care of herself."

"That's not the point."

He stared at the chipping paint on the tall building. He'd never been inside, but a few prospects had. The dollhouse was nothing compared to Macha's nymph lair in the lower level of the clubhouse. Macha didn't whore out their girls, unlike other clubs. It'd go against their rules.

"Kevlar, why do you wear that?"

Frowning, he turned. "Wear what?"

"The vest."

He glanced down to his chest. A day didn't go by where he didn't wear it when he was patrolling. The same could be said about when he was deployed. It was hot as hell but served a purpose.

"Protection, you know that." He smirked. "Kinda how I got my nickname."

"Right, and we used to give you shit for it." Hawk tipped up his sunglasses, the sun momentarily beneath a cloud. "But we don't anymore, do we?"

"No."

"How long has Nikita been an FBI agent?"

"I don't know. Since she graduated college, I think."

"And do you think her boss worries about her every time she tracks down scumbags?"

Kevlar faced forward again, already knowing where the conversation was headed. "No. She's a trained operative who can handle her own."

"I bet when she started, her boss used to, though. I'll bet you fifty bucks they had a pool going on about whether or not the pretty Latino chick would make it a year without cracking." Hawk pulled out his pack of cigarettes and lit one. "Just like the pool we had about you."

Kevlar whipped his eyes to him. "Seriously?"

"Yep." He grinned. "I won too."

"Great, what's your point?"

Hawk offered him the pack. "My point is Nikita doesn't need you to save her. She can save herself." He jutted his chin toward the four-story building. "Yeah, she needed you the other night, but I'm damned sure she'll never drink on the job again unless she pours the glass herself."

Waving aside the cigarette, he nodded once. His brother was right. Kita had lasted years in the FBI doing the same shit and never needed him to save the day. She'd probably been in just as many close scrapes as the one with the Cutthroats. He'd trust her. It was his only option.

"You're smarter than everyone thinks, you know that?"

Hawk offered him a crooked smile. "Yep, sure do."

Chapter Eighteen

NIKITA

THE CUTTHROAT DOLLHOUSE WAS SET UP LIKE A pyramid. The dolls were kept on floors two through four. The first floor was set aside for MC parties, where all dolls attended. It also served as a gateway for visitors. The Cutthroats advocated prostitution, taking a portion of any earnings off the top and gave just enough to the dolls to keep them sated.

Nikita and Mandi easily skirted a group of Cutthroats. The last thing they needed was noisy bikers chattering at them. Finding the back staircase, Nikita took the lead. Her handgun safely stowed in the small of her back gave little reassurance. If they were caught and questioned, her mag would do absolutely nothing in the grand scheme of the operation. Still, she felt naked without it.

Attaining the second floor, they peeked through the porthole window. New dolls stayed on this floor. They were the cheapest too. The rankings and prices went up with each floor. The best of the best girls were at the top, and that's where they were headed. Juliet was the best—according to the club—and they needed to see how much information had already been lost to the Cutthroats because of her murky loyalties.

They reached the third floor and spotted several bikers in the hallway. If they had more time, they'd carefully question a few members, but she wasn't optimistic. Voices drifted from below, and they hurried up the stairs. Mandi stopped on the fourth floor and checked the hall.

"You ready for this?"

She grabbed her gun and nodded. "Yep. Let's find our mole."

Mandi swung open the door, and they rushed into the hallway. Room 444 was their destination. To their surprise, the door was ajar. Motioning to Mandi, Nikita entered quickly and scanned the room for intruders. When her eyes rested on the bed, her gut dropped. Juliet lay naked with a syringe in her arm, eyes wide open, and pale white.

"Shit." She hurried over and checked for a pulse.

None found her, and Nikita shivered at the temperature of the body. "She's been dead at least a day."

Hunkering down, Mandi examined the wound. "She didn't insert this."

"How do you know?"

"The angle is all wrong." She stood. "I've seen this shit before when I worked undercover in narcotics. Somebody killed her and made it look like an overdose."

Putting away her gun for the time-being, Nikita paced. "Who? Pillar? One of her marks? It doesn't make sense. Why would the club kill her? She put the bull's-eye on my back in the club and fed us bullshit info."

"Maybe she didn't."

Mandi held up her hands. "Think about it. What if Diablos was the one who has it out for you, not the Cutthroats? You have history with them, right?"

Suddenly, one of her father's sayings haunted her. "If you don't run with Diablos, Diablos will chase you."

"What?"

She shook her head and glanced at Juliet's corpse. "Just something my father once said to me." Grabbing a sheet, she covered the deceased woman. "Let's get out of here."

"What about the body?"

"We can call the sheriff, but I think the club will move her before a deputy gets here." She walked to the door and cautiously glanced out. The stairwell door opened, and a Cutthroat stepped out, followed closely by another man in leather. Squinting, she made out the familiar devil emblem on the other man's jacket. "Diablos is here. We gotta go."

Mandi nodded, and they hurried to the western adjoining door. Each room had them in case of emergency. Usually, the dollhouse madame or a Cutthroat was on the other side, ensuring their investment. It made Nikita sick to her stomach but it wasn't something she could do anything about yet. She was organized crime, specifically motorcycle clubs. When she returned to headquarters, she'd pass along the intel about this setup. Without a doubt, the Cutthroats had more prostitution hovels in Colorado.

They managed to make it to the adjoining room before male voices boomed from Juliet's room. Both women paused and glanced toward the noise.

Mandi held up her finger and leaned closer to the door. "They're speaking Spanish," she said, ear to the wood.

"We can't stay." Nikita checked the hall and let out a breath at the vacancy. "All clear."

Slipping into the hallway, Mandi followed Nikita to the stairwell. She opened the door, and both women screeched to a halt. On the other side, three MC members stood waiting. Two with Diablos cuts, one with Cutthroats.

"Look what we have here," the curly-haired Diablos said. "Where you two off to?" His eyes slid over their clothes, and he clucked his tongue. "You're not dressed for work, *chicas*."

"Headed to the store," Mandi piped up. "My period started and I'm out of supplies."

The three men took a step backward as if they'd catch it.

"What about you?" the curly-haired Diablos asked, running his knuckles across Nikita's cheek.

She instantly recognized him as the same man who spoke with Pillar the night of her attack. Her eyes dipped to the sergeant at arms patch on his jacket and her stomach dropped. None of this was a coincidence.

"Always travel in pairs."

The men laughed, and the sergeant's dark eyes skimmed her body. "You could make an exception this time, Nikita, couldn't you?"

Surprise mixed with panic flowed through her veins. She met Mandi's eyes and recognized the fear just beneath her tough facade. The duo acted fast. Mandi gut-punched the Cutthroat while Nikita kicked the head Diablos in the balls. They took out the last Diablos together, the short man fumbling down the steps.

"Let's go!"

Rushing down the stairs, Nikita winced at the sound of a gun firing. She pulled Mandi away from the open stairwell. "Go! I'll keep them back." She fired upward, the bullet bouncing off the railing and making a clinking sound.

The bikers hollered for backup, shooting rounds toward her. Nikita picked up her pace, grateful Mandi was one flight ahead of her. So long as they both stayed away from the opening, they'd make it out alive.

She reached the bottom floor and a voice boomed down to her.

"Muerte looks forward to your visit."

Nikita gritted her teeth to keep from yelling something back at her father's henchman. Instead, she pushed through the door and sprinted toward Mandi, who waved furiously at her from the entrance.

"You okay?" she asked as they ran outside, not daring to look back.

"Yeah, I'm good. You?"

"Not a scratch." They made it to the alley, their salvation in sight.

Hawk and Kevlar revved the motorcycles, the loud rumble sure to attract unwanted attention.

"Go! Go!" she urged, hopping on the back of Kevlar's bike.

The Macha men quickly rolled out of the alleyway. Casting a glance behind them, Nikita swore at the sight of the Diablos sergeant standing at the back of the dollhouse, a smug grin on his lips. One thing was certain, they couldn't return to the dollhouse.

Chapter Nineteen

KEVLAR

"YOU'RE SURE YOU'RE ALL RIGHT?" HE LOOKED TO Doc, who nodded for the third time, annoyance evident in his eyes.

"She's fine." Doc smirked and picked up his medical bag.

Kevlar searched Kita's amber eyes, not believing his brother. The man wasn't a licensed doctor, after all. *He could be wrong.* There could be an injury somewhere and she just didn't know it.

Kita placed a hand over his on her thigh. "I'm not hurt."

Doc left them alone in the bedroom, sounds from the clubhouse drowning out the click of the door.

"But my father knows where I am."

Her soft words sent a shock straight to his heart. "How?"

"I don't know yet." She sat cross-legged on his bed, wearing a pair of black pants and his white T-shirt. "One of the men we encountered today was the Diablos sergeant. He told me Muerte expects my visit." She ran both hands through her silky black hair. "I think this is all connected."

Kevlar moved onto the bed, not giving a damn that he still wore dirty boots. He needed to be near her, breathe her in. "He's closely following your career."

"Yes. And now, I believe he's the one who laid out the Cutthroat's breadcrumbs for me to follow. He knew I'd eventually get the green light for an investigation." She leaned against the wall, eyes fixed on the ceiling. "He set it up perfectly."

"But what about the loose ends? Juliet? The Cutthroats? It doesn't make sense."

"Exactly." She lolled her neck to face him, head resting on the wall. "I can't put all the pieces together. I need my father to give me the missing ones."

"But that means—"

"Visiting him in prison, yeah." She went silent, shoulders sagging.

The severity of her statement knocked the wind out of his lungs. Once he'd found out her parentage, he'd read all about Estevan Morales. From the outside, the man was a shrewd business owner with a loving wife and daughter. The truth more than came out during the trial. Estevan Morales—Muerte in the club—had a dark side to his business dealings.

The homemade chicken and noodles from dinner churned in his stomach merely thinking about the secrets her father kept. Secrets that destroyed their family. Secrets that destroyed her hopes of a normal life. *Secrets that destroyed us.*

"I swore I never would." She let out a sad laugh. "But he knew. Somehow, he knew I'd go after MCs like his." She picked at her thumb cuticle. "So he created the perfect mousetrap."

Kita crawled off the bed and paced. "Who knows, maybe all the MCs I arrested were under his control." Her arms flailed in the air. "Have any of my collars been my own, or has my father set them up from prison?" He kept watching her slowly descend into a spiral of all Spanish, face animated the faster she spoke. For ten minutes, he let her vent, fume, and everything in between. Every now and then, he caught a few phrases, but the majority were foreign to him. In the Army, he'd learned the native languages of Iran and Afghanistan. That knowledge didn't do him any good here and now.

Kita stopped pacing and stood with her hands on her hips, looking lost. He reached over and wrapped his arms around her waist, pulling her to the edge of the bed.

"What can I do to help?"

She smiled wearily and cradled his jaw. "You're already doing it."

Her lips closed over his in the next instant. Kevlar's hands gripped her ass tighter and matched her fervor. Her tongue delicately tangled with his, the taste of coffee lingering in her mouth.

Tugging her onto his lap, Kevlar reveled at the softness of her skin combined with toned muscles beneath her clothes. She'd always been on the muscular side, never sickly skinny. His fingers dug into the flesh on her hips. It was one of his favorite spots to touch. He held complete control over her body here.

"Come with me," she whispered against his lips.

Easing back, he scanned her face. "Where?"

"To New York. I must see him. Talk to him." She brushed a hand over his short hair. "And I want you with me."

"I'll go anywhere with you, Kita." He kissed the point of her chin, then her lips. It only took a split second for her to cup his face and overwhelm him with kisses. Hers were the best he'd felt in years. No one compared to Kita. She was in the back of his mind no matter where he went or what happened. Being apart from her again would break him.

"Kevlar, you're gonna be late to church again," Rubble called, fist pounding on the door three times. "And we got shit to discuss."

Begrudgingly, he broke free from Kita's candy lips. He traced them with his finger, adoring when she darted out her tongue to lick him. "Stay out of trouble." He kissed her soundly and stood, cursing the hard-on he couldn't use until later. "I'll be back after church."

She bent her legs beneath her and tugged on his belt, eyes filled with mischief. "Don't stay away too long. I'd rather have an audience than go solo."

His cock jumped in his jeans and Kevlar growled before grabbing the back of her neck and ravaging her with his lips. Only after she let out a soft moan did he recoil to sanity. He walked to the door and met her gaze. "Don't you dare. You know I like to watch."

***

All through church, Kevlar couldn't get Kita out of his mind. She might as well live there with how often she crept into his thoughts. Reaper outlined their role in the upcoming winter games. They were a few months out, but preparations had already started in Snowshoe. The club liked to be ahead of the extreme winter games whenever possible so they could stockpile funds for low months.

"The last matter is the Greenback Cutthroats and the FBI."

He lifted his eyes to the club president. The shift in the dynamics of the room was harrowing. No one liked to involve Feds unless it was absolutely necessary. While the club did nothing illegal, some of their methods skirted the gray lines of right and wrong.

"Kevlar, why don't you fill us in." Reaper nodded at him.

Glancing around the room, he caught sight of curious expressions alongside pissed ones. The prospects stood lined against the walls, seating only available to members. "Nikita Mor—Stockdale"—he was still getting used to the alternate name—"and her partner, Mandi, need us to continue as backup only. The FBI can handle the Cutthroats, but having a local MC at their side will be beneficial."

"Why're they taking down the Cutthroats now and not later?" Doc piped up.

"The Cutthroats and Diablos are working together." A collective grumble of anger filled the air. No one liked Diablos. They were bad for business. He held up his hands. "But the FBI is confident they can disband the alliance."

"How're the two connected? They seem like an odd fit." This from Brewer, the club's bar manager.

"Human trafficking. Women from what the FBI uncovered." He saw several brows raise, and more than one head shook from side to side. Macha would never condone ill-treatment of women. Their goddess and patron forbid it. The club respected and appreciated women—a rarity in the MC world.

"I've heard enough," Hawk said, standing. He looked around the room and nodded. "We're in. No way we let the Cutthroats or Diablos get away with this shit." The rest of the bikers shouted in agreement.

Kevlar met Rubble's gaze. The man predicted such a response. Macha protected those who couldn't protect themselves. He'd joined the brotherhood because of how different they were compared to other MCs.

"What's the next step?" Reaper asked, bushy white brows furrowed.

"Kita and I are going to New York to meet with one of her contacts in prison."

Rubble's mismatched eyes suddenly snapped to him. "Who?"

He swallowed the urge to lie to his brothers. They deserved to know every gritty detail. "Estevan Morales. Her father."

The roar of voices nearly drowned out the gavel pounding on the solid table. "Everybody shut it!" Slowly, the room died down to a dull whisper. "Kevlar, this is news. Why haven't you told us before?"

Sweat trickled down his chest and stomach, tickling him subtly. "I only found out recently. This won't hurt the MC, I swear."

Reaper exchanged a glance with his sergeant at arms, then nodded. "Be certain it doesn't. Our club's been through hell this year. We don't want to tangle with Diablos. They're worse than even the Twelve Brothers."

A round of "Ayes" echoed in the room.

"Macha is helping the FBI take down the Cutthroats and hopefully Diablos in the process."

Kevlar skimmed his eyes from one brother to another. "After that, we're done."

Reaper concluded church and the club dispersed as quickly as they gathered. The involvement of Kita's family earned him glares from Snoopy and Klink. He didn't care. Macha's underlying laws won over the bikers. They'd keep women safe, whether they were innocent or not.

***

"Where are we going?"

Kevlar laced his fingers in Kita's and grinned back at her. "You'll see." He opened the clubhouse door and started toward the garage.

"Please tell me you're not going to show me a garage. I've seen those. Many of those."

He chuckled and shook his head. "Nah, I know you're well-versed in that shit." He led them through the garage and to the side door. Stopping there, he grabbed a helmet and handed it to her. "You still ride, right?"

A confident smile crossed her face. "Does a bear shit in the woods?" She quickly pulled on the helmet. "Now, where's the bike? I've been itching to ride."

"Well, you could always ride me to ease that urge."

Kita propped her hands on her hips, the sass evident in her stature and face. "Still a smartass."

He playfully swatted her ass. "Yeah, you do have a fine ass." Before she could respond, he pointed to the motorcycle parked outside the door. "That one. Rubble and I just put her back together the other day. It's one of the 'Macha originals' as he likes to call them. That guy can make anything mechanical."

Standing back, he watched Kita carefully inspect the bike. Her tight leather pants tempted him to say "screw it" to the ride and simply strip her then and there and fuck her against the motorcycle. He let out a steadying breath. It wasn't about him. Kita was tense and if memory served him, getting out on the road helped relax her. *If not, there's always sex.*

"All right, Kita, you ready?"

She swung her long leg over the bike and patted the seat behind her. "Born ready, baby."

He shook his head. "You really think I'm riding bitch?"

Nikita offered him a seductive grin. "Promise I'll make it up to you."

Eager to see exactly how she'd fulfill her promise, Kevlar hopped on the back and strapped on his helmet moments before the motorcycle lurched to life. In that moment, he didn't care if he looked like a pussy. *Damn, this girl has me whipped already.*

She took it easy the first few blocks. Once they were safely out of town, Kita didn't bother to abide by the posted speed limits.

They zipped along the open road, swerving around cars. Only once did he feel the need to grab her hips. Which, of course, led to Kita laughing and picking up the speed another notch. He didn't give a damn if he died riding bitch with this woman. She could have his entire life if she wanted it. He'd gladly turn it over for another moment like this with her.

The motorcycle hugged the curves perfectly. Kevlar made a mental note to relay the test ride to Rubble later so they could work out some of the shifting kinks he felt whenever Kita's foot switched gears.

After thirty minutes, she pulled over and hung her helmet on the handlebars. She easily slid off the bike, years of doing the act second nature to her. Kita around motorcycles mesmerized him. There was so much about this woman that he didn't know. He dismounted and followed suit and walked over to where she stood at the edge of the road overlooking Snowshoe.

"This place is beautiful." She turned slightly and met his gaze. "I see why you love it here."

Kevlar swept his eyes over the valley and surrounding mountains. "It's more my home than any place I've lived before." He jutted his chin to the left. "Macha's snow lodge is up there. Here soon, the place will be crawling with tourists and extreme sport enthusiasts. It's kind of fun to be around, honestly. Club life is never boring."

She pushed back her long hair, the wind catching it behind her shoulders. It looked like a perfect modeling shot. A sexy woman in leather and a rocking body that he'd beg to touch. He could come on this image of Kita alone.

"Don't ogle unless you're planning on doing something, Macha man."

The slight smile on her face made him take a step closer. He carefully slid his arm around her waist, his hand dipping between the fabric of her leather pants. Goose bumps lined her skin on his contact, and she leaned closer into his chest.

"Don't tempt me, woman. I'll take you here and now."

Kita turned toward him, gorgeous eyes pinning his boots to the dirt. "Prove it."

He didn't need to be told twice. In one swift

move, he swept her off her feet and marched her to the haven of trees nearby. Pushing her against the tall trunk, his lips teased the side of her neck. Kita arched into him, his cock already swelling at the thought of what would come next.

Wrapping her legs around his waist, Kita grazed his head with her nails, the sensation sending shivers up his spine.

Easing back just enough to catch her lips beneath his, Kevlar's pulse quickened at the tantalizing moan that escaped Kita. Foreplay wasn't happening this time. He needed her fast and hard. The gleam in her eyes told her she wanted it equally as rough.

He unzipped his pants, and Kita barely slid her green underwear out of the way before he sheathed up and his cock plunged into her wet pussy. Their breaths hitched simultaneously, and he swore at how ready she was for him. It'd never get old. He'd never get sick of fucking this woman.

Kita's pussy gripped him hard, but he pushed through the temptation for release and pivoted his hips. Her tongue tangled with his, possessing him more with each thrust he completed.

From the edge of reality, he heard a car whiz by. As much as he didn't care where he fucked Kita, he did care who watched. She was his and no one else would get the pleasure of watching her come. Picking up his pace, he didn't relent until she cried out his name, the sound echoing among the trees. She felt too good, milking him with her orgasm that he gave in to his own.

Breathing hard, he searched Kita's eyes and mirrored her lusty smile.

"Told you not to tempt me."

Kissing his chin, she wiggled her brows. "I'll have to tempt you more often then."

Another car, this one slower, made Kevlar zip his pants and set Kita on the ground. Once she was properly covered, he grabbed her hand and led her back to the motorcycle.

"You wanna drive back?" he asked, and she sprinted toward the bike, slowing only to hop on the back.

"Nah, I'll let you chauffeur me around for a change." She pulled on her helmet, and he simply stood there for a second, relishing the moment. A sexy woman who not only knew how to handle a motorcycle but also him was someone he couldn't let go of a second time.

Chapter Twenty

THE DRIVE FROM JFK AIRPORT TO FISHKILL, NEW York, was prettier than she deserved. Rolling hills quickly changed to mountains, creating curvaceous roads and plenty for her to soak in while Kevlar drove the rented sedan.

She glanced over and noticed him trying to find a decent radio station. It wasn't happening, the hills interfering with a rock and roll station he found in the city. They'd been on the road coming up two hours. Towns morphed together the closer they came to their destination.

Kevlar slowed the car off the ramp and flicked on the turn signal. Her eyes fixed on the large green sign with Fishkill Correctional Facility written in bold lettering. A white arrow pointed them to the right, and she let out a breath.

"Hey, you doing okay?"

She met Kevlar's light brown eyes with a mixture of concern and trepidation. "Not really, but I have to do this."

He reached over and squeezed her hand. "Well, you're not alone."

She laced her fingers in his and pulsed back. Facing forward, she saw the tell-tale signs of the prison. A patrol house stopped their entry past the gate. After chatting with the guard, they continued on the curving road letting out at a visitors parking lot.

"This is it." He shut down the car. "No turning back."

Nikita stared at the brown building ahead. From the outside, it didn't look so daunting. Settled on the top of one of the hills with greenery surrounding it, the prison gave off an eclectic vibe. If the electric wire was gone, it'd resemble a mountain retreat. She double-checked her phone and saw the approval come through the head office to allow Kevlar to join her. Normally, protocols wouldn't allow for it, but she needed another set of eyes and his military background served enough good cause for her boss to allow it.

"Let's get this over with."

They made it inside the doors without any hassle. That came when Nikita flashed her badge at the front room. "I called this morning about a visit. Agent Nikita Stockdale."

The guard squinted his eyes at her badge. "FBI, huh?" He typed on his keyboard. "Here it is. What's ol' Estevan done now?"

"Nothing." She glanced toward the cameras. "Yet."

"He FBI too?"

She looked to Kevlar then back. "No, he's with me." Before the guard could refuse, she added, "He's been cleared through the DC office."

The man kept his eyes glued to the computer screen then nodded. "Yeah, I see it now. Just need his ID."

Kevlar handed over his driver's license and three minutes later they were issued badges. A guard escorted them through the maze of hallways to the rooms used for both interrogations and visits. The familiar hum of prison life greeting them at every turn. She tried not to think of how many people she'd put in prisons like these. The hallways were cold, the smell one she'd never forget. *Bleach and overcooked food mixed with odor and must.* She hid her shudder, not wanting Kevlar or the guard to see how the place affected her. The guard buzzed their entry, three chairs, and a table awaiting them. The guard left, then returned minutes later with a man in tow.

"I'll be outside the door," a guard stated, ushering in the prisoner and securing him to the table with cuffs. "If he's any trouble, just call out."

The air in the room seemed to evaporate the moment Estevan Morales stepped inside. Nikita gripped the edge of her seat, not sure how to start this conversation. She was almost relieved when he spoke first.

"Mija, I've been waiting for you to visit me," her father started, a broad smile on his face.

That spine-chilling voice sent shivers throughout her body. "*Papi*, you look well." And he did. She hated how good he looked. Other than a plethora of gray in his otherwise black hair, prison had treated him better than most. Playing nice disgusted her, but she'd learned long ago that her father did more talking if he was in a good mood. Their history and her FBI training warred against each other, much like the way her heart and stomach were in that moment.

"The thought of you kept me young." His dark eyes slid to Kevlar. "And you brought a friend, how sweet."

"You remember Tucker, don't you?"

Estevan narrowed his eyes and slowly nodded. "*Sí*, the name sounds familiar, but I don't believe we've met." He reached for her, chains rattling. "Tell me, how have you been? How's your mother? I want to hear everything."

The guard turned around and peered in through the window. Being given a private room wasn't normal, but she'd pulled a few strings to speak without others listening. *One of the perks of being in the FBI.*

"You know full well how I've been and how Mamá is." She tightly gripped the folder on her lap. When the guard offered it to her at the front, it came as a surprise but one she didn't mind. The more she stayed ahead of her father, the better. She pulled out the packet and emptied the contents. "The guards confiscated this last week."

She held up one of the newspaper clippings and prayed her hand wouldn't shake. "This is me, Papi. You've been watching me."

Estevan took the article and scoured it. "Sí, mija, I wanted to know you. Since you never visited, I had to find out who you were on my own." He tossed the paper back to the table. "I'm surprised, of course, but my daughter, an FBI agent, is an achievement on its own." He puffed out his chest, pride evident in his voice. "You've done well too."

She couldn't reciprocate the emotion in his eyes. It grated on her nerves the longer she kept his gaze. This wasn't the man from her childhood. Hell, she wasn't even sure she knew her father. Her childhood in Diablos seemed like a dream, not the nightmare she later discovered it was.

"I never would've guessed it." He chuckled. "My daughter, a Fed. That's been hard to explain in here, mija." He shook his head. "But your name change helps keep you safe. Too many club members have uttered your name, though." Estevan looked to Kevlar, then back to her. "Better watch your back. We wouldn't want anything to happen to you."

Keeping her father's gaze was harder by the second. The subtle threat wasn't hard to translate. "Why did you choose the Greenback Cutthroats MC?"

His smile remained fixed, not a muscle moving. After years of interrogations, he'd surely built up a threshold to such questions. "I don't know what you're talking about."

The familiar accent grated on her ears. He'd always had it, but now it sounded more defined as if he spoke nothing but Spanish while incarcerated.

"Fine, let's talk about Diablos. Who's running your club?"

He shrugged. "Why would I know?" He lifted his hands, but only as far as the cuffs let him. "I'm shackled to this prison, mija. I have no contact with Diablos."

Kevlar's body tensed beside her, and she reached over, squeezing his thigh once.

"Someone from Diablos came after me." She stared into his eyes, waiting for him to break his indifference. Instead, a slow smile crossed his face.

"Mija, you abandoned me fifteen years ago. How else could I get your attention?"

"You put our family at risk back then, but you couldn't just let us go." She gritted her teeth, resisting the strong urge to slap him.

"You betrayed me." He spit across the table, missing her by inches. His fatherly role quickly evaporated, and a hardened criminal replaced him. "You and your worthless mother. I had to get my vengeance. You're lucky it took me so long to catch you in my snare." Sitting back, his easy smile found him again. "It's been years in the making. I tried so many times, but you never took the bait. You never made the connection. Until this MC." He glared at Kevlar. "I wonder why. Perhaps, because your emotions are in play, sí?"

"I hate you."

"Fine, hate me all you want." He leaned closer over the table. "But hate me from the Diablos presidency seat."

Nikita reared back, his words punching hard. "Excuse me?"

"Run Diablos, mija. You were made for the job." He chuckled. "Hell, when your mother couldn't produce any more children, I groomed you to take over."

"No, you're wrong." She looked to Kevlar but his face was etched in confusion. Rubbing her hands on her thighs, she wracked her mind for an explanation to his statement.

"Am I?" Estevan clucked his tongue. "Remember all those trips we took? How excited you were to be part of my world? I remember them like they were yesterday."

Wracking her memories, she pulled up ones that matched. Plenty of worldwide locations, but nothing ever stood out about the trips. She was fully aware of the MC but never knew the inner workings of their transactions. "I was your companion because Mamá couldn't travel."

"No!" He shook his head. "Your mother refused to go with me, mija, so I took you wherever I went." He searched her face. "Don't you remember playing in Ireland? Those weren't games. Those were battle plans. Ones you helped create."

Her blood went cold. That she remembered. It'd looked like a game, a fun one with tiny motorcycles and stickmen. *There'd been a map.* She bit her lip. *Fuck.*

"Ah, you remember, good. The Twelve Brothers MC adored having you around." His dark eyes lit. "We even discussed merging our clubs with a marriage."

From the corner of her eye, she saw Kevlar's jaw tighten. Meeting his eyes, she saw the rage there. It equally mirrored her own. Shaking her head slightly, she wasn't sure if he could keep his temper sated. She couldn't return to the purpose of their visit. Not until she understood how he went from a seemingly loving father to a maniacal criminal mastermind. The truth of the matter was that her father had always been like this. She'd just been too young and naïve to see it.

"How did you keep the club's business so secret?"

Nikita pushed down her disappointment with herself and her father and pressed on toward the reason she was there. "I never knew how violent Diablos truly was until the trial."

"You saw what we let you see. Your mother kept you away from the darker sides of the club."

"Surely I asked questions." She couldn't recall any. She only remembered happy times. Riding motorcycles with her father and his friends and playing with the other MC children. That was all she could think of when it came to Diablos.

Estevan nodded mindlessly. "You did, but I sent you off to a boarding school with children of similar familial backgrounds. The goal was to bring you home after a few years. Gently integrate you into MC life." He furrowed his brows. "But I never got the chance to hand over Diablos to you. After boarding school, it became clear you were too much like your mother. Carefree and stupid." He shook his head. "I'd hoped to bring you back into the fold once you'd gotten it out of your system but...."

"That's when you were arrested."

He meshed his fingers together. "And the rest is, well, history."

Nikita exchanged a glance with Kevlar. His face remained void of emotion, but beneath, she saw the fury in his eyes. She felt the same. The same plus disappointment. Her childhood hadn't been as innocent as she thought. There was so much she didn't know and desperately wanted to hear. *But I can't.* The reason for the trip wasn't to understand her past but to save the future.

"Call off your sergeant."

"Why would I do that?" He pointed to their chairs. "It got you here. After fifteen years, I'd say it was long overdue."

"It almost got her raped," Kevlar seethed.

Estevan chuckled. "Please, my men would never allow that."

"But they did," she confirmed. "And they shot at me."

"But not to kill." He clucked his tongue. "Never to kill. They know better than to hurt my heir." He sat back, eyes fixed on her every movement. "Take over Diablos, mija, so I can finally rest. I haven't had one day since I've been born. I'm tired."

"No. Now tell me about the women Diablos and the Greenback Cutthroats are trafficking."

He sighed, looking bored. "Why would I? I've nothing to gain and everything to lose."

Thinking over the last few years, Nikita tried to recall a tidbit of information she could leverage that her father would care about. Finally, an idea came to her.

"Tell me about their dealings and I'll visit you again."

"Kita, don't—"

Her glare silenced the rest of Kevlar's plea. She needed her father to hand over the details. If promising another family session would get her there, she'd deal with the repercussions.

A dashing smile covered her father's face. "There's my girl. What do you want to know?"

Chapter Twenty-One

KEVLAR

Parking the sedan, Kevlar did his best to ignore the scowl on Kita's face. He tried for the last two hours to make conversation with her. She hardly said a whole sentence, opting instead to stare out the window, lost in her mind's world.

"Kita, baby, you gotta talk to me eventually." He rested his forearms on the steering wheel, eyes focused on her frazzled hair and matching face. The meeting with Muerte was harder than he expected. More so simply keeping his jaw clenched and fists curled while he watched Kita wrestle wits with her father.

Unbuckling her seat belt, Kita gathered her purse onto her lap. "Should I even believe what he said? He could've made it all up."

His mind screamed the same, but he was an outsider. He'd never met her father before that day.

"It's possible, but we won't know until we track down his information." Reaching over, he rubbed her knee. "I'll be here for you, no matter what." He searched for her eyes, but she avoided him. "Can you at least try to enjoy these last few hours alone together before all hell breaks loose?"

He tickled her side, a smile gradually spreading over her lips.

"All right, stop before I smack you." She giggled, swatting at his hands.

"You'd never hurt me."

She cocked an eyebrow and he laughed.

Leaning over, he moved her hair behind her shoulder and playfully bit her neck. "You know you missed me all those years. You wouldn't hurt me now."

Kita's smile turned sad. "I really did." Her fingers traced his lips and rested on his chin. "I thought about finding you. I had the resources."

He wiggled his brows. "Did you now?"

"But I couldn't." She looked away. "I was worried you'd be mad at me."

Kevlar's heart squeezed. "I admit, I was mad but not because I stopped caring for you." He gently tilted up her chin and pressed his lips to it. "I was hurt. I didn't know if you decided we couldn't be together or what."

"Shit, I'm sorry. I never thought that." She closed her eyes and pressed her forehead to his. "The opposite actually."

"I looked for you, though, Kita." He had to tell her the truth. Too much time had passed without her knowing his feelings. "Off and on. Mostly before I was deployed. The Army kept me busy. It was a blessing in disguise honestly. Took my mind off you and how much I missed you."

She let out a strangled sigh and grazed his lips. His pulse soared the longer their mouths intertwined. She never tasted better. Cupping the base of her neck, he lightly nipped her top lip then the bottom.

"We should get inside. Our flight leaves in an hour."

Regretfully, they left the car, taking their carry-on bags with them. After going through security, Kevlar waited near their gate, eyes darting to where Kita ordered two coffees for the plane ride to Colorado. She was third in line, a family of tourists and a businessman ahead of her.

When his phone vibrated, he dug it out of his pocket.

Rubble: You on your way back?

Kevlar: Yep, boarding soon. Everything good there?

Bubbles popped up on the other end then disappeared. He lifted his gaze and noticed Kita paying, adding a five-dollar bill to the tip jar.

A loud buzz brought his attention back to the phone in his hands.

Rubble: So far. Watching Cutthroats now. They're acting shadier than normal. Klink saw them take a backroad up the mountains. I'll bet they dumped the doll's body. Sheriff hasn't found anything yet.

He cringed at the thought. There were too many hiding places in the mountains to dispose of a body, especially when no one else would be looking for the woman.

Kevlar: Shit. Not good. Be back ASAP.

Rubble: Keep an eye on that girl of yours. I have a feeling she may be in trouble.

He put away the phone, pumping his leg up and down. A noise from the coffee shop caught his attention, and he glanced toward it. He couldn't find Kita. Immediately, he stood, panic lining his gut. By now,

Diablos knew of their visit. If the MC didn't like what went down, they might retaliate regardless of their president's wishes.

Standing, he walked toward the last spot she stood. "Kita?"

He picked up his pace, rounding the shop. His heart skipped at what he saw. Kita was inside one of the touristy airport stores, perusing the knickknacks. Resting his back to the coffee shop wall, he swore. His nerves were getting the better of him. Every time she left his sight, he worried about her. It wasn't healthy, but he couldn't help it.

"Hey, I found these cute little key chains." She held up the Statue of Liberty pin-up dolls. "Mandi's going to love it." She grinned and handed him a cup of coffee.

Lifting it to his nose, he inhaled the heady scent of caramel macchiato. If any of his Macha brothers asked, he'd deny specifically requesting it with extra caramel.

"Did you want a souvenir?"

He shook his head and sipped the coffee. "Nah, I'm happy with you."

"I'm not a souvenir." She bopped him on the nose and walked by, her jasmine perfume filling his nose and reminding him exactly why he couldn't walk by a flower shop without thinking of her.

"You're one to me." He looped his arm around her shoulders. "But I swear I'll never toss you in a junk drawer like all my other souvenirs."

Her light laughter drifted through the airport terminal. It calmed him more with each step.

"Ladies and gentlemen, flight 783 to Denver has been delayed two hours." The voice over the speaker repeated the bad news in three more languages before looping.

"Sounds like we're stuck here for a while." Kita plopped into an open seat, propping her boots on the divider between chairs. "What ever shall we do?" She sipped her coffee, amber eyes like beacons to him through a storm.

"What're you thinking, Kita?" He licked whipped cream from his top lip.

"We have time to burn and plenty of places to hide in this big airport." She stood, swinging her bag over her shoulder. "You coming?"

Kevlar watched her ass sway back and forth with each step, her hips begging for his touch. He couldn't look away if he tried. Grabbing his bag, he hustled after her. A door with Under Construction stuck to it caught his eye.

Slinging his arm through hers, he led them through the door, pleasantly surprised it was full of unclaimed luggage. "This will work just fine." He shut the door and turned around to see Kita sitting on the edge of a table, legs swinging back and forth.

"What do you have in mind?"

He sauntered toward her, dropping his bag and setting his coffee aside. He'd need both later. For now, he craved the addiction Kita's touch provided. Their lips met in a frenzied embrace, her legs wrapping around his waist and pulling him into her.

Shoving up her shirt, he pushed up her bra and latched onto her breast. Her sharp intake only intensified when he pulled her nipple between his teeth and sucked. Back arched, Kita moaned and frantically reached to unbuckle his jeans.

Not willing to let her win so easily, he pushed her chest, kissing her as he did, until she lay on her back. He tugged on her jeans, rolling them over her hips, taking the lacy underwear with them. The scent of her arousal hardened his cock even more. He'd bust right out of his jeans by the time he was done with her.

Placing a trail of kisses down her stomach, he paused below her hips, senses tasting what lay between her legs. He ran his tongue along the inside of her left thigh, then her right. Kita's small squeal when he parted her sex and inserted two fingers urged him forward. Spreading her legs, he settled between them and met her gaze. With the dim lighting, her sun-kissed skin tone shone beautifully against him.

"I can't get enough of you, Kita." He kept her gaze, tongue darting to her clit. A vein in her neck bulged, her body adjusting to the cold. Kevlar licked her slit, pumping his fingers in and out of her slippery core.

"You taste so damned good." He pulled her closer to his mouth, ravishing her pussy. Her moans echoed in his ears, spurring him.

"God, Kevlar, keep going," she said, each word more breathless than the last. Her thighs clenched around his head, legs shaking.

Increasing the pressure with his tongue, he flicked her clit harder. Kita let out a loud cry, his name tumbling from her lips along with a curse in Spanish. Her orgasm spread over his lips, drenching him with her passion.

"That's it, baby, let me have it all." He stopped pumping his fingers, licking each one clean only after her pussy stopped clenching around them.

Rocking on his heels, Kevlar grinned at the

pleased gleam on her face.

"You get better at that every time, but—" She bent over and kissed him hard, tasting herself on his lips. "I need you to fuck me. I need to feel you inside me." She gripped a handful of his shirt, eyes pleading. "Now."

His fingertips traced her spine, pebbling her nipples to hard points. "Since you asked so nicely." He pulled her upright, positioning himself at her center. Condom in place, he plunged into her without another word.

Kita breathlessly groaned, her face relieved at last. "That's it." She lifted her hips to meet his tempo, gripping him tight at each thrust.

"Never thought I'd fuck you in an airport," he whispered against her neck.

"I never thought I'd fuck you again. Period."

Kevlar paused his motion, eyes meeting hers. He smoothed back her hair; sweat lined her brow in the most beautiful way. There'd never be another woman like Kita. No, scratch that. There'd never be another woman for him. He loved her more than the day she left him a heartbroken kid.

"I don't want to fuck anyone else ever again," he admitted, caressing her cheek with his knuckles.

Her eyes glistened with unshed tears. "Kevlar, I...

I...." She sat up, kissing him softly. "Neither do I."

Those were all the words he needed to hear. Pounding into her pussy, he didn't stop until she came once more. Her release drenched him, smothering his balls with her sweet juices.

Finally, he released his load, jutting hard and kissing her roughly until he was spent.

"God damn, Kevlar," she panted, pressing her forehead to his chest.

After his vision cleared, he took a step backward, stumbling slightly, head still light. Sex with Kita obliterated acts normally natural. Staring at her as she sat there on top of the table, luggage all around her, he swore to never forget the moment. She'd be forever tattooed in his memory.

"We should probably head back to the gate." He pulled up his pants, buckling them but never taking his eyes from her.

"What, no round two?" she teased, pulling down her shirt. Standing, she scoured the floor for her jeans and hopped into them one leg at a time. It was a pity to watch her fine ass disappear into the fabric. He craved more than two rounds with this beauty.

Catching her hips in his hand, he grinned. "What, you've never heard of the mile-high club, darlin'?"

Chapter Twenty-Two

THE FLIGHT TO DENVER WAS UNEVENTFUL, AND Nikita was glad for more than one reason. The main one being she was too exhausted to even react to the flight attendant's question about refreshments.

Thankfully, Kevlar drove from Denver to Snowshoe, her mind spinning over the last twenty-four hours. Coming face-to-face with her father after fifteen years was surreal. The fact that he subtly taught her about Diablos management unnerved her even now. She'd had a happy childhood free of crime. *At least I thought I did.* It wasn't so black and white like she was led to believe. She wasn't dense. The MC scared some of her school friends. She knew they weren't upstanding citizens, but they were her *familia.*

The crescent moon and two stars tattoo on her wrist caught her eye. She and her mother had matching ones to remind themselves that no matter where they went, they still slept under the same starry night. They got them the day after the Marshals left them in Ohio. Unfortunately, they didn't stay there long before being uprooted again. By the time she graduated, they'd moved ten times.

I should visit Mamá. The last time she saw her in person was too long ago. They video chatted often, but with her schedule and her mother's constant moving, even fifteen years later, connecting in person was nearly impossible. Nikita thought back to the trip she made to Athens. Her mother begged her to stop hunting down motorcycle clubs, but she ignored the plea. *Should've listened to her.*

The road curved through a mountain pass, her eyes glued to the scenery passing out the window. Nothing would change the past. She'd come to terms with that ever since seeing Kevlar again.

Sneaking a glance at him, she smothered a smile. True to his word, they'd joined the mile-high club somewhere over Illinois. It'd been cramped in the tiny cubicle but worth every inch of pain. A new memory she'd always hold close to her heart. That was Kevlar in a nutshell.

Frowning, Nikita wondered if that was all he'd ever be. Just a memory. Their lives were dedicated to two very different paths. His skirted the lines of legality in his club, and hers was to put away MCs. *It would never work.*

"Penny for your thoughts."

She chuckled. "You don't want to hear them."

Kevlar adjusted the knob for the heater, eyes meeting hers briefly. "Sure, I do. Wouldn't ask otherwise."

"Fine." She turned on the seat to face him as best she could. "I live in Boston."

He kept his gaze on the road. "Mhmm?"

"You live in Snowshoe."

"Last I checked."

She toyed with the string on her sweatshirt. "I'm going back once I take down the Cutthroats and Diablos."

Silence shot through the truck, the rumble from the road beneath the only sound responding to her words. Snow flurries hit the windshield the higher they drove into the mountains. She kept watching his face for a reaction. Other than a slight switch in his cheek, he gave none.

After two minutes, she faced forward again. The silence roared in her ears louder with each passing mile. Fishing out her phone, she checked the messages from Mandi and her boss. Both were anxious to hear the takedown plan. So was she if she was honest with herself.

"I knew this wasn't permanent, Kita." His voice was soft, acceptance lining the words. Kevlar looked over to her. "It's just... whenever I think about you leaving again, I'm afraid it'll be the last time I see you." He chuckled. "Don't get me wrong, I understand your job and all the shit that comes with it. I'd never give you an ultimatum."

"Kevlar, I...." She didn't know what to say. What was there to say that would make sense?

"It's okay. Let's agree to not talk about it until after we get those bastards and save the women and kids, all right?"

"Deal." She smiled, and her heart lifted when he did the same. Leaving would hurt but staying would be worse. After years in witness protection, the need to keep moving became ingrained in her mind. It was more normal than staying in one place. She wasn't even sure if she knew how to be somewhere longer than a year. Nikita sighed and hoped she knew what she was doing when it came to Kevlar. If she wasn't careful, she'd reevaluate her entire life to be with him.

***

The FBI team from Denver showed up an hour after them, the big white van out of place at the clubhouse despite the electric company logo on the side. The men weren't familiar to her, but then again, she'd barely met them when they arrived from Boston before heading to Cutthroat territory.

"What've you been doing while I was gone?" she asked Mandi, entering the clubhouse meeting room. So far it was empty but would fill up once the MC members arrived. She caught the smile on her friend's face. "Or should I ask, who you've been doing?"

Mandi's eyes whipped to her. "Am I that obvious?"

Nikita passed out the folders Mandi put together during her absence. "You're the epitome of transparent."

"Damn. Thought I was hiding it better." She paused and lowered her voice. "Hawk and I spent a bit of time together. And not just sex," she rushed to say.

Placing the last folder at the head of the table, Nikita waved a hand Mandi's way. "No judgment here, you know that."

"He's actually a really amazing guy." She sighed,

a wistful expression on her face. "I didn't fall for him or anything, but I wouldn't mind seeing him on occasion."

The subject of their conversation strode through the door, Doc and Rubble behind him. Mandi shot her a warning glare and Nikita zipped her lips.

A man dressed in FBI gear came in next, his blue eyes pinning to her. "Nikita Stockdale, right?"

She nodded and outstretched her hand. "You must be Agent Gibson."

"Please, call me Zane. Nice to meet you in person finally." He shook her hand. "My team was briefed on the way and are waiting in the truck. I'll be point on the op itself, you and your partner second."

"Great." She heard more bikers enter the room—gruff voices mingled with one she knew well. "Have a seat." Zane took the seat to her left, leaving her in an FBI sandwich with Mandi on the other side.

Ten minutes later, she perused the room. Plenty of men and women with Macha apparel filled the space. It was almost claustrophobic. A few women were familiar—Dolly, Isa, and Queenie. The rest weren't, but without a doubt, they were dedicated to the cause and to Macha.

Clearing her throat, Nikita began. "Agent Gibson and his team are here to follow the exchange between Diablos and the Greenback Cutthroats. As many of you already know, their partnership is based off the Cutthroats' ability to move trafficked women across the Rockies."

She searched out Kevlar's gaze but came up empty. His focus remained on the folder in his hands. "Macha's role is simple. Cut off the Cutthroats' alternative route through the state so they're forced to take the route that leads to the FBI ambush. Once they cross state lines, we'll take them down."

She nodded to Zane. He stood and quickly went over the specifics. His men would handle the dangerous stuff. Macha wouldn't be anything more than bouncers in a club.

"Thanks to Agent Stockdale—" Zane smiled at her. "—we know the shipment is planned for Thursday, two days from now. Plenty of time for us to adequately prepare."

By the end, Zane and Rubble walked off together, heads bent over in hushed conversation. It made sense. The sergeant at arms needed every last movement to ensure every man in his club was kept safe.

"Nikita, I'm leaving to meet with a potential informant in the Cutthroats dollhouse. It's not for an hour, but I like to arrive early," Mandi said, the room still full but everyone focusing on their own conversations.

She swiveled her chair, brow cocked. "An hour early, huh? I wonder why." She tapped her chin faux thoughtfully. "Oh, yeah, probably because you need to get some dick first."

Mandi rolled her eyes and stood. "Whatever. Don't be hating."

"Be safe."

"Always," Mandi called; Hawk's arm laced loosely around her waist.

The room cleared quickly, Nikita the only one left besides the club president.

"How'd the visit with your father go?"

Meeting Reaper's kind blue eyes, she sighed. "As well as it could've, I suppose."

"My father was in prison too." He leaned back in his chair. "It was tough as a kid to see my old man behind bars."

Interest piqued, she closed the folder and focused on him. His tanned face bespoke years of riding his motorcycle outside without sunscreen, his hands showing signs of arthritis. "What was he in for?"

"Murder." Reaper straightened his leather cut. "I

was about ten years old when he went away. My mom left him and remarried somebody I loathed for the longest time. When he saved my sorry arse from ending up like my old man, I couldn't hate him anymore. As it turns out, he's part of the reason we started Macha." He smiled. "Ireland was a different place back then."

"Why did you and your brother start Macha?" She always liked to hear the origin stories from the MCs she collared. Most of the time, they were dumbass reasons, and she took no pity on them.

"My step-dad was in a motorcycle club. Me and my older brother used to hang out at the clubhouse all the time. It was great for a while. The brothers were always there for each other no matter what happened."

"That's one of the things I like about MCs," she admitted.

"I agree." His smile faded. "But this club saw women as possessions. They mistreated them."

She nodded. It was the sad truth for Diablos and the one she grew up seeing glimpses of in her youth. Women were belongings to MCs. It never sat right as a child. "Most do."

"We decided we couldn't support any club who would do that anymore, so we started our own. One based off stories our mother used to tell us about the goddess Macha." Reaper pointed to the Celtic goddess carved in the table. "We pledged to never cause a woman intentional harm. It's not always possible in our line of work, but we built the club from the ground up with that goal in mind. Never regretted one day, either." He chuckled. "Well, I do miss Ireland. That's my only complaint."

Nikita leaned her elbows on the table. "Why did you come to Colorado anyways? Seems like an odd place to have a sister location."

He chuckled, pushing the chair back. "A woman. Why else?"

"Queenie, right?"

"Yep. She was in Ireland with another man actually, but I won her over." Reaper winked and stood. "Love's worth uprooting your life."

Chapter Twenty-Three

KEVLAR

EVER SINCE THE MEETING, KEVLAR AVOIDED KITA. HE didn't want to. His heart urged him to stomp down to the FBI van, grab her by the shoulders, and kiss her senseless. But he didn't. He sipped his beer, watching Mandi and Hawk flirt nearby. He'd keep his happy ass stationary.

The chill from a cold front tickled his nose, tempting him to go inside. He wouldn't budge. He was preoccupied with the FBI plan and how it would put Kita at risk. He'd never been worried about a woman before. At least not one he once loved. *One I still love.*

"Did she cut you off or are you not talking to her for a reason?" Rubble asked, taking the chair next to him at the table used predominately for smoke breaks.

He finished off the beer. "Nothing much to talk about. I got my hopes up and I had to come back to reality." He looked over to the big man. "Life's a bitch sometimes, ain't it?"

"Sometimes, yeah." Rubble pulled down his sunglasses. "But why are you wasting time wallowing about losing her when she's still here?"

Kevlar harrumphed and looked back toward the FBI vehicle.

"Well, if you're not going to do anything, I will."

"Excuse me?" He whipped his head toward Rubble and saw the shit-eating grin. "Asshole."

"Never said I wasn't." Rubble pushed the glasses back in place, nursing his whiskey. "But honestly, she's got one fine ass."

"You're an ass man, aren't you?"

He nodded approvingly. "Oh, yeah. A girl with a nice, firm, and big ass, and damn, I'm in heaven."

"Christ, you're a horn ball."

"Have we met?" Rubble's smile tilted. "Everybody's got a thing. Take you for example. You like your women tough and with black hair. Always have, brother."

Thinking back over the years, Kevlar had to admit Rubble was spot on. He consistently went for women with dark-colored hair who could fight as good as him. The last woman he was serious about was a fellow soldier in the Army. She'd been tough as nails and had the prettiest dark brown hair.

"Shit, you're right."

"Always am."

Doc and Isa rumbled into the parking lot on the man's Harley. They were ideally matched, her with a princess-gone-dark vibe and him with a devil-may-care attitude. She waved at him, and he nodded in reply. Their conversations were usually limited, but she was sweet. Too sweet for him.

"You ready for the show tomorrow?" Doc asked, arm looped around his old lady's shoulders.

"Hells yeah." Rubble pounded a fist to his chest. "Always ready for action. You know that, Doc."

Isa leaned over and kissed Doc's cheek. "Just keep this one alive, will you? I'm rather fond of my old man."

"Don't worry, he's safe."

Kevlar caught sight of Kita and the head FBI agent coming out of the white van. He didn't like the looks of the Zane fellow. The bastard was too friendly for his liking. Zane placed a hand on the small of Kita's back, and Kevlar's grip on the beer bottle tightened.

"Careful, you'll break it," Rubble warned.

"Yeah, I don't think stitches the day before we take down the Cutthroats is a good plan," Doc chimed in, moving toward the clubhouse entrance. "But if you change your mind, you know where to find me."

Kevlar flipped him the bird, and the couple laughed before walking inside. He pulled out a pack of cigarettes and a lighter. The longer he was apart from Kita, the more he wanted to smoke. What he really wanted was her lips on his, but he'd settle for a taste of nicotine.

"Bum one off ya?"

He passed the box over and Rubble snagged one, inhaling deeply after lighting. "I really need to quit one of these days."

"Yeah, they'll kill us." Kevlar smirked. It was a constant conversation they had. Nothing ever changed, though. Neither of them would quit. Maybe not ever.

Kita looked in his direction, her long hair flowing at each movement. He could smell her flowery shampoo on the wind. It could've just been his imagination, but he swore the soap invaded him on every breeze.

"Don't waste the little time you have, brother."

Kevlar flicked ash into an empty flowerpot on the table, eyes fixed on Kita chatting with Mandi and Hawk.

"Speaking from experience, Rubble?"

The big man slid his gaze over to him. "Actually, yeah."

Before that bombshell could digest, Rubble stood and saluted. "Later."

Even after spending time in the sandbox with Rubble, the man never divulged any relationship information. The recent tidbit made him wonder if he knew his Macha brother at all. *Maybe he's right.* He inhaled again, leg bouncing up and down. *I'm wasting daylight without her when I'd rather be with her.*

Snuffing the cigarette, he moved from the safety of the table and walked toward where Kita stood.

"You got a minute?"

Her amber eyes settled on him, sparking that fire only she could light in him. "Catch you later, Mandi. Try to stay out of trouble." She playfully punched her friend's arm and started walking toward Booze and Tattoos.

"What's up, Kevlar?"

He stopped her just outside the bar, lightly gripping her tattooed wrist. It was a ring of ivy, all black but beautifully designed. "For one night, can we be Tucker and Kita?"

A curse in Spanish slipped from her lips and her mouth gaped. "What?"

Easing her away from the incoming crowd, he settled her against the side of the building. Her jasmine perfume drifted to him, bringing the first time he met her to mind. Cupping the side of her face, he memorized the sharp lines of her nose and jaw softened by her rosy cheeks and matching lips. But her eyes blew him away. They resembled precious gems in the waning daylight.

"I don't want to think about what might happen tomorrow or the day after tomorrow." He traced the rose tattoo on the side of her neck. "I just want to live in the moment." He slid his hand up her side. "This moment."

His lips touched hers tenderly, taking all the time in the world as if it were his to steal. "Please, Kita." Separating for a moment, he took in the blush to her face, her eyes glued to his face, searching it for something she perhaps couldn't find.

Pushing off the side, she grabbed his hand and started toward the clubhouse. Sleep was the last thing on both their minds.

Chapter Twenty-Four

LEADING HIM INTO THE ROOM, NIKITA TORE OFF THE leather jacket she picked up from one of the club old ladies. It was stunning and fit like a glove, but in that moment, all she wanted to feel was Kevlar—*no, Tucker tonight*—inside her in every possible way.

She turned the lock behind her and met his gaze. His brown depths held plenty of lust and a hint of mischief. She could use both to her advantage. Closing the distance, she slowly stripped, mindful of watching his expression change from sensual to pure animalistic. It sent a chill of desire all the way to her toes.

Grabbing him by his shirt, she pushed him toward the bed. He made it, but not without knocking over a lamp. It crashed to the floor, bulb flickering until it burned out.

Their gaze met and both let out a howl of laughter before she jumped on top of him. Clenching his shirt in her fist, she jerked it up and off his body. The pristine abs beneath sent her mouth salivating. It was only made more delicious by his artwork. Varying colors spread across his chest, military tattoos the oldest on his canvas. She kissed each tattoo, some even twice, making her way down his chest.

Dipping her tongue in his navel, she grinned at his sharp inhale. Licking a line down his Adonis muscles to his jeans, Nikita popped the buttons one at a time. Already, she felt his sizeable dick trapped beneath the black boxer briefs. She'd make him suffer for a little while longer.

She shoved the pants aside, his boxers the last article of clothing on his toned body. After running her hands along his thighs, she teased his balls with her fingers getting close but not close enough for him to feel satisfaction. This wasn't the Tucker Dorous of fifteen years ago, just like she wasn't the same bright-eyed girl. If tonight was all they had to be their younger selves, she'd show him every inch of pleasure they'd missed.

"Kita," he breathed, his eyes glued to her, but his hands remaining above his head. The muscles bulged, his desire to move clearly torturing him.

"You can touch me after I touch you." Her hand disappeared beneath his boxers, and he involuntarily jerked against her. "Not before."

Catching his strained facial expression, she wrapped her fingers around his cock, the heat warming her entire body. He had that effect on her. No matter how cold her demeanor, Tucker could bring her to a sultry steam.

Slipping his boxers to the floor, she settled between his thighs. His cock bounced impatiently in her hands. The sheer size of him used to scare her. He'd never been her first, but he was the only man to make her come simply by thrusting. A shiver ran down her spine, merely recalling the impending delight. It was one she desperately wanted to relive as many times as the night allowed.

Darting her tongue out, she licked his tip and purred at the immediate surge of precum. Swallowing it, she licked the length of him. Down one side then the other, her right hand massaging his balls.

She glanced up to see him press his hands together above his head, his face lined with frustration. He remained completely still; his cock, on the other hand, wouldn't stop jumping at her every touch. It was beautiful in a way—the control she had over this muscular man.

Determined to let him out of his misery for the moment, she closed her lips over the length of his cock. A guttural groan emitted from him, the sound sending sparks between her legs. Sucking him to the back of her throat, Nikita gagged but didn't stop. She wanted every inch of him and would get it. She always got what she wanted. If not, she'd never stop until she did.

Stroking the base of his cock while she sucked, the scent of her arousal met her. Without a doubt, she was drenched. Reaching down, she felt the slickness there and hummed her delight.

"Baby, I need to taste you." He sat up, and she swirled her tongue one last time before letting him pop from her lips. She nodded her permission, equally needing him to touch her.

Sitting up, she grabbed the base of his neck and pulled him against her mouth. Their tongues tangled wildly, her teeth grazing his lips. The frenzied kiss only intensified when his hand dipped between her legs. He growled in delight.

"Fuck, yes." Tucker kissed down her neck. His

lips enclosed her nipples one at a time. He pulled them to points, playfully biting until she moaned. His hands stayed near her pussy, never entering but toying with her. It was the same sheer torture he'd endured, and she adored it.

He kneeled on the floor next to her, keeping the back of her legs against the side of the bed. In one smooth move, he perched her on the edge and kissed up her thighs one at a time. The closer he got to her throbbing core, the more Nikita regretted teasing him.

Finally, he nudged his nose in her manicured curls. His tongue darted out, the coolness surprising her momentarily. That didn't last long. His heat met her pussy, tongue flicking over her clit.

His free hand massaged her breasts, and she arched her back. Her act moved him closer, deeper into her, and she closed her eyes at the pleasure he sent through her body with so little effort. Already, she felt the familiar buzz in the back of her mind. She'd come if he kept going, and he would. Tucker never relented. Not until she was fully sated.

His grip moved down to her ass and he pulled her closer, fully against his mouth. A week's worth of stubble around his lips enhanced his most intimate kisses, causing delightful friction. He slipped two fingers in her core, and she groaned. Her sound was only drowned out by his hum of satisfaction.

"This is what I've been missing." He eased away and met her eyes. "Your pussy tastes so fucking delicious. I could eat you every day and never get sick of your sweetness."

His thumb flicked against her clit, and she gripped his head, the orgasm building faster. His warm mouth encompassed her clit alongside his thumb. The combination of his tongue, fingers pulsing in her pussy, and the addition of his thumb on her clit sent her over the edge. Her toes curled when she cried out his name.

"Tucker, yes!"

Her hips bucked wildly, furthering the spiral of indulgence to continue. Tucker was there in an instant, plunging his hard cock into her pulsing pussy before her orgasm subsided. His movement hit her G-spot, milking her ecstasy to begin all over again. Gripping his forearms, she dug her fingernails in his flesh. His brown eyes met hers, the pain clearly turning him on further.

He caught her mouth beneath his, sucking on her bottom lip and pulling. She gasped at the sting mixed with the release he provided. It was the best combination she could imagine.

Her hips matched his in synchronized accord as if they were made singularly for each other. He jutted in and out of her, kissing to silence the sounds she couldn't keep bottled. *Fuck it, let them hear.* When he sucked the side of her neck, she screamed in Spanish.

He didn't bother to mute her any longer. Simply fucked her until her legs shook and her stomach quaked from his cock. She tried to get the upper hand, but he wouldn't allow it. Instead, he settled her ankles on his shoulders and plunged his cock deeper. The position shattered her in the best possible ways, her cum drenching him over and over again.

"Damn, Kita, you're squeezing me so tight." He grinned. "That's some magical pussy you have."

A bead of sweat slid down his forehead and landed on her chest. Giggling, she kissed him hard, eyes wide open. She needed to see it all tonight, even if the pure nirvana killed her.

"I do what I can." She laughed at his strained brow.

"Everything about you is fucking magical." He jutted into her faster, then grabbed her and pulled her off the bed.

Hung precariously in the air, she didn't worry.

Her man could more than handle her. Pressing her back to the door, he started pumping in and out of her again. The door shook, the handle rattling.

Tucker gently held his hand on her neck, eyes homed in on every sound, every movement she made beneath his vicious fucking. It turned her on so much she felt another orgasm spread through her body. Opening her mouth, she tried to whimper, but no sound escaped. Her eyes bugged, the intensity too much for her to handle alone. Seeing her dilemma, he caught her lips in a possessive kiss.

His hips slowed and his breath hitched, his cock swelling and spilling inside her. Nikita drew him closer, letting him rest against her breasts while the stars dissipated from her eyes. Chest heaving, she felt the rapid pulse in his neck. In an odd way, it calmed her. To know he was equally spent confirmed their connection. Tucker wasn't a man she could let slip through her fingers a second time. *But he's only Tucker right now. He'll be Kevlar the moment we step out of this room.*

"Don't do that," he said hoarsely, looking into her eyes. He brushed back her hair. "Don't pull away, baby. Not yet, please."

She offered him a small smile and rested her forehead to his. They were sweaty and gleaming in the waning light. His musky aroma mingled with her jasmine, creating the same overwhelming concoction she dreamed of. *I may never leave the damn room.* The moment she did, she'd leave her heart there.

***

Nikita stretched, tangling her leg between Tucker's. The fan overhead whirred noisily, air circulating around their tepid bodies. She stifled a yawn and looked to see him doing the same. They hadn't made it to dinner, but the lingering scent of roast chicken made her stomach gurgle.

Tucker chuckled and lightly rubbed her belly. "Hungry?"

"Maybe a little." She eyed the time on her phone. It was four hours past dinner. "Okay, maybe a lot."

Hopping to his feet, Tucker pulled on a pair of gray sweatpants that did nothing to hide his generous bulge of a cock.

"You're going out like that?" She propped up on her elbow, eyes focused on the one part of his body that just wouldn't stay down.

A slow smile covered his face. He playfully grabbed his crotch. "Yep, I like to show off every now and then."

"Since when?"

"Since I've been fucking the most gorgeous girl here."

She rolled her eyes. "Also known as, you want to brag to your brothers about getting some pussy."

He paused in the doorway. "I'm the envy of every man out there. Can you really blame me, Kita?"

She couldn't. She'd do the same damn thing if there was a group of her friends outside the door. "Hurry up or my stomach will eat itself."

After a mock salute, he returned minutes later with two cold chicken sandwiches and bottles of water.

Nikita munched on the food, eyes wandering the room. His Kevlar vest hung in the closet, and her curiosity mounted. "Why do you wear the vest?"

He finished his sandwich and brushed crumbs off his pants. "Keeps me safe."

"Duh, dumbass." She rolled over and poked the tattoo of a pinup doll on his left side. "I want to hear the story behind it."

His brown eyes darted to the closet, then back to her. "All right, sure." He pulled up his legs and tucked them crisscross. "A year in Afghanistan, my men and I were tasked to a diplomatic assignment. He was a lower-level guy, but dangerous enough the Afghans wanted him dead for giving the US secrets.

We were supposed to move him incognito. Hand-guns only and no uniforms."

Nikita watched his eyes take on a faraway gleam. He was thousands of miles away in that moment.

"Our intel was bad, and suddenly we were all under attack. Five of my men were shot in the head right in front of me."

She reached over and squeezed his hand. Losing a friend in combat was something she understood all too well.

"Anyways, Rubble and I got the package to the Humvee just as our backup caught up to us." The muscle in his neck tightened and he wet his lips. "A sniper caught Rubble in the arm. While our men were reacting to that, a ground group of assholes came up behind us, and I reacted." He scratched his nose. "I really don't remember all the details. I woke up with my vest full of bullets."

"You saved him?"

"Yeah, him and two other guys." He met her gaze. "Rubble told me later that I threw myself on them."

She let out a breath, a new sort of chill spiraling down her spine. Her Macha man was one of the unsung heroes from the war. His nightmares suddenly made sense. "You dream about it, don't you?"

He nodded. "Along with a lot of other shit that happened. I was lucky to only have a dislocated shoulder after that ambush. A lot of my guys didn't make it."

"But you did, and it must be for a damn good reason." She slid her hand on his jaw and turned his head to face her. "I'm glad you made it home."

His crooked smile melted her heart. He reached up and traced her lips with his thumb. "Me too, baby, me too."

Tucker pulled her against him, nestling her safely to his chest. As badly as she craved hearing more of his war stories, she could wait. For the time being, she was satisfied to merely be wrapped in his arms.

Chapter Twenty-Five

KEVLAR

Rolling over, Kevlar opened his eyes, the fragrance of Kita teasing his nostrils. She lay beside him, hair mussed and makeup smudged. Her lips were parted slightly. Reaching over, he gently touched them. They were so soft beneath his callused fingers. His mind repeated how they felt wrapped around his dick, and the hair on his arms stood. *Yeah, her lips are the best.*

She stirred, moving closer to his warmth. His heart pounded at the sight of her cuddling his arm. He'd chop the damn thing off if it meant they'd stay together like this every day.

His phone buzzed, and he frowned at the interruption. Ignoring that forever would be nice. Ignoring reality would be better. He focused back on Kita. Her chest raised up and down, the swell of her breasts visible in the moonlight. They'd fucked four times. Hell, he'd barely changed the condom before heading into round three. The girl was insatiable. *My girl is insatiable.* A sad smile crossed his face. That's how Kita was fifteen years ago. Evidently, time hadn't changed her sex drive. *Thank the goddess.*

He'd never complain about sex again if she was his. Even after breaking the lamp, their cataclysmic sexual acts made the bedsprings squeak long into the night. If her moans didn't wake his brothers, he didn't know what would. He'd tried to swallow her sounds but eventually gave up. He didn't give a shit. He was the luckiest bastard in the clubhouse. His brothers could go fuck themselves. Knowing them, a few probably did too. He chuckled softly, not giving a damn if they did.

Cock stirring at the thoughts of their bodies connecting, he considered leaving her to dreamland. The soft sigh she made in her sleep changed his mind. He needed her once more before the spell was broken, and they were thrown into reality.

Kissing a trail up her arm, he focused on her neck, the one place she couldn't resist. Her fingernails scraped his head, his beauty no longer asleep.

Glancing at her, he smirked at Kita's closed eyes. Well, maybe she was, but her body wasn't.

Kita wrapped her leg around his waist, compelling him to enter her sanctuary one final time. After this, he'd be lost to her. She was the goddess he remembered and the siren he'd think of for years to come. No woman would have the same effect on him. He didn't even want to try. Kita was his Macha.

Her fingertips trailed his biceps, clenching him but not as tight as her pussy walls milked his hard length. It was eerie how easily she made him come. That was new. Then again, his memory could've faded.

Slowly, tenderly, he slid his cock in her warmth. The other times were fucking. This was lovemaking. A fulfilled smile painted across her face, piercing his heart and shattering his resolve. Her departure was unavoidable. He'd pushed it aside whenever the subject broached. He couldn't after this.

Kita's arms laced around his neck, her lips seeking him out, and he gladly obliged. If this was it, he'd give it his all. No regrets. No what ifs. No fifteen years later repeat. His heart couldn't handle another round of her sweet agony.

To his surprise, she rolled them over, taking over

the position. Her breasts swung delicately in the darkness, pulling him into an alternate universe where it was just the two of them.

Her black hair perfectly accented her caramel-colored skin. From his angle, she couldn't be more beautiful. Her hips rocked into him, a breathy moan sending shivers over his body. He adored how he could please her. The repeat performances only bolstered his growing affection. It was selfish, but he didn't care. His heart knew from day one she was destined to be his for eternity. Convincing Kita, though, that was the difficult part. He'd be content with their time. It's what he had to keep telling himself.

Kita's hands spread over his pecs, sliding up to his shoulders and squeezing hard as she ground into him. Moisture dripped from her pussy to his stomach and down his ribs. Every ounce of her passion was worth the heartache he'd carry the rest of his life.

He gripped her hips, helping her to completion. That damn smile she made right after orgasm got him off. It was enough to make him come on command. He waited until she was fully sated, then tucked her against him, his arm encircling her for the last few hours of mindless sleep.

His phone buzzed again. *Should've turned the thing off.* Glancing over at it, he winced at the bright light. Most were bullshit messages from Rubble and Hawk. He'd give them hell in the morning for cramping his style. They didn't understand. The women in their lives were replaceable. Kita was the only one who wasn't. No woman could ever come within tossing distance of the gutsy Spanish goddess tangled in his tattooed arms.

***

"How's your sister by the way?"

Kita's groggy voice stirred Kevlar once more. He grunted and pulled up the sheet, somehow lost after their last embrace. "She's fine."

Soft tresses of hair tickled his neck, and he smiled. Opening his eyes, he watched Kita drag her long, black hair across his chest, teasing him to react.

"Need more than that, *guapo*," she replied, replacing her hair with her lips.

Letting out a steadying breath, he reached over and grazed his fingertips along her back. "Joci is great. Shacked up with some mobster turned cop with two kids."

"Wow, very nice. When was the last time you saw her?" Kita perched her chin on the right side of his chest.

He scratched his forearm. "I don't know. I was overseas for a long time and came straight to Colorado."

Her eyes dipped to his abs, and she brazenly ran her tongue down until she reached the sheet. Settling there, she cocked her head. "You were never close, though, right?"

"No. My parents sent me to military schools while my sister got straight As." He thought back to parts of his childhood when he was home. "We never had that bond. I don't know why."

"Have you tried talking to her since you returned to Colorado?"

He shook his head. "My sister is a kickass criminal attorney in Iowa, baby. The last thing she needs is her degenerate biker brother to waltz back into her life." Grabbing Kita beneath her arms, he pulled her on to his lap. "Why the family talk? I'd much rather do other activities with you that aren't family-friendly."

Kita smoothed his brow. "I never had siblings. When my father... when he went to prison, it hit me hard. Sure, I had Mamá, but we didn't see eye to eye a lot of the time. I always wanted a brother or sister to share my thoughts with." She kissed the tip of his nose. "You have a sister and barely talk to her. I can't even imagine it."

His heart squeezed at her insight. His family was all sorts of fucked up, but they were still family. After they moved from Ohio to Iowa, something shifted in the family dynamics. He couldn't put his finger on it, but the once happy Dorous family disappeared.

"Tell you what, I'll call Joci after all this is over." He searched out her amber eyes. "Good enough for you?"

Kita rolled him on top of her and kissed him hard. "If you can have a family, you should. Nobody should be alone."

"Then should we talk about yours?"

She wrapped her legs around his waist and pressed against him. "Hell no. Mine is much more complicated."

Catching her lips once more, Kevlar easily maneuvered into her warmth. A satisfied moan slipped from her lips, and he immediately caught it in his mouth. They could talk about anything under the sun and still end up fucking. It was why he loved her so damned much. And why the thought of her returning to Boston made his soul shatter.

Chapter Twenty-Six

NIKITA

Fat clouds threatened snow the next morning. After Nikita's alarm went off at daybreak, she stared out the window, her lips drawn in a thin line. The next hours would either bring brilliant success or glaring defeat. She hoped for the former. Her career depended on a win.

Kevlar grunted from his spot in the bed. The warm blankets and equally heated man tempted her to stay wrapped in the cocoon of his love the rest of the day. Her phone rang noisily. Unfortunately, that wasn't an option. She pulled on her jeans and one of Kevlar's black tees. It swallowed her whole, his cologne mixed with oil and cigarette smoke clinging to the fabric. Closing her eyes, she inhaled the musk, swearing to never return the shirt even after the scent faded.

Sneaking out of the room, she answered in a low voice, "Zane, what's going on? I didn't think we were meeting until nine."

"We weren't, but the Cutthroats are on the move."

Her eyes bugged. "What?" She hurried back into the room and grabbed her shoes. Her rapid movements caused Kevlar to sit straight up in bed, the sheet falling precariously close to revealing his glorious naked form.

"They must've gotten wind we were in town." Zane sounded annoyed, road noise in the background. "I already spoke to Rubble."

As if the man himself heard the conversation, Rubble burst into the room. His bald head was covered with a black beanie cap, mismatched eyes alert. "Kevlar, get up. We need to hit the road."

Not speaking, Kevlar got to his feet, not bothering to cover himself in the slightest. While she couldn't take her eyes off his nakedness, it appeared the other man wasn't fazed in the slightest. Then again, they'd known each other a long time.

"Yeah, he's here," she finally said, focusing on the

conversation. She rifled through the discarded clothes on the floor and found her bra.

"Good. There's a snowstorm brewing, and from the looks of it, they're headed down the alternative route." Zane cursed under his breath. "Let's hope your Macha men are prepared."

"They will be." She hung up without another word and finished dressing. She couldn't give up his shirt, a fact he noticed if the smirk on his face was any indicator.

Kevlar brushed by her, dressed from head to toe in Macha gear. Gone was the Tucker Dorous of the night before. The MC replacement stood in his place.

He tilted up her chin, brown eyes searching hers. "Be safe, Kita."

She swallowed hard at the emotion on his face that he desperately tried to hide. "You too."

Kevlar started to close the distance to her lips, then thought better of it. He turned on his toes and followed his brother out the door and down the hall. Rubble banged on doors as they walked, movement from each room, reacting to the sound of his booming voice. The sergeant at arms wasn't coy in his wake-up call.

Mandi's grumbling in the hallway reminded her

they needed to move. Taking one last look at the room, Nikita bit her bottom lip. It'd been a good night even if sleep hadn't been on the menu. Regret didn't line her gut to her surprise. A yearning for more did, though.

She retrieved a black beanie, much like the ones Kevlar and Rubble wore and inhaled the material. It bespoke of hours with Kevlar. She pulled it over her messy hair and stared at the small mirror near the door. The Macha symbol was stamped on the front, a reminder that she all but joined the club to take down two MCs. Somehow, it didn't bother her. Macha wasn't her father's club. They stood for something else entirely.

I could see myself happy with them.

Shaking her head, she hurried over the threshold. Thinking like that would get her killed. She was a goddamn FBI agent who took down MCs. She couldn't join one. Even if her heart urged her to.

***

From all accounts, the secondary route was abysmal. The curvy roads cut through the mountain pass, sharp turns at every glance. The FBI should've counted on the MC to change up their well-laid plans. Their dual informant, Juliet, was murdered —*most likely for knowing too much*—and the

Cutthroats were playing it safe. Her recent visit to Fishkill Penitentiary could've affected their plan too. She tried to push that thought aside. She wouldn't visit again if he warned the MC. Her father was smart enough to know that.

Nikita rubbed her hands together, cursing the lack of gloves. *Should've grabbed the ones Queenie offered.* She pulled her FBI jacket closer. They didn't have time to chat with Reaper's old lady before hustling to their sedan. Thankfully, Mandi snagged a bundle of freshly made cinnamon twists, courtesy of Doc shockingly enough, along with two cups of coffee.

Snow dusted the windshield and she flicked on the wipers. Puffs of smoke drifted from the Macha truck down the road. From cigarettes or exhaling, she wasn't sure. Rubble, Hawk, and Kevlar were stationed at the first checkpoint. Doc and Cueball were at the third, while she and Mandi sat in the middle. Once the Cutthroats and Diablos shipment came through, the Macha trucks would block the road in both directions, and she and Mandi would swoop in.

Zane set up shop at the initial route in case of a double-back. They couldn't be too careful when it came to these two MCs. They'd skated detection before, and losing them today wouldn't bode well at the agency.

A few vehicles passed on the road. None appeared out of place, which both comforted and annoyed her. The longer they sat there, the less likely their intel was correct. The most recent chatter the FBI received didn't specify when the shipment was being moved. They couldn't risk losing the trafficked women who would most assuredly be sold at the next stop.

"Any of this feel odd to you?" Mandi asked, breaking apart one of the cinnamon twists and taking a bite.

"What do you mean?" She turned in the driver seat, brows furrowed.

"I don't know the whole fast switch seems off." She shrugged. "Maybe I'm being paranoid."

Nikita glanced out the window. No signs of movement from Kevlar's truck. Hell, she could barely see it. The only part showing was the chrome on the front. The rest of the truck was well-hidden behind a boulder.

She checked the time and frowned. It was past the time the two MCs should've traveled through the pass along with a semi. A chill traced down her spine despite the car's warm interior.

Digging out her phone, she called Zane. When he didn't answer, her stomach dropped. Agents always answered. *Unless we've been compromised.*

Turning up the heat, she sent a message to Kevlar.

Nikita: Anything over there?

Kevlar: None.

Tapping her knuckles on the bottom of the steering wheel, she tried Zane again. *Shit, no answer.*

"I think you're right." She met Mandi's worried face. "They must've switched routes."

Before she could call Kevlar to retreat, a bullet whizzed between them and hit the windshield. Glass shattered across the dash, and they hunkered down in their seats.

"Get the fuck out!" a voice yelled from outside.

Nikita glanced over the Mandi, who shook her head vehemently. Another spraying of bullets, this time from an automatic. Clenching her jaw, Nikita closed her eyes and sent every known prayer heavenward. She didn't give a shit which god or goddess saved her ass, just that they didn't die.

The peppering paused, but more echoed further down the road. "Damn, how'd they find us?"

"I'm not sure, but I need to warn the other team."

She felt for her phone and realized it'd fallen

through the tiny space between the seat and console. She struggled to reach it, fingertips grazing it only to push it deeper in the slot. The door handle jiggled, and she looked up in time to see a Diablos biker smash the window with the butt of his gun. Grabbing her sidearm, she fired off a round. It took him to the snowy ground, but where there was one, there were more. A slew of shots fired at them, whizzing by her ears and spraying the interior with glass confetti.

"Mandi, are you okay?"

Nikita snapped her eyes toward her partner and let out a frantic cry. Blood trickled down Mandi's face, a bullet to the back of her head silencing her reply forever.

"No, no, no!" She automatically checked for a pulse even though she knew there wouldn't be one. "Goddammit."

Revenge cooled her blood and overtook her grief. She let off another round into an approaching Diablos, shifting the car into gear. There'd be time to mourn her partner later. Right now, she needed to make them pay.

"Do it and die."

The icy voice, coupled with the barrel of a gun to her temple, paused her grand escape. She shifted back to Park and lifted her hands. He tore away her gun and tossed it in a snowbank.

"You don't want to do this," she warned, sliding her gaze to the man decked out in Cutthroat gear. It was Pillar. The club president himself. *Holy shit.*

He laughed and motioned for her to exit the vehicle. "Oh, but I do."

Nikita stepped out of the sedan, eyes scanning the area. Gunshots bounced across the pass, manly shouts joining. Kevlar's truck was still stationary. She walked toward Pillar, hands high. She caught a glimpse of a tall man in black clothes rushing toward their position, but additional Cutthroats cut off his advance.

"Look, if you let me go, I'm sure we can work something out." She stopped beside the green Hummer with vanity plates. Without asking, she knew the vehicle belonged to Pillar. "My father is—"

"I know who your daddy is, Nikita." Three more Cutthroats joined him. "And he'll pay dearly for double-crossing me."

"What are you talking about?"

He thrust the gun in her chest, beady eyes alight with revenge. "Muerte thinks he can take 60 percent of my haul? Well, he's got another think coming.

He'll give it all back to me or lose you in the process."

"My father won't make the deal." The Hummer door opened, and she reluctantly climbed in. "We aren't on good terms."

Pillar shrugged. "If not, I'll sell you with the rest of the women. Either way, I win."

Chapter Twenty-Seven

KEVLAR

Tires squealed in the snow as one last round of gunshots echoed along the road. Snow fell steadily, making visibility near none. Kevlar kept his gun trained and cautiously peeked around the snow-covered rock. No sign of the Cutthroats. He glanced over his shoulder at his brothers. They were all in one piece, a couple somewhat cut-up from the broken glass. He rested a hand to his chest, the bulletproof vest intact.

Kita's car idled nearby, and he sprinted toward it, the worst scenarios running in his mind. The front and back windshields were cracked with bullets, and a red tinge lined the glass.

Please don't let it be Kita. He repeated the words in his mind. Reaching the car, he noticed the body in the passenger side. He kept low in case of any straggling bullets. Opening the door, he cringed at what met him. Mandi's body was slumped over the seat belt, eyes wide and empty. The blood matted her hair, the scent of death lingering in the car. Her gun lay at her feet, hands limp above it.

He glanced to the driver side. *No Kita.* Panicking, he looked in the back seat and even popped the trunk. Seeing scuffled shoe prints in the snow near her door, his pulse skyrocketed. He followed them and reached tire tracks. *Dammit.*

"Kevlar? What's their status?" Rubble asked, jogging toward him.

He jerked a thumb toward the car. "Mandi's dead." He looked past Rubble to Hawk. The man hadn't heard the news yet, and he wasn't looking forward to informing him.

Rubble pushed up his cap. "Damn. I'll tell Hawk." His eyes slid to the open driver door. "And Nikita?"

"Gone. Not sure which MC took her either." He crouched in the snow, flakes hitting his face sweetly despite the havoc in his heart. "Could've been either one. They all wore the same color."

"I don't understand what happened." Rubble holstered his gun. "The FBI...."

Kevlar looked up and saw the suspicious glint in Rubble's eyes. "You don't think...."

"Yeah, I do." He pulled out his phone and dialed. "We've been played. C'mon, we need to get to the clubhouse."

Standing upright, he reluctantly walked back to their truck. Doc met his gaze, and he sadly shook his head. Immediately, the medic called the sheriff, letting the man know the situation and the dead body.

"I'll stay with Mandi," Doc offered. "The rest of you secure the clubhouse."

Hawk shook his head, his face unreadable. There'd be time to grieve later. Now, they had to defend Macha. "I'm staying here too. Better to stick in groups of two or more."

The brothers knew the true reason behind Hawk's request to stay behind, but none voiced it. Leaving Doc and Hawk behind, the remaining men climbed in the bullet-riddled truck and started toward Snowshoe. There'd be hell to pay. And the Cutthroats and Diablos would be held accountable for it.

Along with anyone else who betrayed us.

Chapter Twenty-Eight

NIKITA

A BLACK BAG HINDERED HER VISION FOR THE DURATION of the car ride. She didn't know the area well enough to map where they were headed, but she timed every turn and curve in case she was able to escape.

Metal rock music blared from the speakers, and she did her best not to react. The FBI trained assets in case of capture, music being one of the torture devices. This method wasn't the worst, but her ears begged to differ. She could barely think straight, let alone hear what the men were saying.

The Hummer screeched to a halt and a hand wrapped around her arm, pulling her out of the back seat. She didn't struggle. It'd do no one any good. She needed to keep alert, and getting whacked with a gun wouldn't get her there.

The ground was hard, but not frozen grass. Footsteps echoed in the space, and she guessed they were in a large garage. A mixture of Spanish and English words were tossed back and forth. Mostly about her *tight ass*, of which she chose to feign naivety.

"In here," a gruff voice said, nudging her forward.

She grunted when large hands gripped her shoulders and pushed her onto a metal chair. The material chilled right through her jeans, immediately making her wish she were back in Kevlar's cozy bed.

The bag slid up, and light blinded her on impact. She winced and held up her hands to shield her eyes. When she finally adjusted to the room, she scanned it quickly. It was empty, save a table, chairs, and a large black TV screen on the wall. The low ceiling, florescent panel lighting, and white walls resembled an old office building, an abandoned water cooler in one corner.

"Where am I?"

Pillar came into view and placed a can of cola on the table. "A private hangar outside Snowshoe. The military used it in the 80s for special ops." He sat in the chair opposite her. "I was stationed here for two months before they shut it down."

"I'm assuming you contacted my father."

"Yep." Pillar smirked. "His sergeant at arms will be in touch soon. Just sit tight, Agent Stockdale. You'll be out of here within the hour."

"Doubtful." She opened the pop and took a drink of the off-brand drink. It did nothing to relieve her thirst for escape. "So, who in the FBI tipped you off?"

Pillar sat with arms crossed over his chest. "Not that easy."

"Then who?"

"Your father. Well, in a roundabout way."

She wracked her mind. She never told her father about the FBI plans. They didn't cement them until two days ago. *Shit...* Nikita met Pillar's humored eyes.

"Put it together, now, didn't ya?"

"The FBI. It was one of Zane's guys."

"Nope, Zane himself," a new voice stated, coming into the room.

She swiveled her neck to see Zane outfitted in FBI gear. He offered her a weak smile, and she scowled. "You bastard."

"Sorry, Stockdale, but I saw an opportunity and couldn't pass it up." He pulled a chair away from the wall and sat next to Pillar. "You were too wrapped up in your daddy issues to see it coming too."

"What do you mean?" Only recently reconnecting with her father couldn't have been the reason for the misleading plan.

"I need to admit something." Zane lifted his shirt, the mandatory Diablos tattoo scarred into his flesh. "I'm your father's sergeant at arms."

The room spun at his words. None of it made sense until that moment. She closed her eyes and fought the urge to lunge at him. It'd be a waste of energy. They'd tossed her weapon, and two against one wasn't good odds with no backup in sight.

"You helped run Diablos from within the FBI."

"Look at you getting one right." He nodded. "I couldn't have done it without you either. You were so determined to make your father pay that you barely noticed when his club always skirted your troops at the last minute. It hasn't been easy, so kudos, kid. You've kept me on my toes."

"How did you get caught up with Diablos?"

"I was one of the agents assigned to your father's case," Zane stated. "At first, I thought he was a scumbag. The more I talked to him, the more I realized how brilliant he was." He grinned. "I mean, he successfully ran one of the largest drug-running

MCs on the East Coast right under the government's nose."

She rolled her eyes. "Great, he's your hero."

"No, he's my mentor. He got me thinking about how easy it'd be to keep Diablos going from within the FBI." Zane tossed a candy bar on the table. "He's also my meal ticket out of here."

"Going somewhere tropical?"

"Actually, yes."

She snorted and shook her head in distaste. "That'll be the first place he looks for you. Nowhere is safe from Diablos."

"You should know. You played right into his plan." The FBI agent preened. "Once I made the connection between you, Nikita Morales not Stockdale, I was practically a shoo-in to the sergeant role. Muerte promised me an assload of money, and he's delivered. Now it's time I step down and hand the reins to someone else." He slapped Pillar's back. "This guy will work, and since your father's VP screwed the Cutthroats on the drug deal, I think Pillar earned the extra money."

"And you get a kickback from the Cutthroats too."

"Naturally. Call it my never-ending finder's fee."

"Then why take me?"

Zane's blue eyes turned cold. "Because the price of my retirement reduced significantly the moment you arrived in Waverley."

"What? How?"

"Because you found out about the trafficking and the FBI took the bait." He grunted. "I'd planned another five years before that cash flow fell through. You sped up my timeline."

"Good, I'm glad."

Zane's left cheek twitched. "You're a pain in the ass, Nikita." His eyes lowered to her chest. "A pretty one, but a pain nonetheless."

"Why? Because I did my job?" If she could keep Zane talking long enough, it'd give her time to hatch a plan.

"Partly, yes. Muerte wanted you to take over Diablos, but I knew you wouldn't. Too goody-good for that." He looked down his nose at her. "Since I'm his sergeant, I went along with his plan and left breadcrumbs for you to take down rival MCs, all the while working my own end game with the trafficking ring. Muerte found out and, instead of killing me, decided to take over. Luckily, it all worked out." He frowned. "Until you dug too deep and that whore, Juliet, opened her big mouth. Can't trust junkies."

Zane glanced at his FBI jacket. "That's when we

partnered with the Cutthroats. It was the one trafficking avenue Muerte didn't control and wanted to. Evidently, Muerte was greedy, and that didn't sit well." He glanced to Pillar. "I honestly don't care."

Rubbing her lips together, Nikita soaked in the information. They were backstabbing assholes only looking out for themselves. *Macha wouldn't do this.* At least she hoped they wouldn't.

"And the farce with the route?"

"We had to get you alone. With that Macha biker hanging around you all the time, I couldn't risk the exposure." He cracked his neck from side to side. "Plus, the Cutthroats needed to let off a little steam. Evidently, they blame you for losing their best whore."

Nikita's pulse thrummed in her skull. "Diablos killed her, not me."

He shrugged indifference. "Juliet was a loose end, and we did what was necessary."

"What about the women?" They were the reason she came to Colorado in the first place. "Where are they?"

Zane and Pillar exchanged a glance. "Herded them on the truck this morning. Our driver leaves in two hours. If Muerte doesn't uphold his end of my retirement pension, you join them."

The thought sickened her more than the blood money they were trying to get out of her father. "How much am I worth to you?"

"Five hundred thousand." Zane smirked at her reaction. "Seven hundred-and-fifty thousand big ones if he wants you untouched."

Her stomach dropped at his insinuation. Everything boiled down to money for these men. It sickened her to her very core.

"I'll pay it, but you have to let the other women go too."

Zane's brows lifted, and Pillar choked on the soda he was drinking. "What?"

"Seven hundred-and-fifty thousand dollars. I'll make a couple calls and wire it to you."

"You're a government employee. There's no way you have that kind—"

"My mother left me a trust," she hurried to say. "Let me go and I'll send the money within the hour."

The two men exchanged glances. For one hot minute, Nikita thought they'd take her up on the offer.

Finally, Pillar spoke. "And risk you alerting the Feds? No deal. Our shipment is worth ten times that at auction."

Nikita's hands curled to fists. She didn't have that

much. Even if she did, she doubted they'd make a deal. The odds were stacked against her, but she had to do something. Sitting complacently wasn't who she was.

In a desperate move, Nikita reached across the table and punched Zane in the face, blood instantly gushing. He reeled back and fell out of his chair. Pillar swung and missed, and she quickly kicked his ankle, bowing his stance, and punched his nose before sprinting to the door. The familiar click of a gun met her ears just as she turned the doorknob.

"God damn, Muerte was right to brag about you," Zane said, walking over to her and opening the door. "But I'm sick of playing. Let's go." He grabbed a handful of her hair and wrenched her head back. "Don't tempt me to fuck you like your Macha man did last night."

"How did you—"

His sinister laugh sent chills down her spine. "You ought to be more mindful, Agent. Bugs are everywhere. Even on your precious FBI jacket." He reached down and grabbed the small electronic device and showed it to her before crushing it with his boot.

Zane led her away by her hair, and she swallowed a pained cry. She wouldn't give him the satisfaction. They didn't bother to camouflage their hideout, simply led her toward a large semi on the road.

"Let's hope your father comes to his senses, eh?" He nodded at a biker with a rifle, and the back door opened moments later.

The crushing stench of bodily fluids and lack of hygiene smacked her face hard. She lifted her hand to her nose. It did no good. The women shied away from the door, marks on their exposed skin. From tasers or knives, she couldn't tell. They were in bad shape, though, that much she recognized.

"You're an animal!" She stomped on Zane's foot, and he backhanded her face.

"No, you're the animal. At least until your father frees you." He hoisted her into the back of the truck and the doors shut without another word.

Turning, Nikita braced herself for the worst. What she saw made horror films appear juvenile.

Chapter Twenty-Nine

KEVLAR

"What do you mean you can't trace her?" Kevlar glared at the FBI agent on the other end of the video chat. They'd tracked the getaway car down the mountain but then lost them at the plowed roads.

For the last hour, Rubble combed through Macha's security footage, trying to see if they'd missed anything. After he came up empty, they reached out to the FBI's Denver location, who then put them in contact with Kita's direct boss.

Randy Penn stared back at him. "Her phone is turned off, most likely tossed. We can't trace something that's not there. I'm sorry."

"What do you plan on doing about it?" This from Reaper, who seemed equally pissed about the ambush.

"Agents from Denver will be there shortly. They'll take over the investigation and bring Agent Riggs home." His eyes clouded. "I'm very sorry this all happened. There will be an internal investigation of course."

Kevlar took a step forward, but Reaper's hand on his shoulder silenced him before he spouted off at the man thousands of miles away.

"Please stand down," Randy said before signing off. "The FBI will handle this."

The screen went black, as did the faces in the room. Macha had been played, and they couldn't pinpoint who to blame. The FBI, Cutthroats, or Diablos. Each one had moles, it seemed. And no one had caught them before it was too late.

"So, what're we going to do?" Doc asked. "I'm sure as hell not standing down."

Hawk nodded. "Neither am I. They killed Mandi. Whoever pulled the trigger needs to be held accountable. The FBI's too busy chasing their tails to do it. We gotta step up."

The rest of Macha's members voiced their opinions, all pro kicking some ass.

Reaper banged the gavel on the table, silencing the rumblings. "Brothers, this isn't what we signed on for." His blue eyes skimmed the room slowly. "But

I know we all want to see Nikita safe." He nodded to Kevlar. "And to finish the work she and Agent Mandi Riggs started."

Kita's purpose for coming to Colorado ran through Kevlar's mind. Her life goal was to save others. Whether it be by putting away dangerous MCs or saving women from being sold into horrific situations, she wouldn't stop until the wrongs were righted.

"Women are precious to Macha," Kevlar spoke up. "This isn't new, brothers. We all but worship the women under our protection. Well, the women Kita was sent to help have no one to protect them. They need us even if to give them the chance at a better life. Our goddess would demand it." He met Rubble's gaze, pride lining the blue and green eyes. "Who'll join me in protecting them?"

A chorus of "Ayes" shouted back to him. For the first time since seeing Kita gone, he smiled. His club would never let him down. It was the one constant in his life. Macha and Kita. He needed both to survive.

***

Sleep evaded him every time he closed his eyes to nap. After being up most the night before with Kita, the main thing keeping Kevlar going was adrenaline. Adrenaline and caffeine. He downed the last bit of the energy drink and crushed the can.

Doc gave him an odd glance. "How many of those have you had today?"

Kevlar grabbed a box of shells and shrugged. "Three, four, maybe."

"And coffee?"

"A few cups." He watched Doc's usually cheerful demeanor turn concerned. "Look, I'm good. I just gotta find Kita, then I'll be great."

Walking over to him, Doc glanced around the clubhouse armory in the subbasement. It was filled with fellow bikers gearing up for the unknown. He took the seat next to him and lowered his voice. "I felt the same when Isa was kidnapped."

Kevlar narrowed his gaze, recalling the situation. He'd just returned from deployment and came back to see Macha preparing for an all-out war with the Irish MC, the Twelve Brothers. He'd never seen the club react like that. Then again, the Twelve Brothers took the daughter of their Belfast chapter's president.

"A Macha princess is worth a whole lot more to Macha than an FBI agent." He cocked his gun and double-checked the safety. "Kita is worth ten times that to any MC with a grudge. Her death would be slow, arduous, and painful. They'll torture her for years just for shits and giggles." He shook his head. "No, don't you dare compare Kita to your Irish princess."

Doc held up his hands but didn't back down. "Look, I get it. Maybe not the same situation, but similar. I was worried sick about Isa, but I also knew she could hold her own. My job was to protect her, and in doing that, I also made sure she could shoot a gun." He jutted his chin towards Dolly, who handed out shells by the box. "And she made sure Isa could fight."

"What's your point?"

"Kita is an FBI agent, brother." He patted his shoulder. "She sure as fuck can defend herself. Hell, I wouldn't be surprised if she had them all hog-tied by the time we arrive."

Kevlar let himself grin. It did sound like something his badass woman would do to anyone who dared hurt her. "Yeah, Kita can take care of herself. Has the last fifteen years." He cursed. "I should've looked harder for her. Should've known she didn't up and abandon me."

Doc pushed back his long hair. "Nobody has that crystal ball, or we'd be filthy rich. For all you knew, she married some prince and was living happily ever after."

He rubbed a hand over his chest, the Kevlar vest in place over his vital organs. It was the one thing he felt naked without after so many years of wearing one. "Never felt right, you know? In the back of my mind, she wasn't living out her dream. But I ignored that feeling. Pushed it down because it hurt too much to think she'd left because of me."

Doc didn't say anything. He simply sat there in silence. In a way, Kevlar was grateful his brother didn't try to talk him out of his thoughts. He'd done it so many times over the years. Coming face-to-face with reality fifteen years later was harder than he thought.

"Thanks, Doc." He nodded and stood. The fellow Macha members were all geared up and ready. Rubble explained their plan once. He didn't need to repeat himself. They all knew the risks and the rewards. Macha didn't abandon one of their own. Macha didn't abandon anyone they could save.

Chapter Thirty

NIKITA

THE SUMMER SHE SPENT ON THE SPANISH COASTLINE kept playing in her mind. Over and over, she imagined herself sunning on the beach, the scent of freshly baked bread and suntan lotion drifting on the ocean breeze. For days at a time, she'd enjoyed the surf and sand, worry the farthest thing from her mind.

Opening her eyes, Nikita winced at the harsh reality. This was not a beach. It wasn't even a hovel. It was a shithole. Her eyes grazed a hole cut in the bottom of the truck bed corner. No, that was the shithole. There were two, in fact.

She shivered, from the cold or her surroundings; she wasn't sure which was the culprit. The wind howled against the side of the truck, sniffling and deep coughs the only sound louder. *The one day I don't layer to stay warm.* She rubbed her hands up and down the sides of her arms, the friction barely denting the cold dead set in her bones after six hours in the back of the semi.

A group of Russian girls no older than twelve huddled next to her. None of them spoke English, and she didn't speak a lick of Russian. She flunked out of it in her FBI training.

One of the girls tugged on the sleeve of her jacket. Her bright blue eyes were hollow, no emotion evident other than despair. It broke Nikita's heart. She offered her a small smile. The girl smelled worse than a pigsty. They all did. Her hair was matted with what she hoped was dirt.

The girl spoke a rapid sentence. Nikita shrugged. "Sorry, I don't understand."

"She wants to know why you're here," another girl said in the group opposite them.

Nikita searched the dimly lit trailer and realized she wasn't as young as the others. In fact, the entire huddle was near her own age. "Oh." She looked to the girl and gently cupped her face. "To save you."

The other woman rattled off her reply, and the girl cracked a hint of a smile. It tugged every heartstring Nikita possessed.

"I think your plan failed if you're in here with us," the other woman said. She moved closer, and Nikita got a good look at her. The blonde hair was cut short, almost as if someone sheared it off violently. "The name's Yasmina, by the way." She nodded to her group. "We're from Ukraine."

"It's not the way I planned, but I'm confident I'll get you all out." Nikita's eyes swept over the women. The youngest she guessed was five. It sickened her to think of where they originated and the sick fucks who wanted to buy them for their personal uses.

"How long have you been in here?"

Yasmina shrugged. "Time is easily lost. Four months or more." She nodded to the women from her village. "I was taken before summer. The ship ride was almost deliberate. The sailors...." Tears welled in her eyes and her voice broke. She cleared her throat, pushing the emotions away. "They abused us any way they wanted. Our captors didn't care."

"Was it Diablos? Did they grab you?"

She shook her head. "A gang back home. They sold us to someone else. I heard them talk but couldn't understand the language." She scrunched her nose. "Sounded weird."

The description didn't help Nikita. Too many languages could be labeled as "weird."

"We were sold separately, then boarded the ship."

It was then Nikita noticed how emaciated the woman looked. The dirty clothes hung off her shoulders, her exposed bones sticking out grotesquely.

"The young girls...?" Nikita couldn't finish the question. Her stomach couldn't handle it.

Yasmina shook her head. "They're untouched. For now. They sell at a higher price intact." She lowered her eyes. "The same cannot be said the older you are. I doubt we'll be sold to anyone but a pimp."

Someone pounded on the side of the trailer, the women inside seized up, and all eyes turned toward the sound.

"Shut up in there!"

Nikita waited until she heard footsteps fade to speak in hushed tones. "Have you eaten anything?" She had the candy bar from Zane in her pocket. It wouldn't feed them all but would help a few.

"Not today. We're fed every third day." She nodded to the giant water jugs. "They give us water daily. It's not always clean, but it's better than nothing."

Those words haunted her. All her life, she'd taken so many things for granted while horrible men and women did this to innocents. She gritted her teeth, determined to stay alive if only to rip off Zane's balls with a rusty fork.

"What did you do before they kidnapped you?"

Yasmina blinked several times before she spoke. "I worked at a bakery. We made the most delicious bread and sweet treats." Her slight smile faded. "I imagine I'm eating at the back of the shop whenever we're fed here." She grimaced. "The food is almost always moldy or rotting. Three girls nearly died from it."

Nikita gripped the underside of her thighs to keep from reacting. She didn't feel mere anger. Outrage was putting it mildly. Just when she thought the situation for these women couldn't get worse, it did.

"I heard them say you'd leave soon." Yasmina handed her a scrap of paper. "Will you tell my mother I'm dead?"

Nikita's face paled. Death was better than the future that awaited each woman and child in the back of the semi. She took the paper and opened it to see a name and address.

"Please."

She nodded, swallowing her tears. "I'm going to get you all out of here."

Yasmina smiled sadly. "You won't. Some maybe, but not all."

"Why do you say that?"

Moving closer to her, Yasmina coughed into her hands. The wheezing sound didn't paint a pretty picture. "Some are too ill to move faster than a turtle." The lilt to her words hitched. "But I think you will escape. The men, they said your father will pay your ransom. My parents couldn't. They were poor bakers. Barely had enough money for rent."

Nikita didn't bother explaining. Clearly, whoever trafficked these women from varying places on the map used extortion and, when that failed, sold the women. If the men were as hideous as she thought, they probably took the money and the girls.

"They hurt you, don't they?"

Yasmina nodded against Nikita's shoulder. "It's not so bad at first. The tasers, I mean. They use other sticks, harder ones the more you misbehave." She shuddered. "But when they take you to... to..."

Wrapping her arms around the woman's frail body, Nikita fought the heat rising in her soul.

"They take turns," Yasmina mumbled. "If you don't do what they ask, it's longer and worse."

Silent tears laced with fury trickled down Nikita's face. She looked around the trailer. More than half were old enough to have been subjected to the horrors Yasmina spoke of. Nikita couldn't bear to think of the other atrocities they'd endured.

The sound of chains being removed from the back door sent the women scurrying toward the front. She could only guess if they didn't, they'd inherit more scars from a taser or baton. The sickly scent of burning flesh drifted to her, and she noticed a girl about ten years old with a healing wound on her arm. The sight pitched Nikita's stomach. She swore to not eat a morsel until these women and children were free.

"Nikita, we've heard from your father." Zane's voice boomed in the long trailer. The sunlight waned outside, casting his shadows in a harrowing manner. "Let's go."

She scrambled to her feet, but not before she passed the candy bar to Yasmina. "I will come back for you. All of you."

Yasmina took the candy but didn't reply. She didn't believe her. If Nikita lived in squalor for months, she wouldn't believe the whispers from a stranger preaching hope either.

Carefully walking toward the exit, Nikita held

her breath. Somehow the smell intensified the closer she got to freedom. The root of some of the stench caught her attention. An unmoving body lay near the door. The girl was bloodied, and the cold had minimally slowed decay.

"You sick bastard!" She hopped out and swung a right hook, hitting Zane square in the nose. Blood sprayed the freshly fallen snow, pink staining the ground.

Two Cutthroats restrained her before she could kick the traitor in the balls. She struggled at their hold, cursing at him in every language she knew.

Zane wiped the blood, smearing it across his upper lip. "Bitch! If Muerte wouldn't pay handsomely for you, I'd let the men have their way with you." He stepped closer, breath reeking of tobacco. "I'll bet they'd enjoy your clean pussy after months of diseased whores."

She lunged for him again but received a knock at the back of her skull. The world slowed to half speed. She sank into the snow, the cold failing to revive her. From the edge of darkness, she heard Yasmina's curdling scream. It was soon joined by others, but she couldn't save them. She couldn't even move.

Chapter Thirty-One

KEVLAR

THEY TRACKED THE TRUCK TO AN ABANDONED US AIR Force base. Judging from the trash strewn along the ground, whoever took Kita left in a hurry. Kevlar walked the entirety of the open space. No signs of Kita anywhere. Rubble and Doc examined a patch of blood in the snow.

"It's fresh," Doc said, eyes meeting Kevlar's. "It could be anyone's."

He hunkered down and reviewed the scene. "It's not."

"How do you know?"

"I just do." He stood and pinched the bridge of his nose. "There was a struggle. If the women have been in a semi in this cold very long, none would have enough energy to take a swing at a club man."

"Why do you think she did it?" Doc asked.

He huffed. "It's Kita. I know her."

"Hey, I ... you guys should see this," Hawk called from across the lot.

Kevlar's gut dropped at the shaky tone. The trio hurried over to where Hawk stood pointing at the ground. Rubble leaned down and brushed the snow off the woman's face while Doc checked for a pulse.

"She's dead." Doc leaned back and covered her with a ratty blanket. "The decay suggests a week at least."

Hawk crossed himself, his spirituality surprising all of them. They'd never seen the man pray, let alone attend a service other than Macha's.

"You don't think they kept her in with the others, do you?"

Rubble nodded. "Yeah, I do."

"Sick fucks."

Klink and Snoopy rushed toward them, faces optimistic. "Hey, we found something inside."

"Hope it's better than what we found outside," Doc mumbled, calling the medical examiner for the second time in as many days.

Snoopy tossed Kevlar a manila folder. Opening it, he studied the documents and photos. "These are all Kita." He handed half to Rubble, who flipped through them.

"And different routes to Mexico." Rubble eyed his men. "We'll need to split up." He grabbed his phone and immediately called Reaper, walking away as the call connected.

"We'll find her," Doc encouraged. "They knew we were closing in."

Hawk pulled up his hood. "That's why they left so fast. Didn't even have time to clean up all their shit."

Kevlar knew they were just trying to help. In a way, they did. His heart wouldn't accept anything other than Kita safe and sound. *And in my arms.*

"Let's roll," Rubble called from the truck. "Klink and Snoop, head toward the route through the Springs. We'll take the southern mountain pass."

Climbing in the passenger side, Kevlar barely got his seat belt latched before Rubble peeled out of the drive, snow spitting up their hasty retreat down the mountain. The bloody snow haunted him, the longer they drove. There was an indentation as if someone had fallen. That's where a smaller spot of blood was. The other looked like spray from being punched. His girl was still putting up a fight.

Good. If she fights, she'll stay alive.

***

They didn't stop except to refuel and buy food. The storm subsided sometime around two in the morning. Fluffy snow drifted across the lanes of traffic, and too many of the cars drove as if they had a pot full of chili with no lid sitting in the front seat. The stop and go traffic annoyed Kevlar, and he was grateful it was Rubble's turn behind the wheel. The man was uncannily calm despite the situation. He'd been in the Marines and was known for keeping a level head no matter what.

"Don't get comfy, Kevlar." Rubble didn't look away from the road. "Pulling off up ahead to switch."

He nodded and glanced to the back seat. Hawk slept with his mouth open and legs propped up on the seat beside him. He made a mental note to check in with the man about how he was coping with losing Mandi. They weren't serious as far as he could tell but losing anyone in such a way was difficult.

"One of my old buddies called me while you were snoozing."

He focused on the traffic ahead. "About what?"

"Evidently, he has knowledge of a trafficking auction in Arizona." Rubble's blue eye locked on him briefly. "He works for Homeland."

"When's it scheduled?"

"Friday."

"Shit, that's in twenty-four hours."

He turned down the heat. "Yeah. If we can't catch up before... you should prepare yourself in case of the worst."

Kevlar shook his head. "Fuck that. I'm not giving up on Kita, and neither are you."

"Kev— "

"I'm cashing in the favor you owe me."

Rubble's face went from worried to expressionless. They both knew what he meant. Kevlar saved Rubble's ass from a sniper bullet in Afghanistan. It was a life debt Rubble swore to uphold. He hadn't planned on ever cashing it in, but he had to. If Macha couldn't stop the semi, he and Rubble would together.

"All right, brother." He lowered his voice and looked in the rearview mirror. "But I can't guarantee everything will be done by Macha standards, let alone legal."

"I don't care the price. Kita is worth it all, plus some."

A faint smile crossed Rubble's bearded face. "All right, all right, you love-struck pussy." He lightly punched his arm. "You really are infatuated with this woman, aren't you?"

"I love her more than I love to breathe."

"Figured as much, but if this all plays out happily, what's the plan? You're Macha. She's FBI. The two don't exactly coexist."

"Not yet they don't." He faced forward, bracing himself for the slow traffic. "But they can, and they will if she lets them."

Chapter Thirty-Two

SHE WOKE FROM BEING BASHED ON THE HEAD TO FIND Zane pressing a bag of peas against his lip. Evidently, she'd gotten more than his nose in her haphazard attack. Her wrists were bound, legs too. They weren't giving her another chance to take them out one at a time.

"Your father wants to speak to you." Zane stood and walked to the door. "Alone."

She spit the combination of blood and saliva on the ground. "Fuck you."

He quickly turned and lifted his hand, but before he could contact her again, a voice rang out.

"Leave her."

She'd know that voice anywhere. It was her

father. Nikita glanced to the screen on the back wall. It came to life, Estevan Morales on the other side.

He tsked. "Mija, you don't look well."

"You should know." She tried pulling her arms free but failed. "You put me here."

He shook his head. "No, Zane did. I never wanted to hurt you."

He looked over his shoulder, the prison cell comfortable looking compared to every other prisoner's. She swore she saw a bottle of wine and a record player in the background. Prison wasn't a punishment for him. It was a vacation. Somewhere safe he could pull strings like the puppet master he was.

"What are you going to do, Papi? Give in to Zane's demands or let your daughter be sold like a prized heifer?"

"Are you asking for my help, mija?" A conniving smile spread over his lips.

Nikita fought for control over the situation. She had no leverage. No backup. No hope. Even if Kevlar found her, they were outnumbered.

"I'm asking what the plan is."

Her head pounded, a result of being hit with the butt of a rifle followed by flopping headfirst into the snow. She hadn't slept in almost twenty-four hours, and the last bit of cinnamon twist came up an hour into her initial stay in the semi.

Her father leaned back and laced his fingers together, resting them on his stomach. It wasn't large like it used to be years ago. Prison apparently didn't bode well for his high-class food tendencies. It was the one satisfaction she felt.

"Run Diablos."

"Never."

She didn't need to think it over. Being sold into prostitution was better than being head of a merciless MC, especially one that condoned trafficking along with a plethora of despicable deeds.

"After you were tried and found guilty, I fought to become an FBI agent. I won't abandon my honor."

Estevan's smile faded. "You'd rather rot?"

"Every time."

"How disappointing." He worried his lips together. "I'd hoped all this would change your mind."

Nikita bristled at his words. *I should've known.* After what Zane told her, it all made sense. "This was all an elaborate plan to make me president, wasn't it?"

"Your mother never understood, mija. She couldn't grasp MC life. Not in its fullest, but you..."

His chest puffed with pride. "You display so much gumption. Our club needs that in their president. Plus, having a former FBI agent on the payroll is good for business."

"Keep dreaming," she muttered, fidgeting in the seat. It was more comfortable than the semi, but she'd prefer freezing in the trailer to this.

"I'll be in prison until I'm too old to ride." Estevan stood and paced the cell. "I can mentor you, and this time, you'll know why and how to put my advice into motion. No secrets, mija. I know it's what you've wanted your entire life."

Nikita clenched her jaw. Her father wasn't taking no for an answer. "When will you get it through your thick skull that I won't ever run Diablos? I'd rather take it apart brick by bloody brick."

"Is that your final word?"

"Sí, papi."

"So be it." Estevan's casual mood darkened. "Remember, you've brought this upon yourself, mija."

The video cut out and the door behind her swung open.

"Let's go, Little Miss FBI Agent." Zane and another man pulled her from the chair and dragged her out of the room. They tossed her bound form in the back of the semi and slammed the door shut. Five minutes later, the truck took off. Thankfully, Yasmina unlaced the rope.

The rumble from the highway reverberated through Nikita's body. Every bump and jostle sent the women tumbling from their uncomfortable spots. Scratchy blankets had been tossed in at the last pitstop. They smelled of urine and feces and gave minimal warmth, but she took one anyway. Rattling chest coughs met her ears every few seconds. If not from a woman, then a child and so on and so forth. She doubted even one occupant in the trailer was in fair health.

Yasmina slept next to her, the group of Russian teens on the other side. Their combined body heat helped take the bite out of the artic breeze, but it did nothing to aid the chill from the conversation she had with Zane and her father.

Ten hours had since passed, and she couldn't guess where they were headed. The only openings of the trailer showed the highway. She'd lost count of the stops. Her stomach grumbled noisily. She didn't regret giving Yasmina the candy bar. The woman deserved it more than her anyhow.

"Your father did not pay the ransom?"

She looked down and saw Yasmina finally awake.

She'd drifted off soon after they left. Nikita couldn't tell if her sudden drowsiness was due to the cold or overall health. Both contributed in her mind.

"Not exactly." She pulled the blanket closer over Yasmina's shoulders. "He wanted me to do something illegal, and I told him no."

"What did he want?"

She shook her head. "To keep this business running." She splayed her hands toward their surroundings. "I'd never do it. They can have me before I stoop to their level."

Yasmina crackled a laugh, then broke into a coughing fit, the sound dangerously close to pneumonia. "You are dumb, but I understand. I would not do what they want either. It's why they took me."

Nikita gathered the woman against her, cleanliness be damned. "Whatever happens, I'll protect as many of you as I can."

The woman didn't reply. Within moments, the ragged, shallow breathing returned, and Nikita prayed it wasn't a sign that Yasmina was waning toward death. She wasn't sure she could handle it.

Come on. I'm not asking for much. Just a teeny tiny opening to kick all their asses.

Chapter Thirty-Three

KEVLAR

THEY FOLLOWED THE DISCARDED ROUTE MAPS TO Arizona. The vast difference in temperature should've comforted him. It didn't. All he could think about was Kita trapped in the back of a semi, most likely freezing from the cold, then sweltering from the heat in a twelve-hour span.

He pulled the truck into a fast-food parking lot and shut off the engine. Hawk and Rubble were passed out after driving through the night. According to Rubble's contact, the auction was going down that night. He glanced at the digital clock on the dash. They had enough time to clean up before picking up the fake IDs and meeting Rubble's government friend.

The scent of fries drifted from the crack in the

window. His body had been jonesing for a smoke for the last five miles. Hopping out, he grabbed a cigarette and lighter. Inhaling the nicotine, Kevlar closed his eyes. Kita was all he saw. Her cheery face and captivating eyes. He licked his bottom lip, desperately hoping to find a remnant of her there. No such luck.

Police sirens caught his attention. He couldn't focus on the speeder chase. Kita's smile swam in his mind and stole him back to every time she graced him with one.

He could only imagine the conditions she was exposed to. Cursing, he blew out the smoke and watched the bustling traffic. It was busier here than in Colorado. He immediately missed the quiet town, friendly residents, and lazy traffic signals. Stomach grumbling, he left the keys in the ignition and, within ten minutes, returned to the truck, burgers and fries in hand. They'd survived off nothing but takeout, and he was already sick of it. What he wouldn't give for homemade lasagna and blueberry pie for dessert.

Climbing in the truck, he was pleased to see his brothers awake. Rubble had his phone to his ear, speaking swiftly. Kevlar handed Hawk a bag of food.

"Who's he talking to?"

Hawk unwrapped the burger and bit into it. "The Homeland guy," he said, stuffing a handful of fries in his mouth.

Kevlar opened his bag and dug out the double patty burger. It tasted nothing like the ones Reaper made on the grill at the clubhouse, but it'd do. *I wonder what Kita's eating.* He swallowed and suddenly didn't feel very hungry. Judging from the near skeleton they found in the snow, none of the women were fed much.

"All right, later." Rubble ended the call and faced him. "Jones has everything we need. Just need to stop by and pick it up." He grabbed some fries and chomped them. "The auction is at a hotel down-town. He said it's in the basement and well-guarded. We'll need to spruce up."

"Then the semi made it there?"

"Yep." He took a giant bite of the burger. "Aerial surveillance caught women exiting a semitruck and moving to the hotel an hour ago."

"How many?" Hawk chimed in around his mouthful.

"At least fifty. Could be more or less. The drone was repositioned shortly after."

Kevlar's heart pounded against his ribcage. She was close. "What will they do in the meantime?"

Rubble slid his gaze to him, an uncomfortable expression on his face. "Prep them."

"As in...." He couldn't say the words.

"It's a human trafficking ring." Rubble shifted in his seat. "They'll make them presentable for auction." His eyes turned toward the street. "I can't imagine what she's going through, and for what? Her dad is Muerte, president of the Diablos MC. Couldn't he spring her?"

"Not if his conditions of release are worse." Kevlar finished the food, which was tasteless on his tongue. None of it mattered until Kita was safe. Even if she never wanted to see him again, knowing she was out of harm's way would be enough for him. *Hopefully.*

Chapter Thirty-Four

HOSES OF COLD WATER DOUSED THE LINE OF WOMEN IN the dark, dank room. The concrete floor told her they were on a sublevel. Probably a lower level beneath the basement. She covered her body best she could, but it was no use. She couldn't conceal her nakedness.

Zane seemed to take a deeper interest in her specifically, shooting the water at her nonstop. She gritted her teeth to keep them from chattering, eyes sending daggers in his direction. He laughed and watched her intently before he moved to the next woman.

Once they were clean, a Diablos member handed out clothes picked explicitly for each of them. Yasmina wore a navy dress, the neckline plunging between her breastbone, showing her ribcage and hint of bosom. There wasn't much left after months of starvation.

Kita tugged on the red gown tossed her way. It was smaller than her usual size but would no doubt fit the rest of the women. With her unusual height and curvy body, she was the only woman who filled out the clothes.

"You'll be the last one up there, Nikita," Zane murmured, adorning her with earrings and a necklace that rested between her cleavage.

"Why's that?"

"Because you're in the best shape. The guests are already salivating at the news of a Spanish beauty up for sale." He ran a brush through her wet hair, droplets sliding down her back. "Once they found out Muerte's daughter was here, well, let's just say you'll bring me the most money tonight."

"You're disgusting, you know that?" She bit down the desire to punch him in the balls. It wouldn't end well for her. Then again, maybe a bruised-up face would deter buyers.

"Don't even think about it," Zane warned as if he'd crawled into her thoughts. "They'll want you no matter how bashed your face is." He traced her chin. "You're worth more alive than dead."

He swatted her ass, then walked away, leaving her to a group of older women who started busying themselves with the hair of the recently arrived.

Once makeup was applied, two Cutthroats brought in trays of sandwiches. The women devoured them within moments. Most threw the food back up, the sustenance impossible for them to handle after weeks or months without proper nutrition.

Yasmina handed her a turkey and swiss on flimsy white bread. "You must eat a little." She nodded to the other women. "They'll regret eating so fast later if not already." She took a smile bite of her own sandwich. Ham and cheddar from the look of it. None of the meat and cheese smelled good. She eyed the bread, realizing it wasn't fresh either.

Kita accepted the offering and managed a bite. It was horrible, but it was food. She slowly chewed, wondering if the rest of her life would be shitty food and shittier masters.

Finally, the MC men entered the room. They were well-dressed in all black. Zane walked to the front of the group, a cruel smile on his face.

"It's time, ladies," he said. "Let's make me rich."

Chapter Thirty-Five

KEVLAR

The sight curdled his stomach contents. Women paraded onto the stage like prized cattle. Men and women alike held up cards with numbers, the auctioneer in a black Stetson preening every time a price jumped.

Kevlar glanced around the room. From the looks, it was once a banquet hall, and judging from the way the hotel staff greeted him and his brothers, the move from legal to illegal trading of humans wasn't unusual. The hotel thrived from the trafficking business just as much as the tradesmen themselves.

The lights were low except for the spotlights on the stage. A red velvet curtain opened to each new woman for sale, then closed once she was purchased. He almost didn't want to know what went on behind the curtain.

Rubble nudged him with his elbow. "See her?"

"No." His eyes scanned the crowd. "But I do see Zane." He nodded toward the FBI agent who moonlighted as a dickhead scoundrel. His jaw clenched almost as tightly as his hands.

"Don't react, brother," Rubble warned. "If he spots us, he'll move Nikita." His blue and green eyes turned soft. "We can't help her if that happens."

Nodding his agreement, Kevlar focused on the auction. Each slam of the gavel took a piece of his heart. Despite the attempts of dolling them up, the women resembled breathing skeletons. Their nationalities spanned the globe, and he was positive their English was limited.

Two hours into the ordeal, Hawk patted his knee. "Hey, I think it's her."

Kevlar turned wary eyes toward the woman on stage. The bright red dress left nothing to the imagination. When she lifted her eyes, a gasp escaped him before he could stop it. The fiery amber eyes could only belong to the woman he loved. Purple bruises lined her arms and neck, and his gut pitched at the sight. Her posture was complacent. Dark shadows beneath the makeup reminded him nothing was as it appeared.

"Yep, that's Kita."

Upon her entry, the crowd hushed, then burst into chatter. A vile smile crossed the auctioneer's face. "And this, ladies and gentlemen, is the pièce de résistance. A lovely Spanish beauty with plenty of sass to make your nights pleasurable and your money well spent. We'll start the bid at one hundred thousand."

A few men heckled her, but she didn't budge. She kept her gorgeous eyes trained on the back of the room. Cards waved, and the auctioneer kept jacking up the price.

"What's the play?" Hawk asked.

Rubble nodded to his government pal two rows away. "Jones will buy her."

"What? That can't be the plan? What about—"

Rubble's glare silenced the rest of Kevlar's complaint. He was right of course. They couldn't be seen until the end. Still, he couldn't let the other women—the children—leave with the bastards who purchased them for God knew what horrid acts.

"Be patient, Kevlar. We'll get your girl."

Yeah, but will she be alive when we do?

Chapter Thirty-Six

NIKITA

HOLY SHIT, SOMEONE BOUGHT ME.

Nikita's eyes flooded with tears, none of them falling. She stumbled backward, Zane dragging her out of the small box taped on the floor. The women were told to not step beyond or face wrath. A few of them attempted to flee and were met with batons to their ribs. She was the last of the girls to be on the auction block. The room had slowly emptied, leaving her alone with Zane until her name was called. Nikita glanced around the darkness, searching for Yasmina. Only Diablos and Cutthroat men met her gaze.

"Five million dollars." Zane chuckled darkly. "Damn, if I'd known you'd fetch such a price, I'd have nabbed you years ago and not bothered with

Muerte at all." He pushed her into a new room, the bright lights burning her eyes. Going from darkness to light and vice versa so often drained her energy almost as much as the entire auction endeavor.

"I thought about taking you back with the other girls, but nah. I won't risk one of them hurting you or you riling them up."

"I can't do this."

Zane shoved her into a nearby chair. The comfort of the plush did nothing to alleviate the murderous glint in his eyes. "I don't give a fuck what you can or can't do. You'll sit here like a good little girl until your master picks you up."

Her gaze dipped to the gun in his belt. *It'd be so easy. One shot.*

"Nuh-uh, don't even dream about it." He moved closer to her face, his nose grazing hers. His eyes dipped down the front of her dress and her gut twisted. "But we do have a little time. I don't think your multi-millionaire would mind if I had a little taste."

She backed away as far as she could in the chair. It did no good. She was pinned between his solid body and the soft fabric; both would soon be her doom.

"But I fucking do."

Nikita's breath caught at the familiar voice.

Surely, it's not....

She looked past Zane and bit her tongue. She wasn't hallucinating. "Kevlar."

His face was dark, gun pointed to the back of Zane's head. "Step the hell away, or I'll put a bullet through your skull."

Zane slowly moved backward, hands raised. She recognized the mixture of defeat and anger in his cold features.

"So you found us. Bravo." Zane mockingly clapped his hands. "But I'm afraid you can't have Nikita. She's been sold."

Kevlar's grip on the gun tightened. "Yeah, to us."

Three more men entered the room, guns aimed directly at Zane. He cursed savagely and tried for his gun. They all seemed to move in slow motion. Zane didn't even get a shot off before four guns peppered him with bullets. The big man fell backward, missing her by inches.

"Kita, oh God. What did they do to you?" Kevlar knelt in front of her. His brown eyes were wide and full of heartbreak. He ran his hands along her body, searching for unseen injuries. She couldn't wince. She couldn't move. The shock from the last twenty-four hours wouldn't let her.

"Kita, baby, talk to me."

Kevlar's voice brought her to life, but her mouth refused to speak. "Shit, she's in shock."

In one smooth move, he swept her into his arms and followed Rubble out the door. Hawk brought up the rear, and she tampered down her emotions at the thought of Mandi. Eyes swiveling to the last man, she didn't recognize him, but she was damned grateful Kevlar brought backup.

He came for me.

She swallowed the veracity behind his actions. He might've done it because of their past, but she didn't suspect so. Kevlar was a long-term commitment kind of guy. Feeling his strong muscles and hearing the whizzing bullets quickly cleared the shocking events from earlier.

They almost reached the exit before she found her tongue. She couldn't just leave. She'd make sure the rest of the women and children had a chance at a better life. He rejuvenated her mission and she wouldn't forget why she was there in the first place.

"Wait! The girls." She pushed at Kevlar's chest. His tried and true vest bounced at her fist. "I promised them."

"There's my feisty girl." He kissed her forehead. "Glad to have you back."

A sudden swell of government agents swarmed the banquet room. Gunshots rang out, along with screams from men and women. She gripped Kevlar's neck tighter, burying her face in his shirt, his familiar bulletproof vest hard against her.

Once they were clear of the bullets, she wriggled out of his arms, and he let her feet touch the floor. The need to save the others superseded her need to be comforted. There'd be time for that later. Her adrenaline was up and running through her veins thanks to Kevlar and his brothers.

"Come on, the rest are being held back here." She hurried down the hall, cursing the dress for her limited mobility. Stopping outside the room, she ripped the hem and sighed in relief.

"Holy shit, she's a badass," Hawk said, amusement lining his face.

She managed a grin. "Does somebody have an extra gun? They took mine."

Rubble passed a handgun to her, and she nodded her thanks. "Don't shoot the women, please. They're scared and most don't know English."

The four men nodded, her underlying plea obvious to them all. Hawk and Rubble burst into the room first. Two shots echoed, and she was glad to see the bodies of two Diablos men fall to the floor.

The mass of women huddled together, some whimpering, others crying.

"You get the girls," Rubble called. "We'll watch the doors."

Hawk fired again at a Cutthroat charging from the hall. "But hurry. There's a shit ton of these guys."

Hustling to the end of the room where the women congregated, she handed Kevlar her gun and held up her hands. "It's okay. We're here to help."

Yasmina broke through the crowd and said something in Russian. A quarter of the women reacted with hopeful nods. "You came back," she said, walking closer. Her eyes were bloodshot, and a new bruise darkened her left cheek.

Nikita pulled her in for a hug. "I told you I would."

Before they could celebrate, angry cries in several languages paired with gunshots sent the women scattering again.

"All right, everybody needs to follow me," Kevlar said, taking charge. It was sexier than hell the way he owned the situation. "We have help waiting outside for everyone."

Bringing up the rear, Nikita waited until the last woman walked through the door to let herself relax. It wasn't over entirely. The shouts from inside told her as much, but the Phoenix night sky was speckled with stars. It gave her hope for the women and children being ushered into emergency vehicles waiting outside.

She turned and watched the group of Russian girls climb into an ambulance. Lifting a hand to her mouth, her adrenaline gradually wore off. Her body trembled as silent tears coursed down her cheeks. *They're safe.* She was safe. Her job was complete. The severity of it all sent her staggering backward.

"Come here, baby." Kevlar's arms wrapped around her, pulling her into his warm embrace. She let the tears flow steadily, relief filling her at long last.

"I thought.... I didn't...." Her lips wouldn't let her finish the sentence.

"Shh, it's okay." He eased back and sought out her eyes. "You did it, Kita. All those women—" He nodded to the mass of women and children once in the semi-trailer with her. "—they all get a second chance." He kissed the top of her head. "Because of you."

Nikita kicked off the absurdly uncomfortable heels Zane had forced her to wear. A quick glance down at her body and a laugh escaped her at the sight of the torn dress, no shoes, and makeup most definitely streaking. "I look like a train wreck, don't I?"

Kevlar swiped his thumb under her eye, taking dark eyeliner with him. "I wasn't going to say anything, but—"

She smacked his chest good-naturedly. It was then that she finally got a good look at the tall man in front of her. He wore a black suit and matching tie, though both were in disarray thanks to the recent gunfight. A streak of blood raced down his left temple, his body otherwise untouched. He looked good. Damned good.

"Thank you, Kevlar. I told you I didn't need your help, but I was wrong. I should've trusted you from the start."

"Yeah, you should've." Tearing off his tie, he tossed it to the ground. "I'm glad I could help." He tipped up her chin and pressed a delicate kiss to the tip of her nose. "You can save yourself, Kita, but every now and then, it's okay to let someone do the saving."

"You're my only exception, Kevlar." Wrapping her arms around his neck, she tenderly kissed him. His arms circled her waist, pulling her flush to his hard body. All at once, she didn't care where she was or how she got there. She deepened the kiss, sighing when his tongue matched hers. The memory of him had kept her sane in the back of the trailer, and she never wanted to be without him again.

Someone clearing their throat broke them apart long before she wanted. She eyed the man dressed in a black windbreaker, an earpiece hanging from his left ear. Without a doubt, he was part of a government agency.

"Sorry to break up your little love fest or whatever, but we need Agent Stockdale to identify the people who kidnapped her."

Stepping away from Kevlar, she rubbed her lips together, the taste of him lingering on her tongue. The next part wouldn't be fun. Neither would the part afterward. But the end... now *that* was what she looked forward to. It was time to put Diablos and the Cutthroats to bed.

And no better person than me to tuck them in tight.

Chapter Thirty-Seven

KEVLAR

Sitting up in bed, Kevlar tried to steady his breathing. He looked to the spot beside him and blinked several times just to make sure. She was there. Safe and sound. He ran a hand over his face, sweat sliding down his bare chest.

They'd been back in Snowshoe for two days. After the FBI swarmed the illegal auction, they stayed in Phoenix a day to sort everything out. Kita spent a few hours in the hospital for fluids and tests. The doctors signed her out with a clean bill of health, but he wasn't convinced.

Kevlar tossed the sheet off him, eyes glued to the end of the bed. Hawk, Rubble, and he gave the agents their statements. It all went smoothly. Kita refused to leave Phoenix until the women were placed in safe homes. Their futures remained up in the air. The government would either extradite them or allow them to stay in the US pending residency. It seemed to appease Kita's need to save them all.

But now, the snow fell nonstop in Snowshoe, a blaring opposite of Phoenix's heat in the same week. He watched flakes stick to the window while his heartbeat pulsed hard. Ever since arriving back in the sleepy town, nightmares invaded him every time he closed his eyes. They all involved Kita, and none ended well. He assumed they'd stop once she was with him, but they didn't. As badly as he wanted to believe the danger was over, his subconscious disagreed.

"Hey, you okay?"

Her warm hand on his chest comforted him momentarily, and he placed a hand over hers. "Yeah, couldn't sleep, that's all."

He leaned over and kissed her temple. That was the extent of what they'd done. His body demanded more but he couldn't. After what she'd been through, he wasn't sure he should touch her yet. He didn't want to hurt her or bring up the pain. She could handle anything, but he wasn't sure she could handle the love he so desperately needed to show her.

"You sure?" She pressed her lips to his deltoid. "You haven't slept much since we've been back." Her black hair fell over his shoulder, the silky strands tickling him. "What's wrong?"

"Nothing." He stood and grabbed a sweatshirt. The four o'clock hour struck, and he pulled sweatpants on next. He was long overdue for a run. "Go back to bed. I'm going to get my miles in."

Kita frowned but didn't argue. She laid back down, drawing the comforter to her nose. Within moments, the steady breathing told him she was asleep once more. In the early morning light, he noticed the faint lines of bruising on her neck. It tore him up inside that he hadn't been there to prevent those.

He snagged his sneakers and slipped out of the room. Clearing his head with ten miles through Snowshoe would help. If not, he wasn't sure what would.

***

Flickers of lights dotted the path the longer Kevlar ran. His breath came out in large puffs of air, the slosh beneath his feet spraying his pants with gray. The longer he ran, the more streetlights waned, and streaks of sunshine broke the horizon. Early morning was the best time to exercise in his opinion. He could watch the world slowly wake and enjoy the freshness of a brand-new day.

Heart pumping fast, he checked his watch and slowed his pace to a jog. He had a few more miles to go before he'd turn around and head back to the clubhouse. The thought of Kita in his bed urged him to abandon that idea. He pushed it aside and turned down the main drag through Snowshoe. If he got back in time, he'd whip up something for his girl and bring her breakfast in bed. She more than earned it after the last week.

A buzz in his pocket reminded him that he needed to check in with the prospects before the garage opened in a few hours. The three men were still learning but had decent skills when it came to fixing vehicles. Without a doubt, he'd suggest at least two of them stay on after they were initiated.

Kevlar waved at the couple walking their black lab across the street. Every now and then, he'd see another likeminded person up at the early hour, but more often, he was alone. Images of Kita filtered through his mind. He'd never forgive himself for letting her get abducted. Even though he helped save her, his club could've done more to prevent the Cutthroats and Diablos trade. He shook his head. *Doubtful.* They'd only heard about the trafficking ring the same time Kita and Mandi arrived.

He licked his lips. *Mandi.* He and Kita hadn't discussed her yet. He wasn't sure how. The woman was Kita's best friend, and she lost her in one of the worst ways. He made a mental note to discuss it with his girl when he got back to his room. While he was all for letting her grieve on her terms, he wanted to be there when she did.

A notification beeped at him in his earbud. Checking the message from a prospect, he smirked. Reaper decided the prospects needed more to do, so he assigned them morning duties as well as their usual club ones. He couldn't complain. It gave him more time to spend with Kita.

Pausing at a four-way stop, Kevlar pulled out his phone and noticed a new text message.

Joci: I missed you too, Tucker. Your nephews would love to meet you. Let me know when.

He grinned. His sister finally texted him back. For a while there, he wasn't sure it'd happen, but it seemed her new man brought Joci back to life. After sending a quick reply, promising to look up flights, Kevlar crossed the street. With a family reunion in sight and the love of his life in his bed, nothing could get him down.

It was around mile seven that he saw them. There were at least two men in the dark green SUV. Curls of smoke escaped the tinted windows, the car creeping closer with every step he took. He picked up his pace, determined to make it back to the clubhouse before any trouble started. He hadn't worn his vest this morning. He never did for his ten miles.

The thought urged his legs faster. If anyone watched his routine, they'd notice it too. *Shit.* He took a turn and heard the SUV's engine rev. Pulling out his phone, Kevlar tried to take a picture of the vehicle behind him. If things went south, at least he'd have proof of an attack later to help the police.

The clubhouse seemed too far away. He glanced over his shoulder and didn't spy the SUV. It was gone. Slowing, he checked the surroundings. Other than fresh snow, the city had yet to fully wake. A few cars here and there could be heard streets away, but not this close to the outskirts of town. *Maybe I'm being paranoid.*

Kevlar turned forward again and cursed. The elusive SUV screeched to a halt in front of him, barring his way. The window quickly rolled down, the bright orange glow of cigarettes inside.

"Muerte sends his regards," one of the men said, a Spanish accent evident in the words.

Before he could react, the man fired his gun. The bullet sliced into Kevlar's side, piercing pain seizing him. The vehicle surged to life and peeled around the corner and out of sight. He looked down and his gray sweatshirt darkened with blood. Pressing a hand to the wound, he let out an anguished cry.

And this is why I always wear the vest.

He blew out a steady stream of air, nothing helping to subside the effects of the bullet. Scouring the ground for his phone, he found it in an icy puddle. Tearing off his glove, he quickly dialed Rubble.

"What the fuck, Kevlar? Do you know what time it is? It's not even—"

"Rubble, I'm shot. Not sure if I can make it back to the clubhouse or not." He peeled back the hand pressing against the wound. A gush of crimson escaped, and he bit the inside of his cheek.

"Shit, where are you?"

"Alleyway between Fourth and Washington." He started moving toward Macha's home base. "Walking up Washington now."

"I'm getting Doc. We'll be there in five."

Kevlar shoved the phone into his pocket and

trudged forward. His feet felt like heavy anvils, each movement jarring the bullet wound. The clouds overhead opened once more and coated him in snowflakes. He was right to worry about Kita. Her father wasn't done with her yet.

But it appears he's done with me.

Chapter Thirty-Eight

"Get them out of here," Doc yelled, ripping back Kevlar's shirt. It was fully red, dripping blood on the floor of the small Macha clinic. Splatters of red coated the white wall, making Kita immobile.

Shit, shit, shit!

Rubble ushered the crowd of fellow bikers out of the room, closing the door and leaving Nikita alone with an unconscious Kevlar and a focused Doc. Her stomach jarred at the sight of his pale skin. His ragged breaths nearly sent her to the floor. This wasn't the indestructible Kevlar she knew.

"Will he be okay?"

She ran her hand against his forehead, his hair always kept so short. She almost wished he'd grow it a little so she could smooth it back. Bullet wounds weren't uncommon in her job, but this wasn't just anyone on the table. It was the man she couldn't live without. If he died, a part of her would too.

Rattling medical utensils, Doc nodded. "He'll be fine once I get the bullet out." He handed her a pair of gloves. "Looks like you get to play nurse today."

She pulled on the latex and swallowed the urge to faint. Blood never got to her. She'd seen plenty of dead bodies, plenty of blood, but none had ever been a person she loved. Not until Mandi. Not until Kevlar. It was why she hesitated in the car before Pillar's goons nabbed her. She'd been caught between realities.

"This might hurt him a bit." Doc met her face, blue eyes concerned. "Think you can handle it?"

No! she screamed to herself, but she nodded, nevertheless. The door opened right before Doc dug into the bullet hole.

"I'll hold him steady," Hawk offered, and neither refused the help.

Returning to the task at hand, Doc expertly extracted the tiny bullet. Kevlar jerked once, and Hawk diligently kept him stationary. She moved when Doc instructed, helping him clean the agitated wound. None of her FBI training could've prepared her for operating on the man she loved.

With Doc's oversight, she bandaged the wound. Her hands shook, but she wouldn't let anyone else do this. He'd saved her, and she would do right by him instead of shying away.

"Very nice. You could pass as an emergency medic." He offered her a kind smile. The little she knew of the paramedic turned biker doctor, she liked. He was a gentle soul when he was around his old lady and a Viking when it came to his brothers. That should've tipped her off from day one.

"I better stick to what I know." She felt Kevlar's forehead. It was hot and clammy.

"I gave him something to fight infection," Doc said, already ahead of her thoughts. "He's strong."

"Just because someone's strong doesn't mean they'll survive."

Doc didn't reply. He washed his hands in the sink and checked Kevlar once more before saying something about finding Isa. She really wasn't listening. She was too busy sorting everything out in her mind.

Rubble and Doc found Kevlar on the sidewalk two miles from the clubhouse. The stubborn ass walked a whole half mile before collapsing in the snow. She woke the instant she heard Rubble yelling down the hall but didn't know what happened until he returned carrying Kevlar's bloodied body.

Nikita sat on the chair next to the hospital bed. Seeing him so lifeless sent her gut in a nosedive. Kevlar wasn't one to ever play the victim or try to get sympathy. He'd never been like that. If she had to guess, the Army reiterated those ideas for him.

She gently traced the scar on his jaw, barely visible with his beard. Since they met, he hadn't shaved it. In her opinion, he looked ten times sexier with the scruff.

"Don't worry, mi amor, I'll take care of this devil once and for all," she whispered, kissing his temple. She couldn't leave right then but soon. *Very soon.* She had someone to visit before she could put the Diablos MC out for good. Her father.

She stayed beside him a while longer. Doc came and checked on him. Rubble, Hawk, and the rest of the MC did as well. It comforted her to know she wasn't leaving him alone. His brothers would be there no matter where she went.

Heart sinking, she stood and surveyed the room. Queenie had flitted in and out of the room, bringing a tray of food for her. She'd nibbled on a freshly made chocolate chip cookie, stomach otherwise sour. Her body hadn't fully recovered from being in the semi-trailer. Neither had her mind. But the instant she saw Kevlar, she'd felt herself heal. At least a tiny bit.

Nikita walked over and grabbed a bottle of water from the mini fridge. Vials of medicines stood out amid the water. She picked up a few and smirked. Macha was well prepared for such events like today.

"How're you feeling?"

She looked over her shoulder and saw Isa walk in. They'd spoken a few times, but nothing more than general conversation.

"I'm better, thanks."

Isa sat in the other open seat, the whirly doctor one. "You're stronger than I would be after such an ordeal."

The Irish accent made Nikita smile. It was light enough she could understand but foreign enough to make the pretty woman appear exotic.

"From what I've heard, you're pretty badass yourself."

Isa shrugged. "Not compared to you, but thanks." She pointed to Kevlar. "Doc says he'll be fine. I can watch him for a bit if you need to get some rest." She tilted her head to the side. "You look tired."

Chuckling, she nodded. "Also known as, you look like shit."

They both laughed, but neither broached the truth. If Nikita were honest with herself, she could use a few more hours of sleep. Kevlar kept her up most nights since Phoenix, and not for the reason she'd prefer. His tossing and turning jerked her awake, but it was his sudden jolts up in bed that concerned her.

"All right, sure." She kissed Kevlar's forehead. "Be back in a while." She nodded her thanks to Isa and meandered down the hall to his room. It smelled like him, the scent intoxicating her until she drifted into a dreamless state.

***

The plane touched down in New York before the sun set that night. She watched the city lights gleam back at her. The pilot came across the speakers, welcoming them to the Big Apple and stating the current weather.

She shivered, her carry-on bag digging into her shoulder. Spiriting away from Macha's clubhouse without telling a damn soul wasn't the best plan, but if she'd told someone, she was certain they'd try to talk her out of it or insist on going with her. She needed to do this alone.

The time flashed on the man's phone beside her. She'd yet to pick up a new one. After Zane took hers, she really didn't think about buying a phone. Her mind had been otherwise occupied.

A flash of memory from the semi entered her mind and she winced at the severity of it. Resting her head on the back of the seat, she closed her eyes and took a cleansing breath. She wasn't at 100 percent. Her wounds, both internal and external, given to her during her short stay with the traffickers were nothing compared to women like Yasmina.

Suck it up, buttercup.

Straightening in the seat, she opened her eyes to see the passengers deplaning. She quickly hopped up and scooted down the aisle. The airport bustled with life. Distant voices mingled into one mass of words, some she knew, others foreign.

Nikita hurried across the terminals and found a car rental. One short stop later, she was in a Jeep heading up to Fishkill Correctional. Her father had some explaining to do. It was better to merely stop by instead of giving him the chance to adequately prepare. After all, she hadn't been given such a privilege.

The prison stood out in the darkness, the spotlights visible for miles. The Jeep easily took to the hills, and before she could register what was happening, she sat in one of the private visiting rooms.

A guard escorted her father in, who, in her opinion, looked astonished to see her. The door closed again, and they simply stared at each other. Her first urge to slap him was outweighed by the curiosity to hear his words.

"Mija, you're... looking well." His face said one thing while his eyes said another. He was disappointed. Why, she wasn't sure.

"Surprised to not see me chained to a pimp?" She narrowed her eyes. "Or did you have some secret deal to get me out of the situation?"

"Ah, mija, you overestimate my abilities from these concrete walls." Estevan pointed to the cell. "Not much can be done from within bars."

"Cut the bullshit," she snapped, and his full attention was focused on her face.

"Do not speak to me like that."

"I'll speak to you however the fuck I want, Muerte." She narrowed her eyes. "You practically handed me to human traffickers. Sex traffickers. Do you have any idea what they do to women? To children for God's sake?" She slammed a hand on the table. "No, you don't. You are too concerned with your bottom line. With filling your pockets and not giving a damn about anyone else."

Estevan's face turned dark red, a vein on his neck bulging. "I did what I did to give you a life I never had."

"I didn't want it if that's how you provided it." She shook her head. "Standing on the corpses of innocents isn't how I want to live."

He clenched his hands into fists. "Too late. You already did. You still do. That trust fund you pull money from isn't from your mother's family." He smiled menacingly. "It's from me."

She thought back to the fund her mother swore was legitimate. She'd made a point to only withdraw funds when it was absolutely necessary. She let out a disappointed sigh. The truth wouldn't be heard within these walls. Estevan would say anything to twist her mind. So, she would do the same.

"Fine, then I'll donate it all to aid women who were in sex trafficking." She shrugged. "It'll do them a world of good. Much better than how I'd use it over my lifetime."

He lifted his finger and opened his mouth.

"Oh, and I've taken care of your sergeant at arms. The only Diablos he sees now are in hell."

Estevan folded his fingers together. "You did me a favor."

"No, I did the world a favor, but you should know, I didn't pull the trigger. Macha did." Nikita sat up a little straighter, the pride from those words bolstering her mood. "Macha took out Diablos. By now, they'll have run them out of Colorado."

His eyes snapped to the door, then back to her. "So, I get new men and invade once more. You won't be rid of me so easily."

She leaned over the table. "Oh, I'm not done, Muerte. I won't be done until every last Diablos is off the streets and in prison." She got as close as possible without the possibility of him grabbing her. The gleam in his eyes told her he'd enjoy nothing more. "And then, I'll track down your offshore accounts. Your offshore contacts. I'll harvest every organ of your sickly body of Diablos scum."

Nikita noticed his eye twitch. Her words were taking root, spreading through his body as if they were infectious. "Then, and only then, will I be done."

Sweat beaded on his brow, his dark eyes a mixture of disbelief and acceptance.

"Don't fuck with me again, Papi." She smiled

sweetly. "You only have one daughter. Remember that next time you make a deal with the devil."

And with that, she stood and pounded on the door. Estevan screamed profanities toward her, but they rolled off her back. She was finished with her father. She'd promised to decimate every MC like his. Nothing was a better goal for her life.

Her gait lighter than on the way in, Nikita breezed through the secured doors and took a giant breath of fresh, New York air. It was finally time for her future to begin. And she knew exactly who she wanted to start it with. It'd take a little time, but she'd get there. She'd get back to him.

Hopefully before he thinks the worst.

***

The apartment didn't look the same. Sure, there wasn't a piece of furniture out of place, and the cleaning service apparently came if the scent of lemon disinfectant told her anything. But it wasn't the same. It didn't feel the same.

Walking in, she flicked on lights, tossing her keys to the table just inside the door. The familiar scent of jasmine filled the room. It was her favorite and one she'd never regret buying in bulk.

The lonely TV sat on an old entertainment center, a dark blue couch and matching reclining chair opposite it in the living room. Using her trust fund wasn't necessary to make her life complete. She'd never been big into shopping—a fact her mother abhorred. Nikita was a tomboy since birth. The extravagance of galas and jewelry never intrigued her. Motorcycles were more her style.

Moving to the single bedroom, she sighed. The landlord would rent out the place within minutes of the ad being placed. She'd dropped him a note on her way in from the prison. Already, she loathed finding boxes and filling them full of her possessions.

A photo of her and Mandi caught her eye on the dresser. She picked it up, sadness creeping into her mind. They'd hated each other their first week together. That all changed when they wore the exact outfit to work. Right down to the Converse tennis shoes. She smiled at the memory. It wasn't one she'd ever forget.

Tracing the picture of them from that day, Nikita let her tears fall. Losing a partner was one thing. Losing a best friend who was also your partner was a whole other sensation. Her stomach bunched, shoulders suddenly heavy. Mandi's family already arranged her funeral; it was the next day. Another reason she had to leave Snowshoe, even if only temporarily.

She put the frame down and opened her closet. Mandi would insist she wore something bright. Every funeral they'd attended together, Mandi sported an ungodly cheery color.

"What? They're not here but I am. I need to celebrate while I can," she said when Nikita questioned her *apparel.*

Finding a flowing red jumper, she pulled it off the hangar and wiped the tears away with the back of her hand. *Mandi would approve.* That much she knew for a fact. Grabbing the matching shoes, she set the outfit aside and walked toward the kitchen.

The moving boxes were delivered shortly after she poured a glass of white wine. She opened every cupboard and found them empty. Dining in rarely happened with her hours. She'd purposefully rented an apartment on a street filled with restaurants that offered delivery and late-night pick up.

She retrieved the newly purchased cell phone and called the Indian restaurant down the block. There were a select few numbers she memorized, her favorite restaurant one of them.

An hour later, she sat with half-eaten curry chicken on one side and six boxes stuffed with the essentials on the other. She'd leave the rest here. The landlord could charge more in rent for a furnished apartment, and she didn't have to worry about unloading the items to someone else.

Nikita flipped on the television, the late-night news droning in the background. Normally being alone didn't bother her. Tonight, though, all she thought about was how much better it'd be to have Kevlar with her.

She stared at the cheap phone, cursing herself for not memorizing his number. Once upon a time, she memorized everything about Kevlar—Tucker back then. It seemed like so long ago.

Standing, she walked over to the last closet she needed to pack. A shoebox on the top shelf made her stand on her tiptoes to reach it. The top slid off, her body catching it before it fell to the floor.

Nikita opened it all the way, ignoring the dust bunnies that somehow accrued despite the closed box. Snapshots of the past met her at first glance. There were some of her mother and her. Others were of vacations as a child. But the ones she wanted to find, she had to dig for. Finally, her fingers touched the Polaroid photos from her old camera. She'd been so damned excited to use it and get the images within moments of the event.

Sighing, she stared at the younger version of herself and Kevlar. They were adorably in love when the pictures were taken. *Funny how you can fall so fast for someone and never really let go even after you break up.*

She traced Kevlar's handsome face. He looked the same. Well, plus facial hair and tattoos.

Grabbing the last empty box, she carefully placed the shoebox inside. There were more personal items, but none she wanted to revisit tonight. Not all of the past deserved her attention right then.

She sealed the boxes and looked at the time. It was nearly two in the morning. *It's midnight in Colorado.* She bit her bottom lip. As tempting as it was to call information and find the clubhouse main line, she wouldn't. Kevlar was recovering and didn't need any distractions. She felt bad for not leaving a note or anything. In hindsight, she should've. If Kevlar woke with her gone, he'd think history repeated itself. *But that's never happening again.* She didn't know when she made up her mind about it. One minute she just couldn't fathom living a life without him.

Nikita changed and crawled into bed. The wounds she suffered from the Cutthroats and

Diablos were still tender, wearing on her energy. Not even a week passed since the horrible events. She made a mental note to check in on Yasmina. The woman more than earned a happy ending. If she could make it happen, she would. She'd been deadly serious about giving her money to someone who deserved it. Her mother would balk of course, but Nikita didn't care.

The noise from the streets below met her, and she chuckled. It sounded nothing like Snowshoe. Somehow, over a very short period, she'd gotten used to small-city living. No traffic horns at all hours or people yelling obscenities after drinking one too many beers. She smirked in the darkness—the last one she'd heard at the Macha clubhouse. *But I was with him and didn't mind.*

Cuddling the pillow next to her, Nikita fell asleep to the thought of Kevlar. The next two days would be filled with more emotions than she'd faced in years. Having him by her side would be easier, but she could do it alone one last time.

Chapter Thirty-Nine

No clouds dotted the horizon at Mandi's burial. Instead, the sun shined brightly, the fresh snow glistening on the grass. The funeral had been short but tasteful, and an hour later, Nikita stood among her colleagues and Mandi's family members, all focused on the mahogany casket with white roses on top. Sniffles dotted the crowd. There wasn't a dry eye in sight. Nikita tried and failed to hold back tears. Mandi wouldn't want them.

"If anyone would like to say a few parting words, now is the time," the minister said, gazing out at the group of mourners.

Nikita's eyes dipped to the snowy ground. She had too many emotions fluttering in her heart but couldn't find the right way to say any of them.

The mourners left after an acapella version of "Amazing Grace," family members taking a rose from the casket before their final goodbye. She couldn't look away. Mandi's little niece, Kaley, was there, big eyes teary. It broke Nikita's heart all over again. Mandi's one request was to make it home for her niece's golden birthday. Nikita hadn't kept her word. Guilt flooded her and she closed her eyes.

A small tug on her left hand snapped her eyelids open again.

"You're Aunt Mandi's partner, right?"

She brushed away her tears and squatted to the girl's level. "Yes. And you're Kaley, aren't you?"

The beautiful girl bobbed her head up and down. She pointed to the cemetery. "I don't think Auntie would like it here. It's too quiet."

She chuckled. Mandi would certainly hate the serenity. "Maybe we should visit a lot and sing her songs."

Kaley's face broke out into a wide grin. "Yeah, I can bring a radio for her and leave it here. She can listen to music all the time." The girl ran off to her parents, jabbering about her newfound plan.

Standing, Nikita didn't try to hide her emotions anymore. She was a wreck and barely unpacked her loss. The next twenty-four hours would be spent doing exactly that.

Turning, she caught a glimpse of a tattooed man walking in the other direction of the crowd, retreating from the Boston chill. A fresh set of emotions rushed to her eyes as he neared.

"Hawk."

The MC man had spruced up. A black suit and burgundy tie somehow looked out of place among his colorful tattoos.

"I couldn't say goodbye in Snowshoe." His eyes fixed on the casket slowly lowering into the frozen ground. "I'm not sure I can do it here either but needed to come. I needed to try."

Nikita took in his watery eyes and pulled him in for a hug. He buried his face in her coat, shoulders shuddering but no sounds escaping him. "You loved her too." It wasn't a question. They both knew the unspoken truth.

From the corner of her eye, Nikita watched Mandi's family pile into the dark SUVs. She'd keep her promise to Mandi by helping her niece in any way she could. A new surge of grief ripped through her, and she was grateful for Hawk, even if only to keep her upright.

***

"Stockdale, I wasn't expecting to see you so soon." Randy Penn lowered his reading glasses and nodded to the chair across from him. "Agent Riggs's memorial was very touching."

Taking a seat, Nikita cleared her throat. Mandi wouldn't have cared if Randy attended. Hell, she probably would've laughed if she saw the man's fake sympathy for a fallen comrade.

"I'm only in town until tomorrow."

Randy lifted his brow. "Oh?"

"I'd like a transfer to Denver." She watched his right eye twitch. "Immediately."

"Ah, I see you've become fond of Colorado." He grabbed a stack of paperwork and glanced at it. "But you can't leave quite yet."

"Why not?"

"With how Agent Gibson betrayed our agency and the circumstances of Agent Riggs's death, there needs to be an investigation on both."

She sat back and crossed her arms over her chest. "I sent my full operation reports as required. If internal investigation has any questions, they can contact me in Colorado."

A peculiar expression crossed Randy's face. "It's not just those two instances, Nikita."

"Then what?"

He pushed a folder toward her. "Your father's identity has called you in to question as well."

She opened the file and scoured the contents. "You're kidding, right? This is bullshit. My success rate speaks for itself." A letter with the header from Fishkill Penitentiary caught her attention. "My father sent the FBI a letter?"

"Yes, a rather detailed one." Her boss turned to the computer and pulled up a memo. "While he spelled everything Agent Gibson did to aid Diablos, he also mentioned your visits."

Nikita's head spun. Her father wouldn't let her live her life. He had to jut in his ugly face whenever possible. "I didn't do anything illegal."

"No, I'm not doubting you." He shrugged. "But these orders are above my head. Until you're cleared for duty, you're on leave."

"Are you—"

"It's nothing personal, Stockdale. It's completely normal." Randy offered her a small smile. "Should everything come back spick and span, I'll personally push through your transfer to Denver."

Standing, she nodded. "All right, thanks." She made it to the door before Randy stopped her.

"Nikita, let me be the first to say we'll miss you in Boston." He smiled, this time seemingly genuine.

Despite not liking the man much, she returned the act. "Thanks. Boston has been good, but I need great."

Chapter Forty

KEVLAR

"SHE LEFT? AS IN UP AND DROVE AWAY?" KEVLAR glared at Rubble, who stood there and took his wrath head-on. "And you did nothing? Why the hell are you the sergeant at arms if you can't keep tabs on...." He paused. What was Kita to him? She wasn't his old lady. She wasn't his girlfriend. She was the ex he wanted to sleep beside for the rest of his life.

"Brother, she's an FBI agent. If she wants to sneak out undetected, she'll do it under anyone's watch." Rubble lit a cigarette. "Probably shouldn't smoke in the recovery room." He shrugged. "Oh, well. Want one?"

No, I want Kita.

He declined and swung his legs over the side of

the bed. Doc advised him to stay put. Since when did he listen? *Never.*

"Thought you were taking it slow."

"I am." He got to his feet and swallowed a grunt. "If I wasn't, I'd be climbing into a truck and searching the streets for her."

"Don't think she's in town." Rubble blew out a stream of smoke.

Turning, Kevlar eyed him. "Why do you say that?"

"'Cause her bag's gone." He searched for an ashtray but came up short and used an empty pop can instead. "My guess is she went back east."

Suddenly, walking back to his room seemed more difficult than running a marathon. He staggered backward slightly, his arm shooting out to catch the bed.

Rubble's gaze settled on him. "She'll be back, don't worry."

Kevlar sat again, defeat creeping into his mind. "And how do you know that? Did she leave a note for you?" he asked sarcastically. "Because she sure didn't leave one for me."

"Nah, but I have a hunch about her." He grinned. "A good one." He smoothed his long beard and walked to the door. "Plus, she left her spare gun. No woman as badass as yours forgets her sidearm."

A millisecond of humor filtered through Kevlar. It was quickly replaced by skepticism. A left behind gun didn't mean jackshit. He blew out a noisy breath and leaned back into the bed. Doc's connection with the local hospital had its perks. This bed and the drugs in his veins being two of the better ones.

The sound of the clubhouse drifted down the hall. Somebody—*probably a prospect*—was begging for a blowjob from one of the nymphs. He chuckled at the desperation in the man's voice. He'd never been that bad up for a hummer.

Snoopy and Legs were arguing down the hall. The mixture of Spanish and English intensified as did their volume. They'd make up and fuck like bunnies soon enough. It was a constant for those two.

Klink and Cueball were betting on a pool game. From the sound of it, Cueball was living up to his name. Then there was Doc and Isa. The creaking of bedsprings told him everything he needed to know.

The rest of the sounds mingled together, creating a sweet symphony of Macha life. Queenie and Reaper's voices from the kitchen, Rubble's throaty chuckle, Dolly's cursing, and Brewer egging her on.

This was home. It was the place he'd dreamed of every night of his deployment. Now that he was back, he wasn't going anywhere. The sole thing that'd make it completely home was Kita. She was missing from his perfect ending. He didn't believe in the bullshit fairy tales, but he'd make an exception for her. She was as fiery as Macha herself. And Kita fit perfectly with him.

Closing his eyes, Kevlar let himself drift to sleep. The nightmares didn't invade his mind to his relief. Instead, he dreamed of Kita and a future that involved them together.

***

Three days passed since Kevlar was shot. Doc changed his dressings, Isa once or twice when he was busy. Evidently, Doc's old lady was honing her role, and that involved learning the ropes of first aid. He didn't really mind. It gave him something to look forward to other than the lack of messages on his phone.

Glancing at the rousing game of pool, Kevlar waited his turn. The impromptu tournament started when Dolly and her nymphs bet against Cueball and Klink. Of course, the two men couldn't turn down the chance to make the women eat their words. Thus far, the two bikers were the ones shoveling in the shit.

"You heard from her?" Reaper asked, handing him a tumbler full of whiskey.

He gripped the glass and took a long swig. "Nope."

"She'll call."

"She doesn't have a phone." He set down the drink. "And even if she did, I doubt she memorized my number."

Reaper chuckled. The club president could usually help him feel better nearly all the time. Tonight, he failed. The only mood Kevlar could conjure was gloomy.

"Keep your chin up, boyo. Never know when somebody will surprise you." He greeted Queenie with a smooch on the lips. Their affection usually comforted him. Not tonight.

"Yo, Kevlar, you're up, brother." Rubble waved at him.

Standing up, he noticed the pain from the bullet wound somewhat subsided. Then again, Doc did force-feed him a strong pain pill five minutes earlier. That combined with the MC-made whiskey, he could probably get shot again and not feel a damn thing.

He took the offered cue stick and broke. The balls scattered across the felt table, none making in a pocket. For the next fifteen minutes, he and Dolly shot pool. He finished his whiskey and had another by the time the game ended, and he walked away victorious. The win temporarily raised his spirits.

Klink and a nymph named Tilly took up the next game, leaving him plenty of time to wallow. Well, in his current position, he couldn't remember what day it was, let alone why he was sad. It was a kind reprieve after the last week.

Hawk walked in, stealing the attention from the pool games.

"There he is," Cueball said, hugging him. "Where you been?"

Kevlar wondered the same. Hawk all but disappeared two days ago. He didn't realize the absence until right then.

"Out and about," Hawk replied, skirting the question and walking to the pool table. "I have next winner."

Watching him, Kevlar recognized sadness rimming Hawk's usual smile. He understood then where he'd gone. *Mandi's funeral.* He gritted his teeth, willing himself to refrain from asking about

Kita and if she was there too. He grabbed another drink, the night growing darker by the moment.

Hours later, Rubble had to help him down the hall. He staggered drunkenly, both men singing an Irish tune loudly. Kevlar didn't give a shit when Isa scowled and told them to shut it. Neither did Rubble, who merely laughed and kept walking down the hall.

"Okay, try to throw up in the trash can," Rubble said, clapping a hand on Kevlar's back. "I ain't cleaning up after you."

Kevlar saluted his oldest friend in the club and opened the bedroom door. It took a few seconds for his eyes to adjust to the darkness. Once they did, he blinked, then rubbed his eyes. No matter what he did, she was still there. Kita was back.

Chapter Forty-One

NIKITA

"Kita?"

She flicked on the recently fixed lamp beside the bed. The shade was taped together, a friendly reminder of how they'd busted it during sex. She planned on making a grand appearance, but after seeing Kevlar drunk off his ass, she opted for a more private reunion.

"Yeah, it's me."

He laughed and clumsily kicked off his boots. "Nah, I'm dreaming."

She watched him strip. The act seemingly difficult given his healing wound and tipsy state, but she didn't move to help him. The flight into Denver and subsequent drive through the snow wore her out. All she wanted to do was fall in his arms and go to sleep.

Seeing him with his brothers, she'd accepted it wouldn't happen. At least not yet.

"You're not, but you probably should go to bed." She muted a giggle when he tripped over his feet and flopped onto the bed.

He let out a pained grunt and rolled over. Other than his green boxers, he was completely undressed. Crawling over, she pressed a kiss to his arm. It was so warm beneath her mouth, a vast difference to the bitter cold outside. It wasn't even Christmas, but Snowshoe lived up to its name with frigid temperatures.

"Fuck, you're really here, aren't you?"

She nodded against him, lips moving along his tattoos.

"How long?"

Propping up her head on her fist, she tried to catch his gaze. He wouldn't give up his beautiful brown eyes to her. She didn't blame him. After all, she'd left without a word. If the tables were reversed, she'd be wary too.

"Indefinitely."

"What?" He craned his neck to meet her face now, gaze searching her. "What did you say? I'm a little wasted and want to make sure I'm not making this all up."

"You know, you were drunk when we met." She smiled reminiscently. It was a cliché, but she met the love of her life at a party beside a keg of cheap beer.

"Yeah, I remember. You wore this short blue mini skirt. Every guy in the place was drooling over you." He cupped the side of her face. "And you wanted me. Nobody else."

"I still do, Kevlar." She nibbled on the top of his lip. "I chose you then and I choose you now."

"You sure? Because I hear those East Coast MCs are— "

Her lips silenced the rest of his snarky reply. He quickly overtook the embrace, his tongue invading her mouth. The taste of whiskey mixed with cigarettes was purely Kevlar.

"I love you, Kita." He broke free to say, thumb running across her bottom lip. His eyes shone in the dim lighting. "I know you said you never wanted to be part of an MC again, but I was kind of hoping you'd change your mind."

"I love you too, Kevlar." She grabbed his chin and pulled him to her mouth. "And don't you dare propose to me when you're drunk."

He smirked. "It'd complete the circle, baby. It doesn't get any better than that."

She pressed him into the mattress and carefully

straddled him. "I think I'd rather keep traveling the circle." She kissed down his neck. "That okay with you?"

He nodded and gasped the lower she kissed. "As long as you're mine, Kita, I don't care what happens next."

Sliding down his boxers, she paused and looked up at him. Even with a white bandage covering the bullet he took because of her, Kevlar Dorous was breathtaking. He had been from day one. He'd be until the day she died. She'd run from her past when she really should've been running to him instead. It was a mistake she'd never make again.

Lesson learned love earned.

***

"Kita, wake up."

Groaning her displeasure, she fluttered open her eyelids. Kevlar hovered above her in bed. Darkness hung behind the window shade, but wanes of new light from the day threatened to make an appearance.

"Why? What's wrong?"

"Nothing. I realized I forgot to give you something."

She sat up, keeping her sleepy head on her fist. "And what is that?"

"This."

Following his gaze, Nikita took in the shimmer of her handgun. "Um, thank you?" She grabbed it and put it on the side table. "I think it could've waited until morning, babe."

"Jesus, Kita, did you look at what was on the gun?"

She cocked her brow. "What'd you do, clean it?"

He laughed and crawled out of bed. She couldn't complain at what she saw. Kevlar naked was wonderful to see any time of day or night.

He knelt next to the bed, retrieving the gun. Holding it up, he offered it to her again. This time, she noticed the sparkling glint of a diamond.

"Oh my God." She sat up, eyes darting to the ring attached to the gun by a string.

"It's unloaded, but the diamond isn't." He met her gaze. "And neither is our love. We've been through hell, fought the devil, and walked out. Yeah, we both got a few burns and scars along the way, but I think it's worth it. I think we're worth all the drama and firefights."

She rubbed her lips together, her stomach swirling at his words.

"Be my old lady, Kita. I can't promise any more gems like this, but I can promise to love you every day. Even when you're a badass bitch who can kick my ass." He smiled and unlatched the ring from the gun. "What do you say? Be my old lady and boss me around?"

It was a question she didn't have to think over twice. Closing the distance to his lips, she tugged on the back of his neck until he was fully on top of her on the bed.

"Si, mi amor. I'll be your old lady and kick your ass any time I need to."

"I think you'll enjoy that." He smiled against her lips. "And so will I because it sounds like heaven."

From Diablos to heaven. Yeah, she could get used to that. Life with Kevlar wouldn't be boring. She wrapped her legs around his waist. A life with her wouldn't be either. It was why they were perfect for each other. Both ideally flawed, that their love canceled each other out to create perfection.

"You are so getting laid again," she murmured.

Kevlar slid into her warmth. "Already ahead of you, baby."

Laughing, she rolled him over and thoroughly kissed him. She no longer wanted to take down every MC. Macha was the one exception. Just like Kevlar.

TIME SEEMED TO BLUR OVER THE FOLLOWING MONTHS. Christmas came and went, as did the unexpected murder of Kita's father. The investigation remained open, but he doubted they'd ever discover who murdered the great Muerte Morales.

Kevlar lifted his gaze and grinned. Kita was in the kitchen with Isa and Queenie, preparing for the upcoming winter games by baking cookies to sell at the lodge. The news of her father's death brought a visit from her mother. After learning of what Muerte allowed done to their daughter, he was certain Rose had something to do with her husband's death, but they never spoke of it. He'd leave it alone. It was best for everyone.

Kita smiled at him, then went back to adding

blue sprinkles to the snowflake-shaped sugar cookies. They were married last week, Reaper officiating. He could officially call himself a married man with an old lady hotter than the rest. It hadn't sunk in completely. The new tattoo on his finger caught his eye. Kita had one too. The symbol they agreed neither could remove, no matter what they endured.

The scar on his side wouldn't ever completely go away either. He kept the reminder there on purpose. He needed to see it every now and then to remind himself of the past and what their future could become.

"Kevlar, you ready to go? Hawk and Doc are already at the lodge."

He looked over at Rubble in the doorway. Snow pelted his face, already red from the elements.

"Meet you outside in a second." Standing, he stretched lazily. After spending the day ensuring the Macha women were well taken care of, he was ready to get out and let loose.

Walking into the kitchen, he kissed the top of Kita's head. "You coming to the lodge later?"

She grinned up at him, flour smudging on her cheek. "Yep, and we'll bring some cookies for you too."

"Okay, make one of the prospects drive." He

nodded to Isa, the cute swell to her belly one he'd never put in danger. "Don't want anything to happen while I'm gone."

The three women looked at him incredulously and giggled. "Please, I think we can handle a little snow," Isa stated with a snort, her Irish accent tickling his ears.

"And if not, I'm always packing, baby." Kita patted her side. Sure enough, her FBI issued gun was safely hooked to her belt. It only made him hotter for her. She wasn't a prissy girl who was afraid to stand up for herself. She'd kick anyone's ass given the chance.

Kevlar kissed Kita until both Queenie and Isa cooed giddily. Pulling away, he scanned his old lady's amber eyes. They were glazed with lust. Just the way he wanted them. "Don't stay away long. I have a room reserved."

She swatted his ass. "I'm not that kind of girl."

"No, but you're that kind of woman."

Kita blushed and flipped him her middle finger. "You're right. Good thing you know better."

"Nah, I just know you." He waved at Queenie and Isa. "See you all later."

Kevlar left before the lure of Kita's body swayed him otherwise. He needed to spend some time with his brothers after being in a sex bubble with Kita the last few months. He wasn't complaining one bit, but his brothers were.

Stepping out in the storm, he pulled up the hood of his sweatshirt under his cut. The parking lot was full of snow again even after he plowed it that morning. Shrugging, he climbed into the waiting truck. There'd always be time for chores. Right now, he was off to help initiate a prospect. It was his first in years, and they were all looking forward to the prospect's initial step to being a full-fledged Macha man.

Rubble handed him a cigarette.

"Actually, I'm quitting." He slapped his arm. "Got the patch and everything."

Rubble's face went from surprised to teasing. "Fucking women. They'll get every last one of us."

"I can guarantee it, but they're so worth it."" He buckled his belt and turned on the radio. "What about you, brother? Any lady catch your eye?"

Clearing his throat, Rubble shook his head. "Nah, I'm too fucked up for somebody special." Before Kevlar could argue, the big man added, "Plus, I enjoy nymphs way too much to settle down."

Kevlar snorted. "I believe that's what Doc said, and now he's expecting a baby with his old lady."

Rubble turned the steering wheel. "Yeah, that's another reason. Women want babies."

"Shit, sorry." Kevlar cursed himself for forgetting his best friend's deepest secret. "But hey, not all women are the same." He nudged him good-naturedly. "Especially Macha women."

"Yeah, maybe."

Watching snow pepper the windshield, Kevlar eyed the burly man beside him. They'd gone through hell overseas and even in the States. If anyone deserved a happily ever after, it was Rubble.

"Did I tell you Queenie bought a bakery in town?"

He shook his head and gave Kevlar side-eye. "What? Why? Macha has enough businesses."

Kevlar shrugged. "Dunno. I think it has something to do with Yasmina. She can't run the place by herself and Queenie's too busy at the lodge this time of year."

"Then who's running it?"

They slowed behind a snowplow and he smirked. "Not sure, but she's damn pretty."

Rubble lifted his brows. "A nymph?"

"Nope." He chuckled inwardly. He and Kita met Jupiter Quinn last week. Evidently, Queenie felt compelled to help her. Somehow, Kevlar knew the newest mystery woman in Snowshoe would be right up Rubble's alley.

"What you smiling like that for?"

He nodded to the lodge up the mountain. "Just excited to see my girl."

Rubble rolled his uniquely hued eyes. "Macha have mercy."

Kevlar didn't reply. He was too busy watching the massive lodge come into view. It was the club's best moneymaker, but he had a hunch the newly purchased bakery would get plenty of Rubble's business soon.

Nikita

The city of Snowshoe fell delicately against the backdrop of the mountains. From Macha's Snowshoe Lodge, she could see every inch of the town, plus the snow resort the club ran during the winter. It was packed full of tourists. Most were preparing for the winter games that'd start in the next week. She was thrilled to be part of the event despite snow never being one of her favorite pastimes.

Placing the freshly baked cookies and pastries on

the welcome desk, Nikita nodded proudly. Baking had never been her strong suit, but she quickly found she wasn't too bad at it.

Her phone buzzed from her back pocket. Checking it, she noticed the coded message from her new boss in Denver. The internal investigation was put to bed shortly after her father's murder. Being transplanted to Colorado was the best move she'd made.

Except for Kevlar.

The man of the hour laughed, drawing her eyes to him. He and his brothers recently arrived back from God knew where after part of their Macha initiation. She didn't ask about it. None of the women did. But if she wanted to know, Kevlar would tell her. They had the kind of relationship where no secrets were kept for long.

A guest walked in, his small daughter clasping his gloved hand. For a split second, Nikita felt sad. Once upon a time, she and her father frequented a lodge in the Swiss Alps. But that was so many years ago. She and Kevlar flew back for her father's funeral. Her mother even made the transatlantic flight to watch her husband's body descend into the firm ground. It made sense. She'd had to see the actual body herself before she accepted the truth.

The death of Estevan "Muerte" Morales didn't come as a surprise. She dedicated every waking moment away from Macha to taking down the MCs her father associated with. Thus far, she found plenty of scumbags to put away.

Sitting by the large wood burning fire, she thought back over the last few months. All the women they saved from the trafficking ring were safe either at their original homes or ones in the States. It came as a surprise when Yasmina insisted she stay in Snowshoe after a short visit. Apparently, the woman wanted to help the MC who saved her. With Yasmina's tender heart and knowledge of baking, Queenie purchased a shop in the middle of town that very day. It was something Nikita could get behind every time. Plus, she liked having the woman around to talk to now and then.

True to her word, Nikita set up a foundation for the women who were trafficked with her, plus more. There was plenty of money thanks to her father's will, which left his entire estate to her. She couldn't think of a better way to right the wrongs he inflicted on so many innocents. Diablos was successfully disbanded thanks to her FBI and MC resources. She kept an open file for the few Diablos members that managed to leave the United States.

A boisterous laugh caught her ear, and she grinned at Hawk chasing Mandi's niece, Kaley. The club flew Mandi's family out for an extended stay at the lodge. Mandi would've been proud to see Hawk fawning over the five-year-old. Nikita made certain to keep in contact with the little girl over the last months. The few times she flew back east, the duo even visited Mandi, radio safely stowed near the ornate gravestone.

The Greenback Cutthroats somehow escaped the wrath of the FBI. At least most of the members did. A select few were dragged to jail and were awaiting their day in court. From last she heard, the Cutthroats were president-less and actively looking for a new one. It gave her pause to think that someone else might take over the organization, but another part of her hoped the club would turn around and live within the scope of the law. *At least most of the law.* So long as they kept off her radar, she'd leave them be. If that ever changed, she'd be the first to put her FBI-issued boot up their asses. Love didn't make her soft; love enhanced her intuitions instead.

Nikita focused on the orange flames. Her time with Macha taught her many things. Mostly how to let herself love again. Kevlar had the most to do with her transformation. She loved that man more with each passing day. It physically hurt to think about a time they wouldn't be together. She made it a point to put him first, not her job, a big adjustment for her and the agency.

Kevlar became the person she told everything to. Just like when they were young, dumb kids. She grinned behind her fist. He even helped her with some FBI operations. When it came to MC information opening MC doors, he was irreplaceable. She could do it on her own, but now she didn't need to. Worrying about the future didn't keep her up at night anymore. Not with Kevlar watching her six at all times.

"You ready, sexy?"

Turning, she smiled at Kevlar's handsome face. The scruff on his cheeks was fuller, as was the hair on his head. That'd been her only request. She needed something to grab onto, and he hadn't complained in the slightest.

"I am." She stood, taking his outstretched hand. "You didn't abandon that prospect in the mountains, did you?"

Kevlar's lips parted, but he didn't answer. Instead, he led her to the winding staircase and into a woodsy themed room. The lock clicked in place, and she tore away his shirt in the next instant.

"Somebody's eager," he teased, unlatching her bra.

"Likewise." She bit the side of his neck and he groaned.

His eyes grazed her naked torso, concentrating on the newest tattoo on her skin. It was the only one done with colored ink. Seeing his focus, she traced the sketch Isa made of a new rendition of the goddess, Macha. Her hair was black, but instead of ghostlike features, bright blue eyes stared back at anyone who dared see the tattoo on her ribs. The goddess sat directly below her left breast, controlling the skin above her heart. Kevlar brought color to her heart, and the tattoo was evidence of it if nothing else.

Nikita leaned forward, pressing her breasts against his chest, lips grazing his collarbone.

"Shit, baby, you drive me wild."

Leading him by his pants to the bed, she pointed to it. "Good, now get up there. I'm gonna ride you hard."

"Promise?"

She jumped on the bed. "Oh, yeah. You know I don't lie about you, Kevlar. You and sex."

His lips descended on hers in a lust-fueled fury. She barely got the condom in place before he thrust into her. Sighing with pleasure, she dug her fingers through his hair and rocked her body against his. They had fifteen years of lost time to make up, and they weren't about to lose one more moment.

WE HOPE YOU'RE LOVING THE WORLD OF MACHA MC. You won't be waiting long until book three releases. Be sure to follow Skye for regular updates and release news.

WANT MORE LOVEABLE BAD BOYS? CHECK OUT Appointed by Fate, book one in her bad boy romance trilogy.

Acknowledgments

So many thanks to my readers for helping me pursue Macha MC and their assortment of colorful characters. I couldn't have penned a word without your support! I also want to thank my publisher, Hot Tree Publishing, beta readers, and editors for catching those little flaws I overlook.

Skye McNeil began writing at the age of seventeen and has been lost in a love affair ever since. During the day, she moonlights as a paralegal at a law firm favoring criminal law.

Skye enjoys writing romantic comedies and cozy mysteries novels that leave readers wanting more and falling in love over and over. She writes contemporary and historical novels ranging from sweet and sassy to steamy and sultry.

Her constant writing companions are two cats and Australian Shepherd. When she's not writing, Skye enjoys spending time with family, photography, volleyball, traveling, and curling up with a cup of coffee and reading.

WEBSITE: WWW.SKYEMCNEIL.COM

FACEBOOK READERS GROUP: HTTPS://BIT.LY/2WE93R3

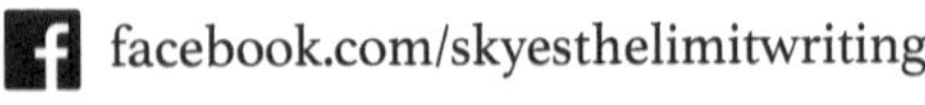 facebook.com/skyesthelimitwriting

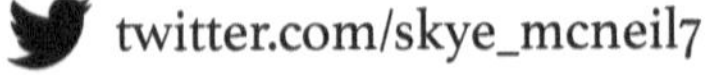 twitter.com/skye_mcneil7

instagram.com/mcneilskye

bookbub.com/profile/skye-mcneil

About the Publisher

Hot Tree Publishing opened its doors in 2015 with an aspiration to bring quality fiction to the world of readers. With the initial focus on romance and a wide spread of romance subgenres, Hot Tree Publishing has since opened their first imprint, Tangled Tree Publishing, specializing in crime, mystery, suspense, and thriller.

Firmly seated in the industry as a leading editing provider to independent authors and small publishing houses, Hot Tree Publishing is the sister company to Hot Tree Editing, founded in 2012. Having established in-house editing and promotions, plus having a well-respected market presence, Hot Tree Publishing endeavors to be a leader in bringing quality stories to the world of readers.

Interested in discovering more amazing reads brought to you by Hot Tree Publishing? Head over to the website for information:

WWW.HOTTREEPUBLISHING.COM

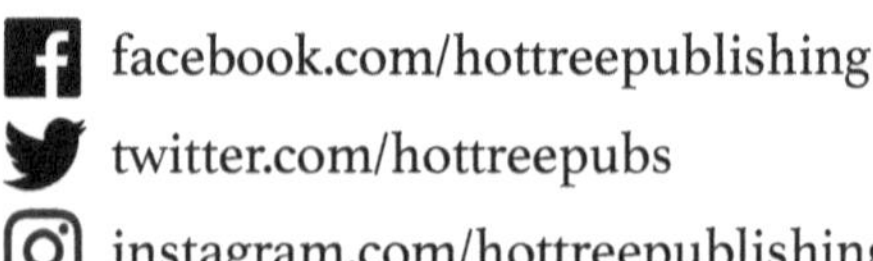

facebook.com/hottreepublishing
twitter.com/hottreepubs
instagram.com/hottreepublishing

9 781922 359490